Black Ink Publications Presents

Yolo 5
A Novel By

Sa'id Salaam

First Edition April 01, 2017

Printed in the United States of America

This is a work of fiction. Names, characters, places, and incidents either are products of the author's imagination or are used fictitiously. Any similarity to actual events or locales or persons, living or dead, is entirely coincidental.

Email: saidmsalaam@gmail.com and/or blackinkpublications1@gmail.com

Facebook: Free Sa'id Salaam

Cover design and layout by: Sunny Giovonni

Edited by: McIntire Edits

Acknowledgements

Bismillah Ir Rahman Ir Raheem
As always, First and Foremost All praise and worship is for
Almighty God, alone, with no partners. I bear witness that there is
nothing worthy of worship except Him.

Dedications

To the women in my life: my mother, Diedra, my grandmother, Rainey Mae, thank you for staying by my side and always being in my corner. I love each of you!

To my kids: Jessica, Ervin (ErvG), Derrick (Ra). I go hard to pave the way to make the way easier for each of you. Love you, Dad

To the readers: Thank for all the love and support you all continue to give to me and my family.

Team Salaam! Next!!!

Chapter 1

"Where is it? You can't hide from me..." Shyne insisted as she searched her mother's room. She hadn't been able to find her diary ever since she'd gotten caught reading it.

She knew she had no business reading it, on so many levels. First, it was none of her damn business what was inside the diary. It was personal and private, so no one should be reading it. Yolo used the tiny book to express her deepest thoughts and fears. Secondly, because it gave the girl the craziest dreams.

First she'd had a dream about *Growing Pains*, where her mother had died and she and her brother had ended up in foster care. It was an adventure all in itself, as the two struggled to find their father and make it back home.

Next she'd dreamed of *School Daze*, with her and Sun trying to navigate their way through high school and then college. Once they graduated, they'd both married their childhood sweethearts, Asad and Bryonna, and then joined the *Family Business*. They both became trained killers going around the country killing people and ridding the world of people who needed dead.

The dreams turned into nightmares when everyone that she loved was killed. Having her mother snatch her from her sleep was the best thing to ever happen to her. Seeing her mom and dad alive and well was the perfect ending to her dream, which would make one hell of a book or movie.

Shyne, of course, didn't believe a word she'd read in the diary. While some of what her mother had written rang true, most of it was so outrageous that it was beyond believable. For instance, a DC 2000. A device that snapped people's heads off. Come on now.

"Maybe in her..." Shyne said, rummaging through her mother's closet. She tossed a shiny ring aside and it snapped closed violently. Good thing she hadn't put it around her neck, because there was indeed such a thing as the DC 2000. She climbed on a pile of shoe boxes, some filled with shoes, others with guns and reached the closet's shelf.

"Jackpot!" she cheered when she found what she was looking for. She pumped her fist, but it was way too much movement for the pile of shoe boxes. It sent them and her tumbling down, causing her to land on her head.

Shyne was unfazed by the spill. She got up and tried to cover her tracks by putting the closet back in order. Diary in hand, she rushed from the room and stashed it to read later. Not a moment too soon, either, because her mom, dad and baby sister had just arrived home.

"Hey, Ma, Dad, um...baby," Shyne huffed, out of breath.

Both parents instinctively sniffed the air for traces of smoke or gasoline.

"What are you up to?" Yolo asked, scrunching her face. She knew her children and this one was crazy.

"Me?" Shyne reeled, pointing at herself like the question was ludicrous. "Why I'm not up to anything. How's my darling baby sister?"

"Yeah, she's up to something," Killa nodded and walked away. He found his sons in the den and joined the video game already in progress.

"Where's Grandma?" Yolo asked. She thoroughly enjoyed having the older woman living with them. The Murda and Malice threat was dead and stinking, along with the dead couple, so technically, she was free to go home, but no one said anything.

"Cooking!" Shyne cheered. Even crazy kids loved when their grandmothers cooked dinner.

****

"That was dope!" Killa sighed after taking his last bite of dinner. Like Yolo, he too was glad to have her around. Having a live in babysitter, cook and security guard freed him up for Killa Season 3. The world was full of bad people who badly needed to get fucked up.

"Dope!" Rico cheered, followed by the rest of the kids.

Diedra beamed brightly as she basked in the compliments. She missed the Bronx, who could blame her, but home is where the heart is, and hers was right here with her family, so she wasn't going anywhere. "Well, them dope dishes ain't gon' wash themselves," she shot back, deflecting the praise.

"Shyne!" all the boys sang in unison. They may have gotten away with it if Sun hadn't opened his mouth.

"Yo, that's women's work. Let Shyne do it," he ordered and leaned back, crossing his arms like the king had spoken.

"I'm out," Killa blurted and bolted. He knew what was coming and wanted no parts of it. He could hear his grandmother and Yolo reading him the riot act as he departed.

"Yeah, yeah, yeah. Take that!" Shyne tossed in like a rapper's hype man as Sun got chewed out. In the end, he would end up cleaning the kitchen by himself. "I'm going to do some reading. Talk to y'all later."

"What you reading, Granddaughter?" Diedra inquired as the women left the dining room.

"A paranormal, romance, sci-fi, fantasy book," she said, summing it up pretty well.

Yolo missed it since she and Killa had a date with a crooked cop. She had just chopped Malice's cockeyed head off and now the cop who'd sold them out had to pay.

"He's home," Killa announced as Yolo walked into their bedroom. He turned the laptop to Yolo so she could see as well.

"I like that shirt! You want one like it?" Yolo admired and asked.

"Maybe in blue," he replied since red wasn't his color. "Let's make the call."

"Let's!" she cheered and retrieved a second phone. This one was connected to the hundred pounds of semtex, high explosive that they'd laced his brownstone with. She and Killa shared playful banter with the cop until it was time to go. Yolo then hit him with her trademarked *Okay, bye-bye* and hit the switch.

"That was so cool!" Killa cheered at the bright explosion. They shared a quick high-five in victory. "How about we celebrate?"

"Six weeks, remember?" she sang. Her vagina still had an *out of order* sign on it from giving birth.

"Oh yeah," he groaned until another idea made him smile. "Guess, I'll just have to settle for some head."

"Okay. I'll be here when you get back," she said sarcastically. Yolo was one of those *don't call me, I'll call you* types when it came to head. She enjoyed it, but did it on her own terms. Odd, since she didn't mind asking him to lick her cookie jar.

"Guess, I'll take care of it myself," he sighed and took his erection in hand. Yolo felt sorry for him and reached into the nightstand for the lube and squirted some into her palm.

Killa and Yolo made out like college kids while she stroked and twisted his shaft. Their tongues swirled in each other's mouths around their moans. Killa let out a grunt as he busted a nut. He was asleep seconds later.

"Mr. Don't Call Him Killa for Nothin'!" Yolo quipped at her snoring husband. The thought of being not just a wife, but *his* wife overwhelmed her. She smiled so hard that her cheeks hurt. Still, she had to get up and wash the semen and lubricant from her hands.

Yolo giggled and blushed at her reflection as she washed. It had been some day. Some week, as a matter of fact, so she decided to record it in her diary. She dried her hands and headed to the closet, her new hiding spot.

"That damn Shyne!" she fussed when her search came up empty. She grabbed a belt, marched down the hall and barged into her daughter's room. There, lying open next to a sleeping Shyne, was her diary.

Shyne was tossing and turning in her sleep with a wide smile on her face. Yolo twisted her lips at her child and decided not to wake her. Instead, she collected her diary and let her enjoy her dream.

Chapter 2

"Yesss!!!" Shyne cheered when she realized she was grown again. It may be just a dream, but she planned on enjoying it. First things first, so she found her husband. "Asad! Where you at, baby?"

"In here. What's up?" he called from his office. Shyne rushed in hunching the air and attacked him. "Again?"

Asad could only hang on for dear life as his wife gave him the business. This was probably why they had so many kids. The way it ended probably meant that another one was on the way.

"Ooh, ooh, what's up with my mom and dad? Sun? Rico?" she asked frantically, finally remembering her dead family members.

"The kids are with your parents, and Sun and Bryonna are expecting us for dinner since you and Sun have a business trip tomorrow."

"What kind of business?" she cocked her head and dared. She crossed her fingers then quickly uncrossed them since she didn't believe in luck or chance.

"Family business, whatever that is..." he answered.

Shyne was so happy that she attacked him once more, setting off round two. Yes, this was exactly why they had so many children.

****

"Sup. Yo, what the hell is wrong with you two?" Sun greeted and asked when he opened his door for his sister and brother-in-law. "Her hair all wild and you look sleepy."

"As salaamu alaykum," Asad greeted, ignoring the question. The last second back shots did have him a little sleepy.

"Hey, girl. Where's PMB?" Shyne said to Bryonna.

"Girl, stop calling my child puppy, monkey, baby! She's at your mom's with your kids," Bryonna replied.

"Yolo...a grandmother! This I have got to see," Shyne chuckled.

"Well, it'll have to wait until we get back from Memphis," Sun reminded.

"Oh yeah, Memphis. Family business...in Memphis," she repeated and winked. *"Who's in Memphis again?"*

Sun shook his head and took his twin outside to fill her in on their next target. A child porn pusher named OJ, who was about to get squeezed.

****

"Too old," OJ said, turning his nose up at an eight-year-old. *"After six, maybe seven, I really ain't got no use for them."*

"Come on, OJ, please, sir. I really need the money," the mother pleaded, pushing her child forward. She danced from foot to foot hoping to make the sale. The girl had just cost her money on food and clothing. Money she could use on what was more important to her, getting high.

"Eh..." OJ said, turning his nose up. Every second that passed reduced the price a few dollars. *"I'll give you fifty bucks for her. Can't do much when they that old."*

"Sold!" the pathetic parent proudly proclaimed and pushed her child forward. Yeah, it was pretty fucked up, and she was going to get fucked up for it. Her and OJ once Killa's kids rolled into town.

"That must be X and Rico," Sun said when a late model car pulled into his driveway.

"Xavier! Rico! They're alive?" Shyne swooned and took off towards the car. She tackled Xavier as soon as he stepped out.

"Help!" X called playfully as his sister smothered him with sisterly love. Rico just shrugged like, *'better you than me.'*

"Don't ask me," Sun shrugged when his oldest sibling looked to him for help. *"See you guys inside."*

****

The next day, the killer siblings met up at Atlanta's Hartfield International for the short flight to Memphis. The team worked like a pack of lions when on a kill. Each one had a job to do and did it.

Sun was his father's son and as such, he made contacts in every city possible. He always made sure that they had accommodations, cars, guns and of course weed. Rico was his father's son too and as such had a chick to stick it in, in every city. Shyne was her mother's daughter and as such was fucking crazy. She had all the gas stations and propane places mapped out. X wasn't Killa's by blood, but had still picked up his cool demeanor, so he just cooled out until it was time to murder something.

"I hope you got us separate rooms," Shyne huffed indignantly. The one time they'd all been forced to share a room in Kentucky still left a bad taste in her mouth. Sun and Xavier had smoked and farted nonstop while Rico had had a pussy parade all weekend.

"I got us separate hotels!" Sun shot back. "Me and X are in the Western while you and Lover Boy are in the Marriott," he explained and then explained why.

She and Rico would have the pleasure of killing OJ, their main target, while Sun and X would go after deadbeat dads and malicious mothers. Rico had bagged a social worker who worked for Child Protective Services so he had a list of some really, really fucked up parents. At the top of the list was Shawna, who'd recently sold her eight-year-old daughter.

Sun took them to their rentals so that they could head to their respective hotel rooms and rest up until show time.

****

Show time!" OJ shouted with a clap of his hands, starting the show. The show was a lingerie show for sick fucks who liked seeing four- and five-year-olds in thongs—yeah, it was some real sick, Jon Benet type shit.

"The fuck!" Rico groaned and turned his face as the first angelic child pranced out.

"Easy...take it easy," Shyne growled through clenched teeth. The men and women in attendance drooled and cheered while taking pictures and making videos. "Remember to get all their phones."

"Why? The fire will take care of them, won't it?" he asked.

"Oh yeah!" she smiled, looking up at the sprinkler system. Most of these pedophiles were probably going to hell. Today they would get a taste of what was to come.

"Well, set it off, cuz I can't take much more of this shit! Plus...I got a date!"

"Don't you always, Mr. Trojan Man?" Shyne shot back with a giggle.

Their back and forth banter kept their attention off the sick sights on the stage. The first act came to an end and it was it was now time to move.

"Y'all, lil' bitches, hurr' up an' change!" OJ shouted and clapped. He kept the little girls terrified so that they'd do whatever he asked. His latest purchase, the eight-year-old, was too old for the stage, so he had her working as a maid until he could get her into kiddie porn.

"Hello?" Shyne called out as she wandered backstage. Meanwhile, Rico chained and padlocked the front doors.

"Who are you? The bidding doesn't start until after the third act," OJ fussed. "Not unless you tryna make me an offer I cain't refuse."

"I am! Can we talk in private?" she answered and asked so the children wouldn't see what was coming.

"Step into my office," he said, leading her into his office. He let her enter first so he could take a peek at her ass. Just like she knew he would, which allowed her to strike.

"Ouch! What the fuck was...th-that?" he asked, getting woozy immediately from the strong sedative she'd given him.

"Something to help you sleep. Don't worry, the fire will wake you up," she replied.

He had a million questions, but was too sleepy to ask any of them. Instead, he blinked a few times and went to dreamland.

"Okay, girls, get dressed! Regular clothes, and hurry!" Shyne shouted compassionately at the shell-shocked children. They heard urgency in her voice, not anger, and knew that their ordeal was over.

"Okay, come on, girls," Rico said when he reached the rear of the building. He ushered the girls out a backdoor and into a waiting van. Once he'd loaded them up, he then rushed back inside just as Shyne hit the switch.

"Hey! The fuck? My hair! This is gas!" the gawkers groaned as gasoline began spraying from the sprinkler system.

"Wake him up," Shyne told Rico, who began to kick OJ until he was awake.

"Stop! Hey! What's going on?" he griped and groaned. "Who are you people?"

"Fire department," Shyne replied, getting a kick out of her words. Rico helped him to his feet while holding a gun on him. He knew she was lying when she started to spray him with gas. "Showtime! It's your turn to walk the runway!"

"Move!" Rico barked and poked him with his pistol. He nudged him forward, leaving a trail of gas following behind him. When his guests saw him, they roared about their ruined hairdos and suits. Their roars of complaints were nothing compared to the roar of the fire that erupted when Shyne lit a match. A blue flame traced the trail of gasoline towards OJ. He saw it coming and took off running. He ran even faster as the flames caught up to him. He bounced around the room, setting his guest on fire along the way.

Rico and Shyne retreated through a backdoor and made their escape. The fire department would find the rescued girls and get them help.

****

Meanwhile, Sun and X were having their own fun. They'd divided their list in half, saving the best for last. Whoever got to Shawna first got the pleasure of killing her.

Sun shot, stabbed, kicked and choked his way through his half of the list. He was out of breath when he reached Shawna's drug den in the projects. It was only slightly better than the environment she'd sold her child into.

"Yes!" he cheered, seeing that he'd arrived first. However, his elation was short-lived when his brother screeched to a halt in front of the worn out apartment. "I was here first!"

"Looks like a tie to me!" Xavier declared and raced to catch up.

Sun took off towards the door with his brother hot on his heels. They didn't even bother to slow down when they reached it. Instead, they crashed right through the flimsy front door.

"Mm-mph," Shawna hummed, holding up one finger as she took a pull from her crack pipe. The brothers cocked their heads curiously as she went for a Guinness Book record toke, the drug sizzling loudly in the quiet room.

Shawna went for another record by holding the toxic smoke in her polluted lungs for several minutes. If not a crackhead, she would have had one hell of a career as a pearl diver. She finally exhaled the thin smoke after extracting all the crack molecules from it.

"Damn!" Sun said and began to clap. Both he and Xavier were so impressed at the feat that they momentarily forgot why they were there in the first place.

"Y'all line up if'n y'all want y'all dicks sucked," she said. They would be numbers eighty-four and eighty-five. Another record for the day, shattering her previous record of seventy-five dicks sucked in one day.

"Okay. No, wait..." Xavier agreed then shook his head clear. "That's not why we're here."

"If you here for the girl, you too late! I already sold her," she said, reminding the brothers of what they'd come for.

"Oh yeah!" Sun chuckled and got to work.

He hit her with an uppercut that lifted her off her feet. She was sound asleep before she hit the ground. That is, until X woke her up with a kick to her ribs. The grim brothers stomped the woman until she was almost flat. They then high-fived over the corpse and turned to leave.

Chapter 3

"Can't wait to see my babies!" Shyne cheered as she and Asad rode to her parent's house. They'd died in her last dream so she was eager to see what they looked like as grandparents in this one.

"You know they love Big Mama and Paw-Paw," Asad said, steering the SUV out to the suburbs.

"Big Mama?" Shyne reeled. "I can see Paw-Paw, but Big Mama!"

"Don't make fun of her this time! You know she's sensitive about that," her husband warned.

"About what?" she asked curiously.

Asad twisted his lips like 'yeah right' and kept on driving. She was impressed when he pulled down a long driveway to a stately farmhouse. Her eyes lit up when she saw her kids playing on the front porch. She hopped out before Asad could bring the truck to a complete stop.

"Wow!" Asad said, shaking his head as Shyne tumbled out of the vehicle. She rolled once, popped up and ran toward their kids.

"Mommy!" the kids shouted and ran for their mom. They dove off the porch, knocking her down once more.

"You guys, miss me?" Shyne asked needlessly as they squeezed and kissed her. The sound of heavy footsteps reached her ears, both catching her attention and alarming her. "What the hell is that?"

"That's Big Mama," the kids cheered for their favorite grandma. Shyne opened her mouth wide in shock when her mother stepped out on the porch; waddled, actually.

"There's my daughter!" Yolo sang and threw her large arms open wide. The fat under her arms jiggled and swung freely.

"Mommy?" Shyne asked, scrunching up her face. She hadn't seen her mother yet in this dream, but this was not what she'd expected.

This forty-something-year-old Yolo stood 5'4" tall and weighed a whopping three-hundred and fifty pounds. Her face was similar to the way it always looked, with the exception that it was surrounded by

17

pounds of flesh and fat. Her usual fly attire had been replaced by a muumuu covered in an assortment of colorful, flavorful stains, such as chocolate sauce, raspberry jelly and ice cream.

"Of course, it's your mama! Now, come give me a hug!" Big Mama insisted. "What's gotten into you?"

"Me? What's gotten into you? You're huge!" Shyne exclaimed.

Yolo's face turned down and her lip began to quiver. A lone fat tear ran down her fat cheek as she took off back into the house. The windows rattled as she stomped into her room.

"She said what?" Killa boomed from inside. "Where is she?"

"Paw-Paw mad," Shyne's darling son warned then distanced himself from his mother. Shyne was scared until he walked out on the porch next.

"Girl, what did you say to your mother?" her father demanded.

"Daddy?" Shyne asked and cracked up. Her father was rail thin wearing a pair of overalls like a farmer and she just couldn't take it.

"What's so funny, girl? Shyne! Shyne! Do you hear me?"

"Damn, Daddy, I..." Shyne fussed, bringing things into focus and perspective. Her father was back to normal and she was in her bedroom. That meant that she was ten again and in trouble again. "I mean, you're the best damn daddy a girl could have! I just love my damn daddy!"

"Get off me," Killa fussed, prying the child's arms from around his neck. He had to respect her clean up game so he saved the pop she had coming for later. Knowing Shyne, she would get it before the day was out. "Get ready for school and come eat."

"Okay. I hope Mommy cooked some damn eggs. She makes the best damn... Ouch!" she proclaimed when her Pops popped her backside.

****

"Is she okay?" Yolo asked when Killa joined the rest of the family for breakfast.

"Depends on your definition of okay," he replied seriously.

"Ain't nothing wrong with my grandbaby!" Diedra huffed in protest. Killa twisted his lips up at her, but kept them closed. This was the same old lady who swore her grandson did no wrong, even when he was at his worst. "Here she is now! Come sit next to great-grandma."

"Hey, Grandma," Shyne sang as she snuggled up against the woman. She shot her mother a daring glance like *take that.*

"You can run but you can't hide," Yolo threw out for whoever it pertained to. The boys ducked their heads so no one got on them and kept eating.

"Like your diary?" Shyne asked, melting into her grandmother's side. There was a brief pause followed by a burst of violence.

"Little girl, I'll..." Yolo fumed and tried to come over the table. Lucky for Shyne, Killa scooped her in mid-air and carried her away. "Just let us get a one! Me and the girl, heads up."

"She don't want them problems, Bae," he comforted as he took her upstairs. He knew the only thing that would calm her down was some good loving and that's what she was about to get.

"Just five minutes with her. No guns, no knives..." Yolo pleaded as Killa lifted her shirt over her head. She raised her arms to help him help her. She softened as he got hard.

"You gone be okay?" he asked cautiously since the six weeks wasn't quite up yet.

"Dude, if a person couldn't kill it, you certainly can't," she replied. They both peeked over at the baby monitor screen to make sure the baby was sleeping. She was giving the green light.

Killa took it nice and slow since she'd just had a baby and it was a full house. He kept it nice and slow even when he heard his grandmother leave with the kids to walk them to the bus stop.

"Mmm...you...feel...so good," Yolo moaned along with his slow stroke. Felt so good she didn't even want to fight Shyne anymore and hissed. The end was near when his stroke got choppy.

"Whatever you do...do NOT... Damn it, man!" Yolo fussed when Killa came before she could tell him not to cum inside of her.

"Hmp?" he asked, too late.

"Nothing," she sighed. "Just hope you didn't just knock me up! Again."

"God, I hope not either. We got work to do!" he reminded. They did, too, because the 1-800-Killa inbox was full. There were plenty of people in desperate need of dead.

****

"Dear Killa people, I don't know if this is real or not, but I hope it is because we need help. There's this gang in our neighborhood who's bullying everyone. They beat up the boys and make them join the gang. Their leader, Tip, he touched me..."

"Grrr," Yolo growled as Killa read about the sexual assault of the teen. "Let's go kill him!"

"Him? Let's kill them! All of the leaders so no one can fill the vacant spot," Killa corrected correctly. If they just killed Tip, his partner Grip would just step up. If they killed Grip, then Flea would step up. There were ten original members and they were about to get killed.

Several more bouts of sex in several more positions had Yolo calm by the time the kids made it home from school. She'd planned to cook a big meal and spend the night having family time before they left for Charlotte, North Carolina. That was the plan, at least.

"Sup, Big Mama? Oh, my little sister is up," Shyne said when she came home. She tossed her book bag aside with a heavy thud that made Yolo frown curiously. She wanted to know what was in there, but first...

"Big Mama?" she asked, poking her lip out. She thought she was bouncing back after the baby pretty quickly.

"Huh? Nothing," Shyne replied and smiled at her mother as she took her sister out of her arms. "Hey, little lady."

"Where are your brothers?" Yolo asked, admiring her daughters. No matter how much Shyne irked her, she loved her little girl dearly.

"Fighting the Joneses again," she shrugged, like it was no big deal.

"Where's your dad?" she asked, so she could send him to go yell at them.

"Oh, he's out there filming the fight yelling 'WORLD STAR!'" she replied. "Smells so good in here. What are you cooking?"

"Baked chicken, macaroni and cheese, rolls..." Yolo recited proudly. She had come a long way from cooking kids to cooking for her kids.

"Oh no, Big Mama! You know you don't need no mac and cheese!"

"What? I..." Yolo screeched, looking down at herself. She couldn't get a good view so she took off and ran upstairs to look in the full length mirror.

"You should be ashamed of yourself!" Grandma Diedra said, stifling a chuckle. She'd heard the exchange form the next room and tried not to laugh. "Anyway, get my belt."

"You gonna beat me?" Shyne reeled in disbelief. She'd seen her in action with the boys and she wanted to parts of it.

"Child, no, I'm 'bout to go out and watch that fight!" she exclaimed. "World Star!"

Chapter 4

"Am I getting fat?" Yolo asked, turning side to side in front of the full length mirror.

Poor Killa wasn't sure how to answer her. Sure, she had some baby fat from just having a baby, but he wasn't sure if he should say yes or no. He did appreciate the extra ass cleavage hanging from the bottom of the French cut panties. At the moment, it was making his dick fat.

"Ummm... No..." he said, taking a shot at the right answer.

"Then why the fuck your daughter keep calling me Big Mama? Why she keep telling me not to eat this or that? No bread, un uh, no rice!"

"Ummm... No," he repeated since it worked the last time. The alarm on his phone rang, indicating that it was time to leave. He breathed a sigh of relief and said, "We gotta bounce. Our plane leaves in six hours."

"We may not make it!" Yolo said fearfully. The airport was only forty-five minutes away, but it took half a day to get through security.

"If you get dressed and come on, we will! I'ma say bye to the kids. Meet me at the car," he said and left before he had to answer more questions.

Killa followed his ears to the den where the boys were playing video games. The game and noise suddenly stopped when he got near. He peeked in and saw why. Asad was standing in the corner offering his salah (prayer). Shyne sat staring with a love struck smile on her face while her brothers respectfully paused until he finished.

The chaos resumed as soon as he concluded his prayers. He turned side to side closing out and glimpsed his future father-in-law. "As salaamu alaykum, Dad," Asad greeted.

"Yeah, yeah, Wa alaykum salaam," he replied. He and Yolo had been side eyeing the boy since the day Shyne had looked for him in her bed. "Anyway, kids, Mom and I have to go out of town for a few days."

"Okay!" they all agreed eagerly. They all had some shit to get into while their parents were away and they looked forward to their parents' frequent trips.

Yolo came down to hug and kiss her babies, including Xavier and Rico, but turned her nose up at Asad. "You, stay from under her bed!" Yolo dared the confused boy.

"Huh?" Asad asked, turning to Killa for help only to get a shrug in reply.

"Remember, no rice, bread or sugar, Big Mama," Shyne sang and laughed.

"Big Mama? Cash me outside den! How 'bout that," Yolo dared. Shyne once again escaped injury when Killa pulled her mother outside. Yolo was still popping off all the way out the door. "Sup? Sup, scared? Let me get a one with her! Come on, Killa! Please!"

****

"He looks familiar," Yolo said, furrowing her brow at the man in front of them in the long ass line to get through security.

Killa looked the man up and down to see if he recognized him from somewhere. He took in his high water pants along with is big, fluffy beard, which both spelled Muslim even before he saw the prostration mark on his forehead. A soft murmur could be heard as he glorified God, praised God and declared his oneness while he waited in line. It created a sense of peace that spread to both Killa and Yolo. Only in the remembrance of God do hearts find rest. Only, it didn't last long.

"Excuse me," A TSA agent politely said to the man. He could afford to be polite with two burly cops flanking him.

"Yes?" the brother replied just as politely even though he was slightly perturbed at the distraction. After all, that is the devil's job, to keep you from the remembrance of God.

"Sa'id Salaam, you're on the no-fly list. Your name has been flagged," he announced as the cops seized him. "You're being deported back to Yemen. Take him away!"

"Yemen? But... I'm from the Bronx!" he shouted as he was carted away.

"So... If he's on the no-fly list... How's he supposed to get back to Yemen?" Yolo wondered, scrunching up her pretty face.

"Hope his ass ain't on the no-swim list cuz he gon' have to swim," Killa joked. Now with the peace gone, the two went back to their favorite pastime, talking about people.

"Look at her!" Yolo said, pointing at a dark-skinned girl with green contacts. "Bitch look like an X-box."

****

"Thug Life! The world is ares," Tip screamed. He meant 'ours' but he was so dumb that he even made typos when he spoke. Too dumb to get a job and too lazy to hustle, so he took to a life of crime.

Being a big motherfucker at 6'5, he just took whatever he wanted. The other dumb, lazy niggas in the hood were on some *if you can't beat 'im, join 'im* bullshit after he robbed and beat most of them, so they fell in line behind him to form Thug Life.

The crew started out terrorizing the underworld of Charlotte. They robbed all the dealers until it was cheaper for the dope boys to just pay a tax. Prostitutes had to fuck for free whenever Tip or one of his crew got horny.

On lives the old adage, *Give them an inch, and they take a yard.* Or as Eddie Murphy once said, "Give a nigga a rope and he wanna be a cowboy." Well, the members of Thug Life had turned into cowboys and now had their sights set on working class citizens. Had they stuck to street people, they may have been okay. However, when they started raping teen girls, someone started reporting their asses. The whistleblower didn't call the cops. They called 1-800-Killa.

****

"I love this city!" Yolo exclaimed as Killa navigated the rental car through the city.

"Mmhmm," he replied half-heartedly. The six-week wait was up and his one-track mind led his thoughts to straight between her legs. He reached over and massaged her thigh. Her legs spread so he could go as far as he wanted to.

"Mmm," Yolo moaned when his fingers slipped underneath her panties. Soon she was slippery wet as they moved in and out of her. She closed her eyes and focused on her impending orgasm.

"Damn!" Killa admired when she came all over his fingers. He pulled his hand back and sucked her juices from his fingers.

"Hurry up!" Yolo protested and put her own fingers below. She made herself cum once more before they reached at the hotel. Once they arrived, the two rushed up the stairs to fuck. And fuck they did for the next hour.

"Pleasure before business," Killa chuckled as they snuggled in their post sex glow.

"Ugh!" Yolo protested as the large wet spot grew cold. She rushed to pull the sheet over it so she could relax. "Okay. So now, who's first?"

"According to Ray, Grip is Tip's right-hand man, but he wants the top spot for himself. We can use him to get to Tip," Killa laid out.

"Like I did with Big Rock down in B-more. He shoulda B-more careful," Yolo replied and cracked up.

"That was a classic book, but...a lame joke," he laughed. "Anyway, Grip and Flea can wait 'til after we catch the rest of the crew. I knew exactly where they'll be."

****

"I should pull a Shyne and burn that whole house down," Yolo said as she and Killa drove slowly by a house hosting a Thug Life party.

"Yo, that dream creeps me out," Killa confessed. Hearing their daughter recount the nightmare that claimed them both almost gave them nightmares of their own.

"Yeah, me too... But our baby went in! All of them!" she cheered.

"I do wanna try some of that shit out," he admitted. "Ooh, especially the one at the convention center where Sun beat and bludgeoned all those pedophiles."

"Well, baby, Home Depot is still open. We can go get some ax handles," Yolo suggested.

"No, even better...sledgehammers!" he shouted, pumping his fist. He then stomped on the gas to head to the nearest hardware store.

"Wait. Stop..." Yolo suddenly said, causing Killa to bring the car to a screeching halt. "It's hammer time!"

"Uh oh, uh oh," he rapped along with her as she pulled up the vintage rap classic. They rapped there and back until it really was hammer time.

"9-1-1, what's your emergency?" an operator asked while releasing a deep yawn. Either she was dead tired or extremely bored by the life or death emergency calls.

"Umm...Yes, well, there's a house party on...187 Mockingbird Lane, and well...there are underage girls there...drinking."

"Mockingbird Lane," the woman repeated as she checked what part of town the street was on. It was in the hood so she quickly dismissed the urgency. "I'm sure they'll be okay. We..."

"Well, they're little white girls and..."

"All units respond to 187 Mockingbird Lane! We have a..."

"Works every time," Yolo giggled. A minute later, police, paramedics and firefighters were on the scene.

Only one of the girls was white, but at least the party was broken up. Once the smoke cleared, the Thug Life members sat alone in the house. They still had plenty of weed and beer to enjoy while they played video games. No one bothered to look up at the clock on the wall. If one of them had, they would've realized what time it was.

"Hammer time!" Killa said as he and Yolo got out. He slung the sledgehammer over his shoulder while she carried the shotgun.

They were the only home invaders in town, so the front door was unlocked. The members were so caught up in the game, music and intoxicants that none of them heard death enter the room. The expectancy of death is why people shouldn't post stupid shit on social media. You never know when your last post will be your last post. The one you'll be forever remembered by, like it was written on your headstone.

"I just said *Bitches suck dick!*" one bragged and turned his phone so that his partner could see it.

"Nigga, you spelled dick wrong! It says bitches suck duck!"

"Dick got an 'o' in it?" he asked ready to fix it, but it wasn't to be. He was gonna have to live with it. Luckily, he didn't have long to live.

"It's spelled, d-i-c-k, dickhead," Yolo spelled out before firing the shotgun. The blast hit him in the neck and almost took his head clean off, but not quite. Instead, it left it laying grotesquely on its side hanging on by skin and cartilage.

"That got their attention," Killa chuckled. Yolo held them at gunpoint while he collected pistols from the coffee table and under sofa cushions. "Is that all? Don't lie!"

"Uh...Yeah," Spellcheck answered, shooting a glance downward. Killa followed his eyes and found a Desert Eagle under the sofa.

"Liar," Yolo sang and fired again. This time the shot hit its victim in his ear, flipping the top of his head into his partner's lap.

"Mannn," the man whined at the skullcap in his lap. "What y'all want with us? We just minding our business!"

"That's not what we heard!" Killa teased, trading Yolo the sledge-hammer for the shotgun. She took the hammer and moved closer.

"We heard y'all some bullies who like taking shit that don't be-long to y'all. Now pick a hand, left or right, and put it on the table."

"Mannn!" he moaned again and got shot. Killa put the triangle-shaped barrel to the back of his head and tugged on the trigger. The fifty caliber slug took his face off when it came out his face.

"Too slow," Killa explained as Yolo turned to the next thug. There were only four left to choose from.

"You! Left or right? On the table!" she barked. The man sat the game controller down and stretched his left hand out on the table. He needed his right to play video games and masturbate.

He leaned forward and closed his eyes as Yolo lifted the sledge-hammer with a grunt. They expected a loud howl on impact but didn't get one, mainly because she hit him in his head instead, caus-ing a sickening crunching sound.

"Fuck this!" number three shouted and jumped up to fight back. As soon as he did, he got gunned down, ending the fight.

"Where can I find Grip and Flea?" Yolo asked since the cousins hung together most of the time. She knew the remaining members were too low level to know Tip's whereabouts, so she didn't even ask.

"I'on know!" number two pleaded so adamantly that they had to believe him. Killa gave a shoulder shrug and then shot him too. Now there was only one.

"123 Maple Street. It's they grandma's address! They there err' Sunday for dinner," he said quickly.

"Snitch!" Yolo quipped and beat him to death with the sledge-hammer until stitches couldn't put him back together again.

"Looks like we going to Sunday dinner," Killa announced. "Hope she ain't cooking pork!"

Chapter 5

"Umm...Shyne, what are you doing?" Grandma Diedra asked when she saw Shyne with a shovel.

"Who, me?" she asked, as if there were several Shynes to pick from. She even looked around to switch her gaze from her great-grandmother's.

"Forrest. Shyne Forrest, with the shovel, what are you up to?" she asked again, bouncing her knee to rock the baby.

"Oh. Huh? I mean...Gonna go work in the garden," she replied. She'd looked everywhere else for her mother's diary, so why not try there?

"Okay. Well, pick a few fresh peppers so I can stuff them for dinner," Diedra replied and turned her attention back to the baby. She would have been better off telling the infant to pick the peppers because Shyne was on a mission.

"Ah ha!" Shyne cheered triumphantly when she unearthed the book. It was wrapped in plastic and buried right next to the peppers. She grabbed it and rushed inside to get to reading.

"Hey, where's my bell peppers?" Grandma called after Shyne as she sped through in a trail of dust and dirt.

Shyne threw her hand up and kept moving. "Okay, now where...was...I?" Shyne muttered as she flipped through the diary. She found where she had left off and began to read. She read until she drifted off to sleep and woke up in dreamland.

"Wake up, Honey!" Shyne urged her sleeping husband once again.

"Not again!" Asad moaned. He knew if he didn't give her what she wanted, she would just take it, with her freaky self. "Oh, okay!"

Shyne got what she wanted and went where she was trying to go. Poor Asad rolled back over to get a few hours of sleep before he had to get up at dawn to pray. She turned the TV on to entertain herself until round eight.

"Breaking news out of Longs, Mississippi. An all-white jury just acquitted four white men in the brutal rape and murder of a black teen, although the abduction was caught on tape and DNA from all four men was found in and on the victim. When asked about the verdict, Bobby Jackson, the jury foreman, had this to say...

"How we know she didn't rape them all and kill herself?"

Shyne heard all she needed to hear.

"And me and my brothers coming down there to fuck y'all up. You, the rest of the jury, the rapists, along with whoever else don't like it," she growled.

"Huh? Again? Okay," Asad sighed and rolled over on her.

That wasn't what she'd said, but she wasn't going to complain or turn him away.

****

"Yeah, that's fucked up!" Xavier said, breaking the grim silence that followed Shyne filling her brothers in the following day. They were so hot that the room could have spontaneously combusted. It didn't, but that didn't mean that there wasn't going to be a fire.

"Let me call Bryonna" Sun announced and stepped aside. X and Rico followed suit and called their women as well since they were all headed out on an unexpected trip.

Shyne went upstairs to get one for the road before packing a bag. Soon the Killa kids were in the airport talking about people as they waited to get through security.

"Bitch got Stevie Wonder edges!" Shyne pointed at a woman with missing edges.

"Makes no sense arguing with Stevie Wonder, he ain't letting shit go!" Xavier added. His jokes were the only proof that he wasn't blood related to Killa. Although he looked, walked and acted like his stepfather, he couldn't tell jokes for shit.

Luckily, they made it through security and boarded the plane to Jackson, Mississippi. Sun had arranged two rental cars and four rooms since it might take a while to hunt down and kill sixteen people. The four rapist would be saved for last while the twelve person jury were about to be hunted down and die violent deaths.

"Gas is cheap down here! I might be able to save a few bucks!" Shyne cheered at the low prices of the south.

"Everything is cheaper down south," Rico replied as he drove towards the city of Longs. The brother and sister duo admired the serene scenery along the way. A few hours later, they reached their hotel.

"Yo, I'm mad hungry!" Xavier announced when they all assembled back together at the hotel.

"The whole place smell like BBQ!" Sun cheered, pumping his fist.

"Yeah, barbecued pork! We down south, yo. They put the whole pig on the grill!"

"Everything from the rooter to the tooter?" Shyne asked and cracked up. Her brothers looked at her, shaking their heads.

"Anyway, I saw a Mickey D's on the next block. I'll fly and buy!" Rico offered and was gone.

"I got a buck say he come back with a girl in McDonald's uniform," Sun challenged.

His siblings put their hands behind their backs and shook their heads no.

"No bet!" Shyne declined. They all knew Rico was a playboy who bagged a broad everywhere they went.

Bagging a broad for dessert was on Rico's mind when he pulled up to the fast food joint. There was a cute white girl working the drive-thru and a few more inside. He parked and went in to check out both menus. One to eat and one to beat.

"Welcome ta McDonald's, can I help cha?" another pretty white girl said, flashing a smile and batting her big blue eyes. Rico gave her a

quick once over and decided that she could definitely help him; bust a nut, that is.

"Yeah, let me get four number fours, three cokes and one strawberry shake for my sister," he said, staring into the blue windows to her soul. He could tell she was totally smitten by her love struck stare.

"Huh?" she asked, looking bewildered by the strange words.

"Um...this...is McDonald's...and I...would like some food," he spelled out slowly.

The girl looked around then down at her uniform. Sure enough, it McDonald's and she worked there. "Oh yeah! Okay, coming right up!" she laughed and rang up the order. She let out a moan when their hands touched to make the sale.

"Did you cum?" he chuckled, turning her face beet red.

"Almost," she admitted, nodding up and down. "It don't take much."

"We'll see when you get off. What time do you get off?" he asked, putting proper emphasis on get off.

She heard it loud and clear. "Right now!" she said and turned. She scanned the restaurant until she spotted the manager. "Mary, I quit!"

****

"Here. I'm going to my own room," Rico announced when he returned with the food. He practically threw it at his siblings and rushed off.

"Pay up!" Shyne demanded when she peeked out and saw the blonde girl. They all knew he would come back with a girl and since the town was predominately white, it was safe to say he would get a white girl. The only thing left to bet on was her hair color.

"Hold up! I see brown roots! I win. Now, you pay up!" Sun replied.

"Call it a tie and let's eat!" X ordered like an older brother does. The twins complied and dug in. They weren't the only ones eating.

"Mmm...sss... Slurp. Gag," came from the girl as she slobbed on Rico's knob while he ate.

He frantically stuffed the food onto his face while she did the same with his dick. "So, you knew that girl who got killed?" he asked, twirling her color-treated blonde hair in his fingers.

"Mmhmm," she nodded since her mouth was full. She filled him in and sucked him off at the same time, multi-tasking at its absolute finest. "Shandrikea... Mmm...slurp...gag...went to school with... Mmm...slurp...me. She...slurp...was a good girl."

Rico grew madder as she told him all about the sweet black girl who was raped and killed at the hands of the racists. She also knew the former high school footballers just as well. Well enough to give up their addresses and hangout spots.

He rewarded her by helping her out of her clothes while she slurped. He tossed them across the room since they smelled like French fries. He reached between her thighs and played in her hot apple pie just before giving up a thick milkshake for her to swallow down. He still needed info on the jury, but it would have to wait.

"Get on your hands and knees," he directed, taking off the rest of his clothes and rolling a condom down his shaft as he did.

"Like this?" she asked, arching her back in the perfect position for back shots. Obviously it was a rhetorical question which he answered by sliding deep inside of her.

Rico spent the rest of the night folding the girl up like a piece of paper used in origami. By morning he had the names, addresses and favorite meals of each of the jurors.

"Get dressed. I'll take you home," he offered after they showered.

"Home?" she asked, wondering what it meant. As far as she was concerned, she could live there with him inside of her for the rest of her life.

"Yeah, you know, where you live, with your family," he reminded.

"Oh yeah. Okay, I guess," she sighed and put her French fry smelling clothes back on. "Guess, I'll go to work later on."

"Didn't you quit?" he reminded. *It wasn't the first time a cashier had dropped everything to leave with him and it probably wouldn't be the last. It was, however, the first time one had leapt over the counter, though, and he doubted if anyone would ever top that.*

"Yeah, but Mary's my auntie, so she'll be alright. Besides, her son was one of..."

"Shit!" Shyne shouted at being awakened from her dream. It was just getting to the good part when she was rudely interrupted.

"Excuse me, young lady?" Grandma Diedra asked, raising both eyebrows.

"Umm... I love you, Great Grandma," she sang and smiled.

"Mmhmm," Grandma said, twisting her lips. "Get up so you aren't late for school."

"Okay, you sexy old lady! You go, girl! Work it, girl," she cheered as her great-grandmother left the room. She heard the woman crack up out in the hallway and smiled.

Chapter 6

"DO NOT CUM! Shit!" Yolo fussed when Killa did it again. His pull-out game was non-existent. "Bruh, you get me pregnant and I'ma fuck you up!"

"'Kay," he replied. If that good pussy meant ten more kids then so be it. His life of crime had put millions in the bank so he could afford them.

"'Kay? I'm talking 'bout real stuff and you say 'kay! I got your 'kay!"

"That shit so good!" Killa cheered like his team had just scored. Actually, since he'd just gotten some pussy, his team had scored. "Yo, don't forget we're married now. Plus, we're financially straight. I don't mind having more kids. Be like my cousin Cam."

"Well, you ain't the one who gotta carry and deliver them, so..." she shot back even though she didn't mean it. She'd wanted this man her whole life and she'd gotten him. She would have twenty more of his kids if he wanted her to. "Just no more girls! I can't take another Shyne!"

"You and Shyne," Killa laughed. The two were just alike and best friends. "Anyway, let's get dressed and go kill some people."

"Let's!" she cheered and rolled off the bed. They showered separately to save time since they knew they'd end up fucking again if they went in together.

****

"The fuck?" Tip replied to the news of the massacre. The downside of being a fucked up person is making a lot of enemies. It literally could have been anyone of the dope boys or legit people they'd robbed or extorted.

"That shit was crazy!" Grip reported. He'd happened to swing by to see if the party was still going on and found the crew in pieces.

"Who we hit last?" he asked, scratching his head. He and his lieutenant spent most of the day going back and forth debating on who it could have been.

"The Chinese restaurant?" Flea asked fearfully since it was his idea to extort them. He'd forced them to deliver shrimp fried rice every day for free. They made the free delivery after every member of the family spit in the food.

"Nah, plus that shit be good!" Tip said since he'd just polished off an extra-large with extra saliva in it.

"Yeah, it do. If we ain't have to eat at Granny's, I would've smashed some too!" Grip agreed. "Tradition is tradition, you know."

"I know," he replied even though he didn't. He'd long ago burned all bridges with all kith and kin. He had no loyalty to anything. "Anyway, let's hit the scrip club later!"

"Fa sho!" Flea agreed. Nothing set off Granny's collards like a hot oiled thot. They shook hands and left Tip's secret hideout.

"Guess that's the secret hideout, huh?" Killa chuckled when the men emerged. Putting the GPS tracker on their car sure beat following them around all day.

"Well, let's grab a bite before dinner," Yolo suggested. "How about Chinese?"

"Chinese sounds great," he agreed. Killa actually spoke some Chinese, not a lot but enough to make a deal to make a delivery. They got it to go so they could get to Granny's house before the victims.

****

"Let's try not to hurt the old lady. It's not her fault her grandsons grew up to be scumbags," Yolo suggested as they walked up the walk to the door.

"Mamas, don't let your sons grow up to be scumbags," Killa sang with a country twang. Yolo didn't think it was funny and twisted her lips to prove it. "Oh, okay, we can spare her. I'll tie her up, gently."

"Be nice," she reiterated and rang the bell. The loud yapping of one of those loud as little yapping dogs could be heard immediately. "Hate those fucking loud ass, little yapping ass dogs."

"Be nice to the dogs," Killa teased since he had to be nice to the old lady.

Both agreed, but we'll just have to see how things play out.

"Yes?" a sweet little lady asked while her ferocious one and a half pound dog darted back and forth between her legs baring its teeth.

"Yes... Um...we're friends of Grip and Flea and um... they invited us to dinner," Killa explained while Yolo glared at the dog. She wish she'd worn her fangs to bare back at the mutt.

"Melvin and David have friends?" she wondered with a curious frown. Even she knew that her grandboys were dicks. "Okay, well, come on in. I got a big pot of neck bones just a boiling on the stove."

"Thank you," Yolo said, stepping in in front of her husband since the old lady kept smiling her plastic teeth at him. She didn't give a fuck if a chick was eight or eighty, she didn't play about her man.

"Smells good in here!" Killa lied. The smell of the bubbling pork made the two killers want to wretch and hold their breath.

"OUCH! Hey, that little dog bit me!" Yolo growled when the dog took a nip at one of her ankles.

"That's a lie! My Angel don't bite!" the old lady shot back, like she was ready to fight about it.

Yolo just pursed her lips together and nodded. "You got that," she told both the dog and its owner since she had plans for the both of them.

"Wanna see some pictures of the boys from when they were little?" the lady offered. She took Killa by the arm and led him into her bedroom. "You can stay out here and play with Angel."

"I sure will," Yolo giggled.

The old lady had played right into their plan and didn't even know it. As soon as she and Killa entered her room and closed the door, Yolo got to work. The first order of business was the dog. It snarled and snapped as she scooped it up. She then took it straight into the kitchen and dropped its little yapping ass into the pot of neck bones.

"This is David at age eight," the lady narrated and turned the page of the photo album. Meanwhile, Killa pulled out the plastic ties to tie her up with. "This is David... Let me see yo' dick!"

"Handsome little fel—wait... What?" he asked when her words processed.

"Your dick, is it fat? Lemme see it," she said again greedily. This was exactly why no one from the church stopped by to see her. She'd cracked on the pastor, the deacons, the choir director and every other member who'd dropped by to see her.

"Lady, NO!" he said and began to secure her firmly to her bedpost. All the while, she kept asking to see his dick.

Killa finished his task and joined Yolo back out front. "Where's Angel?"

"Huh?" she asked instead of admitting that she'd used her to season the neck bones. "Why is your zipper down?"

"Huh?" he asked instead of admitting that he'd shown the old lady his dick, with his nasty ass. "They'll be here soon."

****

"Hope this ole bitty cooked some neck bones," Grip announced as he turned onto his grandmother's street.

"And macaroni and cheese," his cousin added, rubbing his hands together in eager anticipation.

The old lady did bake a mean batch of mac and cheese. Killa had just he finished a second helping.

"That was good! You need to get the recipe because yours is kinda wack," Killa confessed.

"Okay, Baby, let me fix you a plate of these neck bones," she offered to get him back. Luckily for him, they were pork and their guests arrived.

"Looks like they're here," Killa replied to the knock at the door. "Go let them in and bring 'em here."

"'Kay," she said, putting a little extra sway in her hips for him. She was feeling and looking sexy when she opened the door.

"Who are you?" Grip asked, looking at her crotch, breasts and then back down at her crotch. "Where's my Granny?"

"Not in my pussy!" she chuckled. "She's in back, come on in."

Both men followed her swaying booty, as if they were being hypnotized by a swinging pendulum, through the door, past the living room and into the kitchen straight into trouble.

"Who are you?" Flea asked the man with the gun. Meanwhile, Grip was still staring at Yolo's body parts. He still hadn't even seen her face.

"I'm a killer named Killa. Now, sit down," he answered and ordered. His tone was pleasant but the gun in his hand wasn't so the two quickly complied. Yolo strapped their ankles to the chairs and then moved on to do the same to their wrists.

"Leave one hand free so they can eat," Killa reminded. It was only right to let the condemned men eat a last meal.

"Oh yeah!" she laughed. Once she finished, she began to fix their plates. She was pleased to see how tender Angel had become. She made sure each got a good portion of dog with their neck bones. They weren't quite sure what was going on, but they were hungry so they used their free hands to eat with.

"Granny put her foot in this!" Grip cheered as he shoveled the food into his mouth.

"Well, I tossed in a lil' something, too," Yolo said proudly. At the same time, Killa placed a metal ring around each of their necks. He then attached a string to the lever on both and laid the ends on the table.

"What's, mmm... that?" Flea asked between bites of Angel and neck bones. Killa nodded at Yolo to give an explanation.

"This, my friends, is the DC 2000," she announced as if it were a game show. "We've added a cord to each so that the two of you can do the honors of killing one another.

"Or you can chose door number two... I shoot granny in her head before I kill you both," Killa tossed in, waving his gun.

"Okay, it's either granny or us, or kill granny and us?" Grip needed to know. He would gladly trade her life for theirs if it was on the table.

"Shoot him," Yolo said, disgusted by his bitch ass reply.

"Nah, let him kill him. Matter of fact, whoever kills the other, gets to... Damn!" Killa laughed. He didn't even get to finish the lie before both went for the cords and tugged them. Both heads flipped off and landed right side up in the bowls of dog and pork.

"No one's gonna win this staring contest," Yolo laughed. "Let the lady loose so we can go."

"'Kay. See you outside," he said, retrieving the car keys from Grip's pocket. It was under a wad of stolen money that he took too.

"A'ight," she said after collecting the DC 2000s. She gave them a rinse under the sink so they could be used again. After all, they didn't want to make anyone sick.

"Sorry 'bout the mess in the kitchen. I hope this helps," he said, showing her the cash. He removed the gag from her mouth then cut the ties that bound her. "Enjoy."

"Park their car somewhere so we can use it to roll up on Tip later. Then...Why is your zipper down again?"

"Huh?"

Chapter 7

"Have you been fighting?" Diedra fussed when her grandkids came in. Their clothes were disheveled and torn, and Rico and Shyne both a knot on their heads.

"Not each other!" Xavier made clear since that would really get them beat up. Grandma Diedra didn't mind them fighting, other people's children that is, but not each other.

"Would have won, too, but they just kept coming. It was too many of them," Shyne explained. She may have just gotten beat up but at least she was happy about it.

"There was like twenty of them and they still couldn't do us nothing," Rico bragged, holding his chin up. He reminded her of Killa at that age. Not quite, though, because Killa would have aired the projects out if he'd gotten jumped.

"They jumped y'all? Who?" the old lady asked with a twinge of violence, causing her temple to jump.

"The Jones family. I shot a one with Mike at school and won, so him and his cousins jumped me after school and I won that, too," X explained.

"And the ones that go to our school was talking 'bout helping so we got involved, too," Sun said on behalf of himself, Shyne and Rico. "Then they had some grown men out here and still couldn't really do us nothing!"

"One of them men grabbed my butt!" Shyne fussed. She blacked his eye in return but she still was hot about it.

"Who?" Diedra asked, boiling with rage. She couldn't wait to report this to Killa when he came home.

"Thomas Jones, Mike's uncle. He like twenty-five!" Xavier said, like he was one-hundred and twenty-five. It didn't matter, though, because unless his birthday was within the next day or two, he wasn't going to make it to see twenty-six.

"Thomas Jones, age twenty-five. Thomas Jones..." she repeated to herself to lock it in so she could look him up. She did and found an address. Now, Killa needed to come on home before she took matters into her own hands. "Must think ol' Diedra won't bust something!"

****

"Bruh!" Yolo fussed when Killa did it again. This time it was her fault since she was on the verge of climax herself and didn't make him pull out.

"Sis," he shot back with a laugh. "Don't worry, Ma. If you get pregnant, I got you."

"Got me how? Like, carry it and deliver it? That shit ain't no joke!" she said even though she had baby names already picked out. At the rate they fucked, it was just a matter of time, not when or if.

"You think I need a haircut?" he asked, changing the subject. It worked and she pursed her lips together while checking out his hairline.

"Probably. Wait 'til we get back," she decided. Yolo reached for her phone and said, "Let me check on my babies."

"I'm not here if they ask!" Killa said fearfully as he ducked into the bathroom. He jumped into the shower and turned the water on.

"Punk!" she called after him just as Sun took her call.

"Yo, Mama!" he shot back and cracked up. The revelry didn't last long before he turned back into a momma's boy. "When you coming home?"

"In a couple of days. You guys taking care of your grandma and sisters?" she asked, already knowing that they were.

"Yes," he replied, deciding not to mention getting jumped or the knot on Shyne's head. "Where's Pop?"

"Hold on," Yolo said, rolling out of the bed. She barged into the bathroom and stuck the waterproof phone in his face "Kids wanna talk to you."

"Sup, yo?" Killa greeted while shaking his head at Yolo. "In a couple of days. You taking care of Grandma, Shyne and..."

Yolo climbed in behind Killa and washed the sex away. He was stuck talking to the entire clan while she showered and got out. By the time he joined her back in the room, she was fully dressed and waiting on him.

"Time to kill," Yolo proclaimed with a wicked smile. It wasn't anywhere near as wicked as the small caliber pistol in her hand.

"Twenty-two Twos?" he asked eagerly. His eyes lit up like a child in a candy store at the notion. He wasn't talking about the classic song off Jay-Z's classic *Reasonable Doubt* album. Their version of Twenty-two Twos was shooting a victim twenty-two times with a .22 caliber pistol. A slow, painful death if ever there was one.

"Indeed!" she smiled happily. She happily watched the handsome man get dressed, dressed to kill, and once he finished, they set out to do just that.

****

"Stop! Wait! No! Hold up!" Little Shanita pleaded as Tip tried to put the top of his dick in her. Her pleas fell on deaf ears as he continued on as if she hadn't spoken. She had smoked his weed and drank his beer, after all.

"Hush!" he demanded. The one thing he hated about his rape victims was their whining. "Shut up and take this dick, bitch! You wasn't saying wait, hol'up when you was smoking my weed!"

Shanita let out a loud sigh and braced herself to be raped. It wouldn't be the first time that someone took some pussy after she'd smoked up their weed. Just as he was about to force himself inside, two strangers entered through the front and back doors.

"Make him stop!" Shanita pleaded to the couple. "I said no!"

"NO...MEANS...NO," Yolo said, aiming the pistol at his earhole.

"She smoked all my weed and... Who is you?" he demanded back and forth between Killa and Yolo. He settled on Killa since he was a dude and would be able to relate. "Bruh, she smoked my weed. Now she wanna call y'all when I wanna fuck!"

"Well, she did smoke your weed, so..." Killa shrugged to teach the teen a lesson. "She didn't call us, though."

"So, get your ass off of her!" Yolo growled while screwing a long silencer on the pistol in her hand. "Can you drive, sis?"

"Yes," she whined as she tried to put her shredded clothes back on. She had to tie knots in her tank top due to Tip having ripped it off.

"Take his car. He won't need it where he's going," Killa said, tossing her the keys. The room went silent until they heard the car pull away.

"One," Yolo announced, firing the first round into his calf muscle. The gun may have been silent but Tip certainly wasn't when that hot lead entered his flesh.

"Yeeooow!" he howled like a Broadway opera singer. He hit a similar note when she hit him in his other leg. "Yeeeooooow!"

"Want some of this?" she shouted over his screams. Killa nodded and reached for the gun, but she pumped a round into his ass cheek before handing it over.

"Wha-what are y'all doing?" Tip pleaded, trying to shield himself with his hand.

"Killing you, duh!" Yolo teased. Killa added injury to insult by firing a round into each palm.

"How many is that?" he asked Yolo as he put one in the top of his foot.

"Six, seven? Man, we gonna have to start over!" she fussed, stomping her feet.

"Six! That's six! Both legs, ass, hands and foot," Tip shouted.

"Seven, eight, nine," Yolo quipped, pumping three more bullets into him. All were flesh wounds designed to hurt not kill. The steady flow of blood from all the holes would eventually kill him. That's why you had to get all twenty-two bullets into him before he bled out to win. Either way, he loses.

"Ten, eleven, twelve," Killa counted, hitting him in both earlobes and the other ass cheek.

"Sheesh!" Yolo fussed, putting foam earplugs into her ears. "Niggas don't be doing all that screaming when they terrorizing the hood!"

She was right, too. Niggas be doing the most when they're running around slinging dope and busting their gun, then they cry foul and play victim when it's time to pay the piper. Tip kept right on crying the blues while Killa and Yolo hit him with twenty-two twos.

"Yay!" Yolo cheered and did a little dance when Tip made it through the twenty-two shots. The celebration was as short lived as Tip when round twenty-three hit him in his forehead.

"Bet he coulda went ten, twelve more," Killa mused as they left the crime scene.

"Perhaps, but I want to get back home to my babies," she pouted.

That was all he needed to hear to cut the trip short and go home.

Chapter 8

"Why, hello, Asad," Diedra sang delightfully when she saw him walk by. She had actually been stalking and lying in wait for the home-schooler to come outside. She even had a plate full of warm cookies fresh out of the oven.

"Umm... As salaamu alaikum," he greeted skeptically. This was the same old lady who watched him like a hawk anytime he and Shyne were in the same room. Shyne's dream about all those damn kids had everybody side-eyeing him. He knew the cookies were a trap, but they were fresh baked chocolate chunk cookies.

"That's it," she cooed when he stuffed three into his mouth. "Eat up, son, and show me where the Jones family lives."

"Okay," he shrugged and accepted the plate. He happily munched as they walked up and over a few blocks. His mouth was full so he just pointed at the rundown house.

Three generations of Jones lived in the three bedroom house. It was obvious that none of them intended to cut the grass, paint the house or pick up the malt liquor cans from the yard. The Jones kids were busy terrorizing at all levels at school while their mom was still chasing cars in search of get high money. Grandma Jones was out at bingo, leaving only one behind.

"Thomas Jones, age twenty-five..." Diedra mumbled to herself as they walked by without even slowing down. One of her great-grand-daughter's vivid dreams came to mind as she scanned the house. They made it back to their own block and parted ways. Asad continued on with his trip to the store while she grabbed the tool box. She found what she was looking for and marched back up the street.

"Grown man fighting my grandbabies and he grabbed my Shyne's narrow little butt!" the lady fumed while fiddling with the gas line. It took a few minutes but in the end, she managed to direct the flow into the house. She let out a lonely sigh as she went into her purse and parted with one of her neatly rolled joints. She grabbed her lighter and tossed both into the mail slot on the door. She rang the bell and rushed off.

"Who? I said, who! Stay out there then!" Thomas yelled from the sofa bed. It didn't pull out or anything, he'd just made it his bed since all the bedrooms were full. He did a double take and blinked at the joint on the floor. Ironically, his older sister was doing the same thing with a pebble that looked like a crack rock.

Both siblings went in for a closer look. She was disappointed when it was just a pebble. He, however, struck the jackpot when he sniffed and saw that the joint was legit. Thomas frowned up as the rotten egg smell of the hissing gas filled the house. He was used to various odors with all the kids that lived in the house, so he thought nothing of it. Instead, he sat back on the sofa and stuck the joint in his mouth. It took a couple of flicks of the well-used lighter to light and then...

"Dang!" Diedra giggled as the explosion shook the ground. It put a happy skip in the old lady's gait. It was just like old times, but that's another story.

****

"Honey, we're home!" Killa proclaimed when they arrived back at the house. It started a small stampede as the kids rushed in for hugs. He had to wait his turn since Yolo got love first. Even X and Rico mobbed her before him.

"Where's my baby?" Yolo asked once she was free. On cue, Diedra came in holding her namesake and handed her over. "There she is, there's my sweet baby!"

"So, what we miss?" Killa asked and braced himself. No telling what this bunch had gotten into during their absence. They'd heard about the explosion and wondered who would take credit for it. Not Isis or Al Qaeda, but Sun, Shyne, Xavier or Rico.

"We ain't had nothing to do with nothing!" Diedra declared, holding her hands up in surrender. "I been right here, all day!"

"O...kay," Killa said curiously. If he didn't know any better...

The kids began to chatter, killing the awkward moment. Grandma slinked into the kitchen to begin dinner while Yolo took her infant away to play.

"We fought the Jones again! All of them!" Xavier informed. "The grown uncle even jumped in, but we ain't gotta worry about him no more."

"He got blown up!" Rico cheered and pumped his fist triumphantly.

"That's what he get for grabbing my booty!" Shyne said, all sassy like Shyne does.

"What booty?" Killa asked, turning the little girl to the side to look. "Nope, no booty there."

"I got it!" X called in response to the chiming of the doorbell. He rushed over and opened the door to let Asad in.

"As salaamu alaykum!" he greeted and waved. Shyne started giggling and fluttering her eyelashes like she did whenever he came in. She was far from boy crazy, but she was definitely crazy about this boy.

"What's been up, my brother?" Killa asked the kid. He made sure to raise his voice and boom down upon him to intimidate.

Asad just giggled in amusement. "Nothing, Abu. Me and Miss Diedra went from a walk. I showed her where..."

"Hey, Asad! Good to see you!" Diedra shouted as she rushed in. Asad opened his mouth to reply, but she shoved a cookie into it and dragged him away.

"What...a...strange...lady," Killa said in wonderment then turned to Shyne to ask, "What does Abu mean?"

"It means dad. He called you dad," she explained.

****

"Damn girl got into my diary again!" Yolo fussed. "I buried it in the garden and she dug it up!"

"Nosey ass," Killa said, as if she didn't get it from her. She was sassy and pretty like her mother, but nosey like her daddy.

"Hmm, wonder where she gets that from," she quipped and began to write. Killa tried to wait until she finished so he could fuck her but sleep crept up and claimed him.

He wasn't the only one. Shyne banged her head gently on her pillow until she fell asleep. She went to sleep on Long Island, New York but awoke in Longs, Mississippi right where they left off...

"Wake up, Shyne, we got some killing to do," Sun said, shaking his sister awake in her dream.

"Hells yeah!" Shyne said, looking around. She popped up and rushed to look at her grown up lady parts in the mirror. Sun twisted his lips as she turned to the side to look at her booty. "That booty, Daddy!"

"Get help, Shyne, but first, get dressed so we can go pay the Johnsons a visit," he said. The jury foreman was Bobby Johnson, but four more of the jurors were Johnsons as well. That would allow them to kill five birds with one stone, a match, actually, since gas was cheap down here.

Killa's kids assembled in one room to go over the plans for the night. Using the info Rico fucked out the cashier, they made plans for the whole jury while the rapists they would save for last. Sun and Shyne would take care of the Johnson five while X and Rico would make a mess of the other seven jurors.

"Last team back buys breakfast," Rico dared. He knew Sun and Shyne would have some elaborate plan to cause a spectacular fire to consume their victims. Meanwhile, him and X planned to ride around shooting jurors in their racist heads.

"Deal!" Shyne agreed before Sun could decline. He'd much rather bust his gun than start fires. "Don't worry, bruh, I got this."

Xavier drove to do drive-bys and walk up shootings. They caught juror number one rocking on his porch. A silent round flipped him over and laid him out. Juror number two lived and died a few doors down. Rico kicked the door down and murdered him on the toilet. Three and four were at the hotel having an affair behind their spouses' backs. Rico crept in their motel room and shot him in his back. The bullet went through and killed her too. Two adulterers with one bullet.

"They up four already!" Sun griped when he read a text from Rico. "You know them two eat like pigs! This gonna cost hundreds!"

"Be easy, greasy," Shyne said, watching through binoculars. "The Johnson five have entered the building."

The building was a storage shed converted into a man cave. It was fully loaded with A/C, a flat screen TV and kegs of cold beers. Only tonight, one of the kegs was fully loaded with hot gas.

"Looks like they got company," Shyne added when two more rednecks rolled up. She would have called it off to spare innocents, but the confederate flag on the truck said they were anything but innocents. Fuck them and every racist like them.

"More the merrier," Sun said when he spotted the flag on the truck. "Birds of a feather, all die together!"

"Okay, bye-bye," Shyne sang and waved before pressing the button.

"Now that's a fire!" Sun cheered when the dark night turned bright orange from the blaze. The men inside burned to death before they even knew what burned them. "'Bout to text this to Rico."

"Hashtag, you lose!" Shyne cackled and pulled off. Rico got the video clip just as they reached the last juror.

"Aww, man!" he moaned before gunning the woman down. They would have to pay for breakfast but luckily for them, they were saved by the bell.

"Shyne, don't you hear your alarm?" Yolo fussed as she barged into her daughter's room. She opened the blinds to let the sunshine in to wake the girl. "Get up!"

"I'm up, Big Mama. Be easy, greasy," Shyne fussed and got a long overdue spanking.

Chapter 9

Shyne watched and listened to her teacher explain the mathematical equation on the board. Her eyes began to blink and get heavy. Soon, the woman's voice became garbled like an adult on Charlie Brown. Next thing she knew, she was eating breakfast with her grown brothers down in Mississippi.

"I'll have another steak and some more cheese eggs, please," Sun called out to their waitress. *Not that she was far away or hard of hearing. Rico just had her full attention.*

"Just gonna run the tab up, huh?" Xavier asked, shaking his head. The twins had already run through two T-bone steaks each and were both going for a third.

"As high as humanly possible," he laughed. This should be their last day in town once they murdered the racist rapists. First, Shyne took the liberty of flying in a ringer to give them a fitting send off to the afterlife.

"Well, you guys do your job and I'll catch y'all later. Just, please, save them for the surprise," Shyne pleaded.

"What surprise?" Xavier asked. His brothers just shook their heads at the smart comment to come.

"Wouldn't be a surprise if I told you, now would it?" she quipped and sashayed out the diner.

"Look, so um... how much time we got?" Rico asked as he and the waitress made googly eyes at each other from across the room.

"A few hours. I need a nap," Sun replied after stuffing himself with the free breakfast. "Our victims get off at five, they'll be dead by six."

"We better wait for Shyne. I don't want no problems with her," X said wearily. Everyone knows that Shyne gets what Shyne wants.

"Good, cuz I got someone to do... Eh... Something I mean," Rico announced and stood.

The girl quickly removed her apron and quit. She caught up with him at the door and off they went.

****

"We need to find another one," Adam suggested to Haney as they worked side by side on the assembly line.

"Another what?" Haney reeled. He hoped that he wasn't talking about what he thought he was, but knew that he was. "As much trouble as we had? I don't know about that!"

"We're white. As long as we get a black one, we can't get in no trouble!" Adam reminded. He threw up a hail Hitler salute to prove it.

Haney let out a sigh but ultimately agreed. "We are white, after all. Call Jimmy and Johnny and let's get us one," he agreed. "This time we gotta get rid of the body."

With that, the four made plans to rape and murder another black girl. Why shouldn't they when they'd gotten away with it the first time? Why wouldn't they when they could get away with it a second time? Well, they would have if Killa's kids hadn't been in town.

****

"What happened? What's wrong? Don't stop! Please, don't stop!" Rico's friend pleaded over her shoulder when he brought his smooth back shots to a sudden stop. At that moment, she would have given him anything she had to make him start again. That was the point of him fucking her to the verge of an orgasm and then stopping.

"I need a favor from you," he said, looking down at her pretty brown ass and pretty, pink vagina wrapped tightly around your dick.

"I get paid tomorrow. You can have it! Plus, I got twenty bucks in tips in my purse. Keep going and you can have that, too!"

"I...need...you," he said each word accompanied by a baby stroke that teased as much as it pleased. "To...lure...someone..."

"Okay!" she agreed to whatever and threw her ass at him. He gripped her hips and threw the dick. The girl collapsed and shivered, slobbered and shook from busting a nut.

Rico spent the rest of the day sexing the sexy waitress into submission. By five o'clock, she was ready to be used as bait. When she figured out who the targets were, she once again offered her paycheck to the smooth, pipe laying Rico. Instead, he laid some more pipe and they both won.

****

"We can just go across the tracks and snatch one!" Johnny suggested when they all congregated over a twelve pack of cheap beer.

"Cross the tracks? I don't know 'bout that!" Jimmy reeled. They were safe on their side, but the blacks would kill them if they caught them on their side.

"We can just post up near the tracks and catch one. Like fly-fishing. Catch us a nigger!" Adam laughed.

They piled into their pick-up and drove over to the railroad tracks that segregated the town into two. One black, one white.

The racist rapists were down to a beer when they finally struck gold. Caramel, actually, since the waitress had honey colored skin and eyes from her daddy sneaking across the tracks to get some black pussy. At least he'd had a relationship with her mother. These fuckers planned to take her, kill her and bury her body.

"Hey, there, nig—oh, pretty lady. What's your name?" their spokesman Haney greeted.

"Carlita," she replied, remembering that Rico hadn't asked even asked her name. His semen was swimming around in her belly, but she'd never even gotten his name, either.

"Where are you going, Miss Carlita? Got time to hand out and drank a few beers?" he asked.

"We ain't got no more beer!" Jimmy blurted and caught an elbow to the ribs from Johnny. "We can get some, though!"

"Actually, I have some beer at my cabin. It's out Route Ten, if y'all wanna go," she said, batting her lashes. Next thing she knew she was in *the back of the truck speeding towards Route Ten. She pointed out the directions and they arrived at the cabin in the woods.*

"Gal, this place is in the middle of nowhere! No one could even hear you scream!" Haney laughed at the inside joke.

"That's the point!" she laughed since she was in on an inside joke of her own. They watched her round ass shift under her skirt as she led them to the cabin. She opened the door and stepped aside so they could enter.

"What the..." Johnny fussed when he saw the gunmen with guns pointed at them. Both Rico and Xavier held double barrel shotguns that could chop them in half.

"Fuck?" X asked, finishing the statement for the confused redneck.

"Carlita, take their truck and go home," Rico told the girl.

She smiled so brightly at hearing her name that the dim room lit up. "You didn't ask me my name," she gushed girlishly.

"It was on your nametag. Now, beat it," Xavier fussed.

She complied and found Sun waiting at her house. He got in the truck and drove it back out to the cabin.

"What you boys want?" Jimmy demanded. He was growing tired of holding his hands up and wanted answers.

"You dead," Rico stated. "And as soon as my brother and sister get here, that's exactly what you're gonna get. Dead."

"I got your dead, nigga!" Jimmy shouted and made his move. He took two steps towards Xavier before Rico fired. The shotgun blew a hole through him large enough to see through. It folded him in half and dropped him dead on the floor.

"What happened?" Sun demanded as he rushed in with his gun drawn after hearing the shot. He saw that his brothers were fine, but one of the victims was dead. "Ooooh, Shyne gon' have a damn fit!"

"He did it!" X snitched, pointing at Rico. Johnny, Haney and Adam went wide-eyed with fear. If whoever this Shyne was was worse than getting cut in two with a buckshot then they were in deep doo-doo.

"Listen, nig—eh, fellas, I'm not sure what's going on here, but we can work it out," Haney offered diplomatically.

Sun nodded in agreement since he too was a diplomat. "Hold my gun," he said, handing the pistol to X. He then turned towards Haney and socked him so hard that it removed his front teeth. They flipped up in the air while he went down. Sun wasn't the type to kick a man while he was down so he just stomped him. Would have killed him too had the door not swung open.

"Y'all just hard-headed!" Shyne whined and pouted when she saw one of the rapists dead and another on his way. The sky went dark behind her as a large man stepped up behind her and cast a large shadow into the cabin. All guns swung his way when he stepped inside after her.

"Whoa!" the big man said, raising his big hands in the air in surrender.

"Who the fuck is that?" Rico demanded, hoping that the shotgun could bring him down if need be.

"Chill, this is Big Bubba...from Rent-A-Rapist. I found him on Craigslist. You can get almost anything from there, you know?" Shyne cheered happily.

"Rent...A...Rapist?" Sun asked and squinted at the odd name.

"Yeah, I do parties, graduations, bar mitzvahs, pretty much any event. Anytime someone needs to be raped, I can handle it," Bubba explained.

"Is that really a thing?" Xavier asked, looking between his brothers for confirmation. They both shrugged since neither had ever heard of such a thing. Shyne had, though, and that's why Bubba was there.

"That's them right there," she said, pointing to the men as Haney climbed back to his feet.

"White boys! I love white boys!" the rented rapist cheered as he rubbed his large paws together. He dug into his bag of tricks and came out with a large tube of anal lube. "They look familiar..."

"*They should. These are the fucks that raped and murdered the black girl and got away with it!*" *Sun growled.*

"*No, they didn't,*" *Bubba said, putting the lube away. That was the siblings' clue to step outside and let him do his thing.*

The killer kids tried to have a conversation over the screams from the brutal rapes taking place inside.

Bubba held Haney in an LAPD choke hold while he raped him. His friends heard his neck snap and decided to just give it up. That didn't stop Bubba from beating and choking Johnny to death while raping him, though.

"*Come on, you don't have to force me,*" *Adam said, dropping to his knees and opening his mouth.* "*I love black men!*"

"*We don't love you!*" *Bubba said, twisting the man's head completely around like a chicken's. He fell dead next to his buddies.*

"*Huh?*" *Shyne frowned when the screaming stopped.* "*He better not be in there making love to them when I paid for rape!*"

"*Yeah!*" *Sun protested, following her as she rushed inside. X and Rico were right behind the twins with their guns in hand.*

"*Sorry. I got a little carried away,*" *Bubba said, lowering his head like he was a child and Shyne was his mother.*

"*Awww, man!*" *Shyne whined when she saw the corpses.* "*I'm knocking off ten percent cuz you didn't save me any!*"

"*Take off fifty percent,*" *he offered since it was fun.* "*My bad!*"

"*Bring me the gas cans and then take him to the airport,*" *she ordered.*

Shyne gets what Shyne wants so her brothers complied. She took her time pouring gas on the dead men, even stuck the spout in their mouths to fill them up with unleaded. She used the last of the gas to make a trail outside to the car. A wicked smile spread across her face as she lit the match and tossed it. She watched the fiery trail of fire as it rushed towards the house, underneath the door and then burst into flames.

"*Yay!*"

"Glad that you could rejoin us, Miss Forrest," Shyne's teacher greeted when she awoke with a cheer. "Principal's office, now!"

Chapter 10

"We should move," Yolo announced as she and Killa relaxed in bed. Both swiped their tablets perusing their different interests. Killa was checking news sites across the country in search of anyone who needed dead. Meanwhile, she was checking sites for real estate out of state.

"Huh?" he asked. He'd heard her speak but hadn't caught the words since a story in Chicago had his attention. Three children had been murdered by gangs and that shit didn't fly with Killa. Everyone knew that Killa loves the kids.

"We should move. Look, it has five bedrooms, an in-law suite, four and a half bathrooms..." she said, passing him her tablet before reaching in his pajama pants to sweeten the deal, if need be. Plus, she was horny anyway.

"Babe, this is in Atlanta?" he reeled. She dropped down and let her lips, tongue and suction speak for her. "I love Atlanta!"

Killa loved pussy, too, so he flipped his wife around into the sixty-nine position. They mutually pleased each other until she came in his mouth. He decided not to return the favor and pulled her down. He put her on her back and spread her firm thighs.

"Sss...Mmm," Yolo hissed and moaned as he slid inside of her. She looked up into his eyes and enjoyed his slow stroke. They traded kisses and pecks as she ran her fingers all over his body.

"Mmm... Shit!" Killa warned. He was right there and tried to pull out.

"Mmm-mph," she declined and held him in place. He wasn't strong enough to overcome her and pull out. No man is, so he pushed in and let go. "Too late now anyway."

"What did you mean, too late now?" Killa asked when his breathing returned to normal minutes later.

"Means you knocked me up again. Congrats, you're gonna be a daddy again. Anyway, can I make an offer on the house?"

"Sure, I guess. Why not?" he said, trying to digest the brand new news. "We still got some killing to do. Next stop, Windy City!"

****

"Yay!" the kids cheered when their parents gave them the news about the move. Killa played the DVD sent by the realtor once they closed. The kids cheered again at the pool in the backyard with diving board and spiral slide. They argued over who got what room.

"Well, that's my room!" Shyne proclaimed when the tour reached the large master bedroom.

Killa was laughing too hard so Yolo explained. "You get your own room, but that's not it. Xavier gets a room and Sun and Rico can share. The other is a nursery for the babies," she said, breaking the other news, but they didn't catch it.

"Hmp!" Diedra huffed and crossed her arms over her chest in protest.

Killa hit the remote to speed up the disk. "And this, this is the separate in-law suite," he said when it reached the fully furnished basement unit.

"Separate entrance? Never know when I might have company," she fussed. She could fuss all she wanted but everyone saw the smile on her face.

"Now, you'll be able to smoke your weed on the patio!" Sun announced happily. Grandma Diedra smoking weed was supposed to be one of those things that everyone pretended not to know about, but Sun had no chill.

"Weed? What weed?" the old lady frowned and fanned herself. She was a quick thinker so she quickly changed the subject. "Did you say babies?"

"Yeah, well... We're pregnant!" Yolo cheered. She expected more cheers but got jeers instead.

"Boo! Boo!" Shyne fussed. She was already tired of her baby sister taking her shine. She wouldn't get any light with another baby coming. That's why she decided, "I'm not moving! I'm staying here."

"Girl, stop," Killa laughed dismissively. Although they intended on keeping the house, their ten-year-old daughter would not be living there alone. He told her so, too. "You're ten, you can't live alone."

"Asad can move in with me. We... Get her!" she shrieked as Yolo stood to come for her.

"Nah," he declined. Luckily for Shyne, her brothers stopped their mother and saved her ass once more. "Anyway, once school's out, we're moving. Your mom and I have to go out of town for a few days."

"You need to visit Chicago. Have you seen the news?" Diedra asked. She knew what they did when they went where they went and she wanted to make sure they went up there to do what they do.

"I have, and we will," he replied. "Keep watching the news."

"I will!" she cheered, knowing it was about to get that much more exciting. The bad people of Chicago were about to meet some bad people who did good.

****

"Aww man," Asad moaned when Shyne delivered the sad news with tears streaming down her pretty face. He didn't have a chance to grieve since he had to console her. Men are the protectors and maintainers of women after all. "Don't cry. Allah will protect us. He always does."

"Okay," Shyne sniffled and stopped crying. Asad said it would be okay and she believed him. He may still be just a boy, but he was still her man.

Diedra spied on them from the next room and felt some kind of way. She'd fallen in love with her husband at their age. They'd grown up, gotten married and lived happily ever after until his death. If she had anything to do with it, those two would too. She would not split them up.

"Hey, you two," Diedra barked, startling the kids as she barged in.

"I'm three feet away!" Asad insisted. He'd made sure to keep that distance after being threatened by Shyne's father, mother and grandmother.

"I need you guys to help me make some chocolate chip cookies!" she said, switching gears on them.

The cookies came out of the oven around the same time that Killa and Yolo reached the airport. They settled into the long ass security line.

"Look at this one," Killa chuckled under his breath, pointing with his head at a woman with super tight jeans on. "A walking yeast infection."

"Bruh, I know that trick! Get a free look at her booty!" Yolo protested.

The woman saw them looking and smiled at Killa. "Hey," she sang and waved, as if Yolo wasn't standing there.

"Hey! Hey what? Hey who? Hay is for horses and just cuz you got a ponytail made from a real pony's tail don't make you a horse! I got yo' damn hey! I'll..."

"Chill, yo," Killa laughed, holding her back. The woman flipped her weave and turned her nose up at Yolo. Yolo glared at the woman for the next hour. She heard her ask the person behind her to hold her spot while she went to the restroom and announced, "I gotta pee."

"So, go pee," Killa shot back, wondering why she was announcing it. Yolo headed off and he went right back to looking for people to talk about.

Yolo marched like a North Korean solider to the bathroom and stormed in. She looked around but didn't see the woman. That didn't prevent her from looking under the stalls until she found the six-inch heels she was looking for. She entered the adjacent stall and climbed over its top.

"Hey!" she sang sarcastically and commenced to beating the woman up. She kept her ponytail as a trophy and left her lumped up on the toilet.

"What are you up to?" Killa asked, twisting his lips skeptically when she returned. She was grinning wickedly and was slightly winded.

"Who? Me?" Yolo asked, pointing at herself as if he could possibly be talking about anyone else. She opened her mouth to speak as the girl came limping by on one heel, missing her ponytail. Killa just shook his head and took another glance at her booty when she passed by.

****

"Mile high?" Yolo offered once their plane was a mile high and the fasten your seatbelt sign went out.

"You really had to ask?" he asked incredulously. When did he not want some pussy? He popped up and led the way down the aisle to the restroom.

They had to wait their turn, but finally entered the cramped space. Yolo rarely wore panties which made for easy access for quickies. She turned and bent while Killa played between her legs with one hand and produced his dick with the other. He entered her cramped space and stroked them both to a quick conclusion. They then returned to their seats and fell fast asleep.

"Hello? Excuse me. Hello?" the stewardess said gently. "Welcome to Chicago. Please be careful, it's very dangerous here."

"It just got a lot more dangerous," Yolo assured her. She and Killa deplaned and set off to right some wrongs.

Chapter 11

"Welp, I'm going to bed," Shyne announced to everyone's surprise. It was just after eight, but she was stretching and yawning like it was midnight. In truth, she was just eager to experience another one of her vivid dreams.

"Well good ni—, dear," Diedra said to her back as she fled up the stairs and into her room.

"Let's see here," she said, flipping through the diary to where she'd left off. She had to let out a little chuckle at her mother's latest hiding spot. She didn't know what made Yolo think she wouldn't climb up the chimney to get the book.

"Where we going?" Grown Shyne asked her husband as he drove.

"To see Big Mama and Paw-Paw. Remember, we promised the kids?" he said, hooking his thumb behind them. Shyne turned and saw her babies watching cartoons on the overhead screen.

"They are so cute!" she gushed over her babies.

"And you are so...strange," he laughed and shook his head. Strange, but still the love of his life. He reached his hand out and she placed hers in it. They rode hand in hand to Big Mama and Paw-Paw's house.

"Looks the same," Shyne said when they pulled up to the house she'd grown up in. She hopped out and freed her children from their car seats. She carried the baby and let the toddlers toddle behind her like baby ducks following their mother.

"Hey, Shyne!" 350-pound Yolo cheered as her oldest daughter walked in. She rocked back and forth in an attempt to stand but was just too heavy. Ten children of various ages scrambled about.

"Are you running a daycare? Who are all these kids?" Shyne asked, looking around the messy room.

"Girl, stop! You know these are your brothers and sisters! Paw-Paw just can't get enough of Big Mama," she said with a chubby chuckle. As if on cue, Paw-Paw came in from the backyard.

"Killa? I mean...Daddy?" Shyne asked of the skinny man in dirty overalls wearing a wrinkled version of her famous father's face.

"Hey, Shyne," he cheered, stretching his scrawny arms out for a hug. She looked at his dirty clothes and hesitated until he snatched her up. He squeezed her tightly and transferred dirt from the garden onto her designer clothes. "Let me have a word with Big Mama, if you don't mind."

"Umm... Okay," she said as he hoisted his wife off the sofa. The whole house shook as they rushed upstairs. It really shook once they got there. "Are they? Oh, hell naw!"

"Why you think you have so many brothers and sisters? They go in!" Asad explained.

Shyne tried her best to tune out the sounds of sex emanating throughout the house. Bits of plaster fell from the ceiling in harmony with the bed's springs singing and Big Mama's moaning.

"They at it again, I see," a voice said causing Shyne to spin around. She squinted at the young woman barely dressed in a pair of tiny shorts hiked up into her crotch. A halter top gave her braless breasts the spotlight above her belly piercing. Smoke from the blunt smoldering between her fire engine red lips wafted up into her elaborate weave.

"Diedra?" Shyne asked when she recognized her baby sister. "Girl, where are your clothes?"

"Clothes? Strippers don't wear clothes!" she insisted and began to twerk. Shyne reached over to cover her husband and son's eyes as her baby sister turned up. "Turn down for what! Un! Un!"

"So, what's the plan? If it was up to me, we would just pass out a bunch of DC 2000s to all the gangbangers and hit the switches at the same time," Yolo offered.

The room went silent while Killa pondered her question and its answer. "Not a bad idea, but too much work. Would have to get them made, pass them out..." he declined. "We need to kill as many as possible as quickly as possible."

"Let's have a cookout! We can poison them," Yolo tossed in happily.

"Poison! That's it!" he said and filled her in on the time he'd distributed free weed to the Black Mob.

"I still need to bust my gun. It's only right," she said to honor the children murdered in the last few days. Killa's sources had identified three shooters responsible for stray bullets that had killed kids.

"And you shall," he laughed, producing a sniper rifle. "Debo Johnson is first up to bat."

Debo was a six foot, six inch bully who ran his block with an iron fist. Literally, since he had one made to sock people with. He socked the wrong one and he came back shooting. Debo shot back and hit a child playing on the swing in the park. We must truly be living in the last days when a child isn't safe in a park in broad daylight. The world would be a lot safer once this clown was removed from it.

****

"Seven, fuck niggas!" Debo shouted when he rolled the dice. They had come up eight, but no one argued with Debo. Plus, it was easier to let the goon cheat you out of your money than to have him snatch your pants off and take it out of your pockets.

"Dang, you win again!" Mike-Mike play fussed as Debo picked up his money off the concrete. He still had more money to donate so he let him roll again. "Bet a hunned!"

"Make it two!" Debo insisted and shook the dice. He stopped when he saw a smile spread on Mike-Mike's face. "What? Let's make it five!"

"Nothing. Okay," he agreed, watching the red dot trace his wide body. It roamed up his face and settled on his forehead. That would have been a great shot until the man yawned and offered another.

"Ooh!" Killa cheered as he watched the dot settle on his tonsils. Yolo fired and hit her mark.

Debo coughed as if he'd swallowed an insect. That is, despite the large bullet blowing the back of his head out. He sank slowly to the ground, sat Indian style and died. The dice fell from his hand and came up seven.

"Eight, fuck man!" Mike-Mike laughed and collected his money. He dug into the dead man's pockets and came out with all the money and weed he'd taken from everyone throughout the day. He wouldn't get to spend it, though.

"Nice shot!" Killa said, clapping when Yolo clapped him too. A head shot split his wig in two. He fell into Debo's lap and died with him.

"Let's go see Bone," Yolo said since Bone couldn't shoot straight either. In his defense, he was cross-eyed, but that's really no excuse. Cock-eyed people shouldn't do drive-bys. No shade to the cock-eyed people of the world, just don't do drive-bys that kill kids.

****

"What's my name? Say my name!" Bone insisted as he delivered back shots.

"Bone!" the girl moaned in ecstasy. He laid some mean pipe, but she always had him hit it from the back; his cocked eye made her giggle and that wasn't a good look during sex.

"And...what's...Bone...doing?" he asked with each pelvic thrust.

"He boning!" she replied and came all over his wood. He looked down to watch the creamy porno. It would be that last thing he saw on this side of life.

"Pull," Yolo ordered when Killa lined up his shot through the open window. It was quite a shot at that distance, but Killa was a real killer. He put a round right in the man's ear hole from two hundred yards away. The shot was so clean that Bone took a couple more strokes after the bullet came out the other side.

"In one ear and out the other!" Killa cheered. He and Yolo shared a high-five before packing up their gear and moving on to their next victim.

****

Smiley was next on the hit list. He wasn't smiling after Yolo put a slug right between his eyes. In the two days it took to kill the child killers, several more children were also killed. Gang wars raged throughout the city. It was time to put an end to them.

"Cookout time!" Yolo cheered when the big day arrived. She and Killa had sponsored multiple cookouts all over the city. Each gang had its own park that it ruled over. It wasn't safe for kids to play in them since rival gangs would often do drive-by shootings at them.

Not today, though, because today everyone was getting a free meal. No civilians were allowed to break bread with the gangbangers. That meant today was their lucky day.

"It is! It is!" Killa replied just as happily. He rubbed his hands together in anticipation. These same gangs had been trying to wipe one another out for decades. Now Killa and Yolo would do it in one afternoon.

The couple separated, going all over the city to distribute poisoned chicken, ribs, weed and malt liquor. By day's end, almost three thousand dangerous men, women and teens were stretched out. The medical examiners declared them all suicides, saving the police a bunch of time and paperwork.

"You're welcome," Killa said, looking down on Chicago as their plane lifted off. It was time to go back to New York to their children.

Chapter 12

"Tuh!" Shyne hissed at her mother and turned her nose up.

"Little girl!" Yolo fussed at the snub. "If you got something on your chest besides them little nubs, speak your mind."

"Ten kids! Really? You think it's cute having all these dang babies?" she replied, shaking her head as if it was just pitiful.

"What ten? The boys, you, and your sister make five and... Damn!" Yolo agreed. They were starting to add up with another one on the way. "We need to hurry and move!"

"Well, I've been thinking about that too, girlfriend," Shyne said.

"Oh, have you?" Yolo said, trying to stifle her amusement. She took a seat so her ten-year-old could fill her in.

"Yes, sis, actually I found an apartment in the city for Asad and me. I'll have to change schools, but..."

"The city is expensive! Did Asad get a job?" she asked as if there were high paying jobs out there for a ten-year-old.

"No, Daddy can pay our rent. He has lots of money!" she said wide-eyed with enthusiasm. "Just tell him."

"Oh no, sis. You're gonna have to tell him about this. Just please, make sure I'm there when you do!" she shot back.

"'Kay, Mommy," Shyne agreed and skipped happily on her way.

"Your daddy gonna whip your little ass, too," Yolo laughed to herself. She was still laughing when Killa came in.

"Sun or Shyne?" he asked in reply to her laughter. X and Rico were a handful as well, but the twins were hilarious. Life in the Forrest household was like a reality show.

"Shyne, but I'll let her tell you, though. So what's up with dude?" Yolo asked regarding a pimp who lived in Amityville.

"Oh, he pimping alright. Got a bunch of young girls fucking for money and he keeping it all while buying them weed, sneakers and lace fronts!"

"Well, them little tramps were fucking for free, but still..." Yolo replied. She had to stop herself from making excuses for the man. Sure, the teens were fucking but the grown man was exploiting them. Besides, killings pimps was fun. Fun to do, fun to watch and fun to write about. Snitches get stitches, and pimps get tortured and cut into little pieces while still alive.

"Well nothing, cuz come Saturday night, he's going to meet the pigs!" Killa growled.

****

"Bitch, what the fuck you doing sitting on yo' ass instead of slinging it?" Pimpin P fussed when he found Young Chili sitting in front of the TV.

"I got my period," the new girl moaned. She was new and didn't quite get it. She was about to get it though.

"Period? Bitch!" the pimp screamed and unleashed a vicious pimp slap. The sound of the slap echoed throughout the house, sending the other girls scrambling to get ready. "Now yo' mouth bleeding, too! Now, get out there and suck some dick! If a nigga want some bloody pussy, sell that to him too!"

"Okay!" Chile reeled, holding her hand up to the spot she'd been hit in. She could feel the welts starting to rise, leaving a pimp slap print in her face.

"Anyone else need the shit slapped out of them?" Pimpin P asked, making his rounds. All the young whores declined and rushed to hit the trap. Once he was alone, he kicked his feet up and changed the channel. "'Bout to watch my stories..."

"That should be the last one," Killa advised as the last of the prostitutes left the house. He backed the van into the driveway and parked it.

"Well, let's go then," Yolo sang and hopped out. Killa admired her round ass in the short dress as she went up the steps. He had to enjoy it while he could before she got big again.

"'Bout to tap that," he muttered to himself, not quite low enough that he wasn't heard.

"Is that right?" she giggled and flipped her skirt up to show her cheeks hanging out the French cut panties she wore. The banter was cut short as she rang the bell.

"Bitch better have my money," Pimpin P fussed as he stood to get the door. Like most pimps, he was a scary little bitch so he checked the peephole before opening the door. He didn't recognize the woman, but she was a woman so he opened the door. "Hello?"

"Hello," Yolo smiled in reply to his smile. Killa smiled too when he stepped from the side and shot him.

"Argh!" the pimp grunted as the electric current surged through his thin frame. His platinum teeth sparked from the Taser before he dropped and peed his pants.

"I'm not touching him!" Yolo grimaced. Killa just shook his head and dragged the man by his feet to put him in the car. The pimp's head took a beating as it bounced on the concrete steps.

"Just pull the trigger and give him some more juice if he wakes up," Killa said, handing her the gun with the wires still attached to the unconscious man's genitals.

"Like this?" she asked, shocking him awake.

"I said *if* he wakes up!" he fussed and shook his head.

"Oh! Well, he's awake now, so..." she said and pulled the trigger again. She kept pulling it and Killa kept shaking his head until they reached the house, the house out east where they kept the man eating pigs.

"Get up, Pissy P!" Killa barked once he parked. The pimp looked like he wanted to protest the name, but the pistol aimed at his face changed his mind.

"What I do?" the pimp pleaded. A lone tear escaped his eye and ran down his cheek. It didn't make it to the bottom because Yolo stepped forward and slapped a spark out of him.

"Now that's a pimp slap!" she shouted triumphantly.

"It was okay..." Killa said, turning his nose up at her effort.

"What? You think you can do better? Be my guest!" she dared and took the gun from him.

"That was it! That was perfect!" the pimp proclaimed to prevent another slap. It didn't work, though, and Killa unleashed another nasty slap that nearly broke his neck.

"Eh... It was a'ight," Yolo said, passing the pistol back to him so she could get another try. The two took turns slapping him until his face felt like it was on fire.

"Just shoot me already," he begged to stop the assault. Come to find out, he didn't like it any more than the girls he abused did.

"'Kay," she agreed and hit him with another dose of the Taser, causing him to drop shaking and slobbering to the ground.

"Okay, he's had enough. Let's let him go," Killa suggested, to his relief. As long as he lived, he could pimp another day.

"If you say so," Yolo moaned disappointedly. "Okay, go on and go, but use the back door."

"Okay. Thank you! I'm sorry for... Whatever I did. What did I do?" he wanted to know, so he wouldn't do it again.

"Pimpin' little girls, playing with their little minds, having them selling their little bodies for you," Killa explained as he reached the back door.

"Oh, that. Oh, okay. Yeah, I won't do it again," Pimpin' P lied without conviction. Probably because he didn't mean it. He actually laughed at their stupidity as he stepped out into the backyard. "Stinks back here!"

"Lights!" Yolo cheered and hit the lights. She then turned her camera on and announced, "Camera!"

"Action!" Killa added, hitting the switch that released the pigs from their pens. Pimpin' P stopped dead in his tracks when the curious hogs began to come out to investigate. They sniffed the air and smelled dinner.

"Uh oh!" the man said, realizing his predicament. He ran back to the door and tried desperately to get back inside.

"They always do that!" Yolo laughed as the man beat on the door as the pigs approached. He let out a blood curdling scream when the first hog took the first bite of him.

"They always say that!" Killa laughed at the opera worthy high note.

"Oh, and didn't you say something about tapping something?" she reminded, turning the camera on him.

Only Yolo and Killa could make love while a man was being eaten alive just a few feet away. They tuned his screams out and focused on their own moans of pleasure. They fucked as if in a race to please the other. Killa held Yolo up by her ass while she rode him in mid-air. The race concluded in a near tie as they came one behind the other.

"Good thing I'm already pregnant," she said as he pumped her full of his semen.

Chapter 13

"Oh boy," Bryonna groaned when she spotted Shyne traipsing toward her with a smile on her face. The strange girl had attached herself to her after some strange dream she'd had. Had she seen Shyne coming before Shyne had seen her, she would've run for cover. However, it was too late, so instead, she pasted a smile on her face and a greeted the girl, "Hey, girl!"

"Hey, bestie!" Shyne cheered and wrapped her into an awkward embrace. Bryonna couldn't hug her back since her arms were pinned to her sides. "I brought an extra sandwich for lunch."

"You should have brought two; you know Miranda always eats with me," she replied, reminding her of her other friend. The one that she had actually *chosen* to be friends with.

"Oh yeah. I keep forgetting about her," Shyne quipped and twisted her lips sarcastically. She let out a sigh as Miranda came into view and approached. Even Shyne recognized that there was something different about the girl. The usually happy child skipped and smiled her way through life. Now she lumbered forward like a zombie with a blank look in her eyes.

"What's wrong with you?" Bryonna asked her friend. Shyne too awaited her answer, wanting to know what had practically lobotomized the girl.

"My dad... He...came into my room and..." she said, filling them in on her traumatic experience. By the end of the story, all three were crying and mad. All three wanted to do something about it, but only one had a killer for a father and a lunatic for a mother.

****

"Grrr..." Yolo growled as Shyne filled her in on Miranda's sordid story. She knew from reading her diary who and what her parents were.

She also knew she'd just gotten the man murdered and didn't have a problem with it. She would do it herself, if she could.

"He's a biggen, Mommy," Shyne informed. She wanted to strangle the man until she saw how big he was. Miranda's father, David, was a 6'5" ex-football player who liked little girls. He was about to get fucked up for it.

"Don't tell your dad," Yolo said, hoping to keep this one for herself. Sure, she enjoyed killing with Killa, but every now and then a girl wanted a solo kill. A little *me time* and murder.

"Don't tell me what?" Killa asked, entering the room as the words still floated in the air. Yolo opened her mouth to explain alternate facts like the white house does, but Shyne spoke first.

"Oh, about my friend Miranda. Well, she's not really my friend, she's Bryonna's friend, but since we're besties, I guess she's my friend too," Shyne said and did a make believe retching action. "Anyway, her dad has been molesting her."

"Grrr..." Killa replied, feeling his blood boil. "Where do they live?"

Shyne gave up all the info she had, including pictures of the man she'd taken when he'd come to pick the girl up from school. The pervert didn't want her riding the bus anymore, afraid she might reveal his sick secrets.

"Welp, guess I'll leave you guys alone," Shyne sang and stood. Her work was done and it was time for them to do theirs.

"Wait..." Yolo remembered with a smile. "Tell your dad about the apartment you found, in the city, for you and Asad."

"Apartment! City! Asad!" Killa shrieked. "Where's my belt?

Shyne escaped without getting touched up, but David, on the other hand, wouldn't be so lucky. He was about to get fucked up.

****

"You look sleepy. Why don't you go on to bed?" David suggested, and when you're 6'5" and weigh 300 pounds, suggestions sound like orders.

"Okay," Miranda agreed, eager to escape his intense glare. Her father had been staring at her lustfully over dinner like he wanted her on his plate.

"Not you! Your mom," he corrected so he could get her alone.

"Me? It's not even seven o'clock yet. I'm not tired. As a matter of fact, I'm wide awake. On second thought, why don't you come to bed with me?" she offered along with her vagina. She was beginning to suspect that something was going on between her husband and daughter.

"Bitch, if I say you look tired, you better yawn! Sick of you back talking me! Now, take yo' ass to bed before I put one of these size sixteens in yo' ass!" he barked and chased her off.

She left because she didn't want his size sixteen in her ass. Who would want a foot that big in their ass? She went right upstairs and got on the computer. It took some searching but she finally found someone who could help.

"1-800-Killa, huh..." she said and began to type. This qualified as an emergency so she used the newest feature on the app. If someone really needed to be fucked up really quickly, you could now use the express button.

****

"Check this out?" Killa announced gleefully when the emergency request came in. He was starting to hire killers in every city to handle the abundance of requests they got, but this one he'd handle himself since it was local.

"Wow! This is no coincidence," Yolo said, reading the address they were getting ready to visit on the screen. The mother had just saved her own since Yolo had *planned* to murder her also. She didn't know if the woman was turning a blind eye to what was happening under her nose or not, so *when in doubt, murder* was her motto.

"Told you!" Killa gloated. He took the big man to be a big bully who bullied his family. He planned to break him down to size tonight.

"Yeah, yeah," she admitted and removed the extra DC 2000 she'd packed for the Mrs. from her bag. She left in the new mini DC 1000, designed to remove body parts like hands, ears, noses and even size sixteen feet. "Wanna fuck before we go?"

"Umm..." Killa contemplated. He was down to fuck anywhere, anytime, but a child was in danger. "Let's handle our business before we get down to business."

"'Kay," she agreed.

They finished packing and eased out of the house. Shyne popped up the second she heard them leave and got down to business herself.

"Let's see here..." she said as she began to pick the lock on her parents' door. Thanks to YouTube, she was a pro at it and inside a few seconds later. She scanned the room wondering where her mother could have hidden her diary this time. She couldn't believe her eyes when she saw it laying atop the nightstand. "You slipping, Ma! Owww!!!"

The mousetrap snapped shut on Shyne's little fingers. She was lucky her father had talked her mother out of a rat-trap; now that would have broken her fingers. She pried the trap open and retreated to her own room with her prize.

****

"So, would you like another drink?" David asked his date, actually it was his daughter, but in his twisted mind, he was on a date.

"I don't like it, Daddy," Miranda whined about the wine he poured her to drink. The last time he'd given it to her, it had put her to sleep and she'd woken up with him on top of her.

"Smoke?" he asked with a seductive smile, pushing a smoldering joint her way. He blew smoke rings in the air hoping to entice the minor.

Meanwhile, her mother got a response to her urgent request.

Open your back door, popped up on her screen. She frowned and twisted her lips dubiously, but what did she have to lose? She could hear her husband flirting with their daughter as she crept through the house. She pulled the door open to find two smiling killers standing outside. "1-800-Killa?"

"Take your daughter and go," Killa advised as they entered with guns.

"This will be a crime scene when you return, so don't let her back in," Yolo added as she followed him inside.

"In here!" the mother said triumphantly as she led the way. She barged in the family room first and covered her child's eyes. "Be quiet and come on!"

"Bitch, I..." David shouted and stood until the guns mad him shut up and sit back down. "What? Who are you? Don't hurt my family!"

"Don't hurt... Nigga!" Yolo fussed and fired a round into his leg.

"You shot me!" David fussed, more angry than scared. He stood and Yolo put another slug in his other leg.

"Chill, yo. Take it slow," Killa warned. "A scumbag like this deserves a nice, slow death."

"You right," she agreed, nodding but still shot him again. Killa just shook his head at his hard-headed wife. "Now strip!"

"Huh?" the man asked. He certainly understood it when he was the one forcing his child to strip. Yolo raised her pistol again, but didn't have to shot when he scrambled to get undressed.

"Oh my!" Yolo blushed when his penis swung free. She turned her face, blinking in embarrassment.

"Now, didn't you say something about a size sixteen in someone's ass?" Killa asked, reading from the complaint on the site. Meanwhile, Yolo began removing items from their bag.

"I just be talkin'. I ain't mean nothin'," David chuckled in an attempt to laugh it off. A failed attempt since neither killer found it amusing.

"Mmhmm," Killa said, slipping the DC 1000 over his big ass foot. He then stepped back and hit the switch. David took the gunshots with grace, but losing a foot was a different matter.

"Yeoow!!!" he howled when his foot came off. Ditto when the other come off.

Yolo took full advantage of the scream and shoved his foot in his mouth. "Talk about putting your foot in your mouth!" she cracked and cracked up. The killer couple high-fived at the corny joke. Killa had a joke too and it wasn't funny, either.

"Pass me the anal lube," he said, picking up the other foot. "Then again, never mind."

No one wants a size sixteen up their ass; especially their own. It took some doing, but Killa managed to get it in. Good thing his other foot was already in his mouth to muffle his screams.

"We should just leave his ass like this," Killa remarked. "This should definitely have learned him a lesson."

"True. One final touch, though," Yolo agreed. She stepped forward and put a bullet in his head. "Perfect!"

Chapter 14

Yolo and Killa left the murder scene and headed home. It wasn't far, but Killa decided to take a little detour. Yolo giggled like a teenager when he pulled up to the park. It was where cheap or broke guys took cheap or broke girls to fuck. They were neither, but were still there to fuck. This way they could get as loud as they wanted and not wake the kids. After all, they wouldn't want to interrupt Shyne's dream.

"Stripper?" Shyne reeled at her sister's twerking. Her three-year-old came over and started flipping dollar bills at her. "Asad, get him!"

"Who?" Asad asked as he too started flipping dollar bills at her. This dream was not going her way.

"Come here, girl!" Shyne fussed and snatched sister aside. She started to take her upstairs, but the sound of their father making love to their 300-pound mother was just too much. So instead, she pulled her outside to have a heart to heart talk with her. "What the hell are you doing? I know Mommy raised us right!"

"She did, but my boyfriend made me do it. He said he would beat me if I didn't!" she said and broke down into tears.

Shyne could see her baby sister in the woman's face and got mad. Flaming mad. "Where is this boyfriend of yours?" she snarled dangerously.

"J-Mo is in the trap, like always," Diedra Junior pouted. "Are you gonna tell our brothers?"

"Nope," Shyne said, ready to handle it herself.

J-Mo spent most of his time in the trap and he was now about to get trapped.

****

"Uh. Uh. Uh. Un huh!" J-Mo cheered as two more young girls twerked for weed. He loved how society, social media and modern music had turned girls into vulnerable and easy prey. If their favorite singer was sucking dick in public and twerking, why wouldn't they want to? If their favorite rapper was a drug addict then why shouldn't they want to be?

The trap was a rundown house at the end of a rundown block. A steady flow of rundown junkies flowed to and from it like worker ants. The money was good and young teens killed the monotony of slinging crack all day. Once he got his hooks in deep enough, J-Mo would put the young girls in strip clubs to make him even more money. Just like he'd done with Shyne's little sister.

That's why Shyne was currently welding the burglar bars shut tight. He was really about to be trapped. In a death trap. Once she finished, she cut the gas line also so the house could fill up with gas, a little trick she'd picked up from her mother's diary. She timed it perfectly and entered the house.

"Hey, guys! I said, hey guys!" Shyne screamed to be heard over the loud music.

J-Mo turned then turned back to the twerk team. The gun finally registered and he snapped his head back around and turned off the music. He looked over at his gun on the table and wondered if he could make it.

"You can try," Shyne warned, hoping he wouldn't. One spark from either gun would set the gas off. In another minute, a spark would definitely set it off.

"What, you supposed to be robbing me? By yourself? Who put you up to this?" he asked, looking behind her.

"Out!" she demanded, sending the young girls scurrying. One made sure to grab the blunt they had been dancing for on her way out. "No, I'm not robbing you. I came for the girls. Cuff yourself and wait five minutes after I leave before you try to get loose."

"I got you, ma. Gon' have you shaking that ass too" J-Mo warned as he cuffed his wrist to the arm of the sofa. Shyne backed out quickly while aiming at his face.

"*Okay, bye-bye!*" *she shouted from the doorway and sprinted to the car. She tore out of there passing the twerkers at the end of the block.*

"*Bitch fucked up! I'ma see you again!*" *J-Mo fussed as he pulled at the handcuffs. He couldn't pull free, but he could just reach his pistol. He stretched and grabbed it off the sofa. A smile spread on his face as he took aim. He died with that smile on his face when the gunshot exploded the gas.*

"Yay!" Shyne cheered in her sleep, while her mother stood over her. Yolo looked at her daughter's swollen fingers and shook her head. She picked up her diary and let the girl sleep.

****

"Good morning, Shyne. Girl, what happened to your hand?" Grandma Diedra reeled when Shyne came to the table for breakfast. The girl had used Popsicle sticks to make a splint for her injured fingers.

"Huh? Nothing!" she said and stuffed food in her mouth so she wouldn't have to talk.

"There's my little mouse!" Yolo sang as she breezed into the kitchen with the baby. The infant darted her little hazel eyes at her family as her mom fixed her a bottle.

The boys didn't catch the joke, but snickered nonetheless. They loved when Shyne got fussed at instead of them. They stayed in so much trouble that they constantly got fussed at. Good thing for Shyne the mouthful of food prevented her from the smart reply that would've gotten her butt whipped before school.

A few minutes later, the house was empty and quiet thanks to the kids having headed to the bus stop. Xavier's bus came last so he made sure to watch over his younger siblings until theirs came.

"Hey, Bryonna!" Shyne shouted, waving her splinted hand. Bryonna tried to duck behind a tree, but it was too late. "Girl, I see you! Come on out!"

"Oh hey, Shyne," she sighed. It was finally dawning on her that they were going to be friends whether she liked it or not. Just like the dream, except she was not marrying Sun when they grew up. She twisted her face at the thought, having just watched him pick his nose. He scrunched his face up at the large booger that came out before wiping it on some kid's book bag. "Ewww!"

****

"Here's one!" Yolo announced as she scanned the 1-800-Killa site. Killers had been posting their resumes in response to the help wanted post. The country was full of so many bad people in need of dead that they couldn't possibly handle the load alone.

Killa was doing some recruiting himself, scanning the internet for vigilante killings. Bad people who killed bad people were okay in his book. If he could unite them, the world would be a better place.

"Looks like Dexter from that series," Killa said, looking over her shoulder. He didn't, but the unassuming white guy had an impressive resume. He was a real killer for sure.

"I like this one," Yolo said of the attached news report of a Cleveland massacre. "Ten men suspected of selling bad dope were killed in..."

"I remember that! I wanted to get them myself!" Killa cheered. The men paid the police and operated with immunity. Since the police wouldn't do anything, Clyde did.

"Pizza!" he replied to the barking man behind the door. The dealer snatched the door open and shoved a gun against his nose.

"We ain't ordered no pizza, white boy," he teased. He inhaled a whiff of the cheese and sauce and quickly had a change of heart. "How much?"

"J-j-just k-keep it," Clyde stuttered and passed off the pies. He walked away with a smile as the man took them inside and slammed the door.

"Sodium cyanide, nice!" she nodded. "Let's sign him up!"

"Let's," Killa agreed. He was the first to join 1-800-Killa, but he wouldn't be the last.

By the end of the day, they had added three more murderers to the team. That allowed them to focus on requests from the tristate area. Good thing, too, since Yolo was pregnant and it was time to move down south.

Chapter 15

"Are you packed? The movers will be here in the morning," Yolo said as she waddled into Shyne's room. She got the answer to her question on her own as she looked around the room. The girl hadn't packed a thing.

"I'm not going!" Shyne insisted and crossed her arms. "I'm staying here with Asad and that's that!"

"You staying here by yourself then because Asad is going with us to Georgia," Yolo shrugged and turned to leave. The nimble little girl rushed in front of her before she could get to the door.

"Whatcha talkin' 'bout, Yolo?" she asked, in her best Gary Coleman impersonation.

"Asad's mom said that he could come down for the summer," she informed. It was a quick fix to a big problem since the kids were inseparable. Even Asad's mother had seen signs of depression in him as the moving date grew near. They'd disappeared when she informed him he could go to Georgia for the summer. Besides, the boy needed a strong man role model in his life and Killa fit the bill.

So, with that being said, the Killa clan packed up their Wyandanch house to head south. The cars had been shipped ahead of the move so the extended family boarded a flight to Atlanta.

Two weeks later, they were unpacked and getting settled into their new lives in their new home. Everyone was happy, except for Grandma Diedra.

"Why is it so hot down here?" she fussed as she watched the boys frolic in the pool.

"Just as hot as in New York," Yolo dared, even though it did seem an extra hundred degrees warmer; especially with a baby moving around inside of her like it was ready to walk out. It was, since she was almost due.

"It was even hotter when you were in Belize," Killa reminded. They knew that the real problem was that she just missed New York and Cameisha. "Besides, we need your help with all these kids!"

"Especially after this soccer player kicks his way out!" Yolo said, putting her hand on her belly. Their words did the trick and Diedra's eyes lit up in wonderment.

"Hope it's a boy, these girls are too much!" she fussed. As if on cue, Shyne pranced out in a two-piece and a pair of large shades.

"Grrr..." Killa growled and took off after her.

She ditched the shades and ran back in the house.

"I was just playing! Ma!" she shouted, trying to escape the wrath of Killa. She did and put on an age appropriate suit. His next target, however, wouldn't be so lucky.

****

"In breaking news out of Atlanta, Georgia, another unarmed black man was gunned down by police. As seen in this body cam video, the man clearly had his hands raised when the officer opened fire..."

"Damn!" both Yolo and Killa cringed as the graphic video was shown on the screen. Killa shook his head and rolled out of bed.

"Where you going?" Yolo wondered since it was after ten. For all the gangster shit they pulled, the two were generally in bed by ten P.M. So were the kids until about eleven when they were sure that their parents were sleep. Then it was their time to play NC-17 games and watch R-rated movies.

"You already know!" he huffed, pointing at the smiling cop on the television. He was already a dead man, but only made things worse when he spoke.

"The black suspect made an improper lane change, giving me probable cause to pull him over to check to see if he was trafficking drugs or white girls for sex slaves. I initiated a stop and asked the black thug to

step out and raise his hands. He complied, but I saw how black he was and I felt threatened and fired," Officer Johanson smiled.

"What?" Yolo fussed and tried to roll out of bed also. Tried but was too big to get without help.

Killa certainly wasn't going to help her because he was too busy laughing. "Yo, you look like a turtle stuck on its back," he cracked. He had more jokes, but was interrupted once again by the news report.

"The District Attorney states that he will not seek an indictment since the man was black and he has had a driving infraction in the past. He was previously ticketed in 1990 for the same offense. He has a long history of changing lanes without using his turn signal..."

"He's a fucking middle school teacher! A coach! A deacon!" Yolo fussed, shaking her head. "Yo, I want in! You gotta let me get some of this! At least the DA... Please!"

"A'ight, after you have the baby. But the cop is about to get it now! Wish we could have brought the pigs. What did you do with them, anyway?" he asked, scratching his head.

"They bacon, baby. I'm sorry. It was last minute, so I sold them to a farmer. He turned them into bacon, chops and..."

"And that is so gross! Baby, we fed people to those pigs! You can't feed those same pigs to people! That's... That's... Ewww!" Killa grimaced.

"Well, that's what they get for eating swine from the rooter to the tooter!" Yolo cracked up. Had a good laugh too, until the contractions hit. "Uh-oh!"

"Uh-oh what?" he asked, even though he already knew. This wasn't their first rodeo, so he already knew she was in labor. "Okay, breathe. Take it easy, breathe."

"Bruh, if you don't get me to the hospital..." Yolo growled.

It was enough to calm Killa. He helped her off the bed and into her robe. Because again, this wasn't their first rodeo, her bag was already packed and waiting in the truck, so they headed down the stairs and got a shock.

"What the... Is someone cooking?" Yolo asked as wonderful aroma's invaded her nostrils.

"Wait here," he said, sitting her on the sofa. He marched into the rear of the house to find out what was going on. "What the..."

Xavier had a full-fledged diner going. He had all the burners going and was cooking to order. Shyne had on an apron waiting on Sun, Rico and Asad while they watched a movie.

"Where's my steak?" Grandma Diedra demanded, sitting behind the boys. Killa just shook his head.

"What?" Yolo asked when he returned to get her. "Where'd you get a steak? Let me have a bite!"

****

"Yesss!!!" Killa cheered when the baby came out with a penis. He pumped his fist and did a little dance in triumph.

"Whew!" Yolo exclaimed at another successful delivery. Plus, because it was a boy. Shyne was bad enough, but little Diedra was also becoming a diva. Couldn't even talk yet but was fussing already.

"Have you picked out a name?" a nurse asked eagerly.

The parents smiled at each other and replied.

"Killa. The world will just have to deal with it!" Killa said smugly while Yolo nodded in approval.

"Malik Killa Forrest," she said formally so the woman could write it on the birth certificate. Killa proudly signed it once she was done. He and his wife high-fived before he turned to leave. "Save one for me!"

"Shoot!" he fussed at the reminder. If it were up to him, that cop and the DA would die tonight, but a promise is a promise, so he would save the DA for later. Yolo would be out of commission for at least six weeks, so he would get a short reprieve. As soon as she was given the green light to fuck, she could also kill.

Chapter 16

"Psss," Shyne hissed when Yolo brought the new baby home the following day. Even baby Diedra seemed to turn her nose up at the new addition to the family. The boys, on the other hand, were thrilled at having another brother.

"He can stay in my room," Xavier offered. He was already sharing with Asad for the summer, so what was one more?

"Thanks, but he'll take the crib," Killa replied. At this rate, they were going to need a bigger house.

"She..." Shyne said, pointing at their little sister, "can sleep in the den."

"Or... With you," Yolo added. Shyne threw a fit and stormed out the house. Yolo shrugged and went about her business. The novelty of the new baby wore off and the boys rushed back to their playing. They alternated between the pool and video games while Killa manned the grill.

Killa was basting chicken when Yolo joined them outside. She stopped and took in the surreal sights and sounds of her happy family. It was far cry from the foster home she'd grown up in. Also a far cry from the Black Mob's mansion. As much as she'd loved the late Mr. Grimsly, she had to admit that he had contributed to her lunacy. Not as much as Casper, who Killa had turned into bird food.

"What? And what is that?" Killa asked when he turned and saw his wife in a daze.

"What is what?" she snapped from embarrassment. She quickly knocked the warm tear away and played it off. "You sure you know what you're doing? Don't burn our dinner!"

"Girl, stop! I'm a beast with this thing!" he bragged, twirling the tongs on his finger. They came loose and sailed into the air and into the grass.

"Yeah, you are, baby," she laughed and kissed his cheek. "Your daughter come back yet?"

"My daughter, huh? Not yet. I'll go get her in a few. Would hate for her to get kidnapped."

"Hate it for the kidnapper!" Yolo cracked up and went back inside.

****

"Damn babies!" Shyne fussed as she stomped through the upscale neighborhood. She was so busy griping that she didn't notice the van creeping behind her. The creep behind the wheel had locked his little beady eyes on her narrow butt as she walked.

"Sweet," the creep murmured as he retrieved his pink penis from his pants. He pulled on it with one hand as he drove with the other. A block later, Shyne turned and looked directly at him. That was enough to send him over the edge. He skeeted on the steering wheel and took off. He was delighted to see a new girl in his neighborhood. He usually had to drive across town to find little black girls.

"Weirdo," Shyne huffed about the strange man. She didn't see what he'd done, but his googly eyes had creeped her out. She decided it was time to head home. "May as well since that damn baby ain't going nowhere!"

"Where were you?" Sun demanded when Shyne returned an hour after leaving.

"You ain't my daddy! I don't answer to you!" she hissed and turned her nose up.

Asad and Rico appeared as she did. "Where were you?" Asad asked. It was the same question, yet got a different reply.

"I just went for a walk. Ten blocks that way, two blocks left and straight back," she recited as if he were her daddy since she obviously answered to him.

"Soup's on!" Killa called from the back. His work was done so Yolo and Grandma Diedra fixed the plates.

The family had a lively conversation over dinner, then moved to the den for dessert and a movie. Life was great, unless you were a racist cop who'd just gunned down an innocent, unarmed, black man. In that case, life was short.

****

"So, how do you feel now, after taking a life? The life of unarmed black man at that?" the therapist asked softly. Officer Johanson had been invited to a special support group for officers just like him.

"Well, to be honest... I feel great! I've wanted to kill a black man since...since...middle school," he admitted to a round of applause. "We'd shower in gym class and I'd have to look at all those long, thick, black cocks and I couldn't wait to join the force to kill one of them. I pray to God I can get another one!"

"The fuck!" Killa winced as he eavesdropped on the meeting. He'd been following the cop for two days, waiting for the chance to murder him as brutally as possible.

Now it looked like he'd stumbled across a treasure trove of crooked cops who rejoiced in murdering unarmed black men. One couldn't join the group if their victim had a weapon. He listened as they joked about the paid leave they'd received after doing the deed. Paid vacation as a reward for taking a life. The rest of the country may hold rallies and protest, not Killa. They don't call him Killa for nothing. He was about to kill all of them.

Killa retreated from the meeting to get tag numbers for the six officers in attendance. The counselor too for facilitating the fuck shit. Johanson was at the top of the list. The rest he would wait to share with his wife.

****

Officer Johanson may have hated black men, but he sure loved him some black vagina. Who could blame him? After all, black vagina is a marvelous thing. That's why he was a frequent flyer with a couple of escort services. Killa hacked into his computer and sabotaged his next date. He thought he was meeting with Bombquisha, but instead made a date with death.

"Sup, my nigga?" Johanson practiced as he drove to the motel. He used to let the escorts come to his house until one stole his watch. She'd tipped herself for the verbal abuse he heaped on her while he short stroked her.

He arrived at the motel and made his way to the room. He instinctively pressed his ear to the door and listened for danger. Hearing none, he stood and knocked. A ghetto girl with a gold lace front and gold tooth pulled it open.

"Bombquisha?" he asked, licking her black body up and down with his eyes.

"Yeah, white boy. Come on in," she spat and turned. Her black ass cheeks hung out of her red panties, stealing his vision. "Hope you eat ass."

"Of course!" he shot back as if everyone did. Everyone doesn't, but he certainly did.

The rent-a-hoe peeled off her panties and propped herself up on the bed doggy-style. The cop moved close and sniffed her ass, just like a real dog would. He then stuck his tongue out and went to work. He was enthralled with the black vagina that he didn't hear the door ease open. Partly because Killa made sure to oil it before he got there.

"Be careful, you don't want to suck a turd out of there," Killa warned, announcing his presence.

"'Kay," he agreed and stuck his tongue right back in her ass. He stopped suddenly when he realized they were no longer alone. He spun to see a gun with a long silencer attached in his face.

"Hol' up, white boy! Let Bombquisha get a nut!" the escort insisted.

"May as well," Killa shrugged and pushed him forward.

"May as well my ass! I'm a cop!" he shouted as if it meant something to either. Killa and Bombquisha both laughed at his whining.

"Fine," Killa said, raising the gun back to his forehead.

"Wait! Wait! I'll do it!" he insisted and dove back in. He ate her ass as if his life depended on it. It didn't because he was still going to die.

Bombquisha moaned and thrashed as he sucked a nut out of her ass. He was an expert ass eater, as most racists are. He even ignored the tiny pieces of shit that came out.

"Good looking out, white boy!" she laughed and got dressed to leave.

"Tell Leroy I owe him one. You too," Killa told her as she walked to the door. He and the escort service owner went way back from New York.

"Naw, this was on the house. Fuck da police!" she said and left.

"Bruh, I'm unarmed," Johanson pleaded, sticking his empty palms out. He'd left his gun in the car since he'd only come for some sweet black pussy. Sweet black pussy ain't never hurt nobody. However, the pursuit of it certainly has. It had in the past and would again tonight.

"So, was that father...you...gunned...down," Killa replied, punctuating each word with a silent round. They weren't .22s either. The heavy .40 caliber slugs knocked chunks out of the man.

Killa made sure not to hit anything vital and also refrained from a head shot. No, the cop was going to die slow. He took a seat on the adjacent bed to enjoy the show.

"At least your hands aren't cuffed behind your back," Killa growled. The cop had cuffed his victim's hands and let him die slowly on the hard, hot asphalt.

The holes in the cop's lungs prevented him from speaking. He moaned and fought the good fight for survival but lost. A rattle came from his throat as his wicked soul left his body. Killa gave a curt nod and then departed.

Chapter 17

"Sup, Big Mama?" Shyne greeted when Yolo came down stairs. "Are you pregnant again yet?"

"Get help, little girl. I'm not fooling with you this morning," she shot back. She knew her baby was feeling neglected and needed some attention. "Get dressed after breakfast cuz we're going out."

"All ten of us?" she asked, twisting her face up. It was proof that she was feeling overwhelmed.

"No, just us two. A girls' day out, shopping, hair and nails, lunch and a movie," Yolo replied.

"Ooh, I wanna come!" Sun pleaded, walking in on their conversation.

"To get your hair and nails done?" Shyne fussed with her hands on her hips.

"Aww man!" Sun pouted and crossed his arms. That's how Killa found them when he walked in. He took one look at their long faces and turned to leave.

"Un uh. You need to take the boys somewhere to do something," Yolo protested. "Grandma is watching the babies and Miss Shyne and I are having some girl time."

"Girl time?" he repeated. Shyne tried to flip her hair and turn her nose up. Her afro-puffs didn't exactly flip, but he got the point. "Guess I'll take them to the gun range."

"Yay!" Sun shouted and rushed to tell his brothers. Xavier, Rico and Asad also broke out cheering and did the happy dance. Now, it was Shyne's turn to pout again.

"What?" Yolo fussed, wondering what could be eating the spoiled diva now.

"I want to go to the gun range too!" she pouted.

"Well, that's what I meant by girl time, but we gotta go get cute first. Don't we? Can't be busting our guns looking scruffy," Yolo sang.

96

After breakfast, the family dressed and went their separate ways. Diedra was more than happy to have the babies to herself. Killa loaded the boys up in his SUV and off they went. Meanwhile, Yolo and Shyne dressed in similar summer dresses and sandals. Each stuck a flower in her natural hair before meeting up in the living room.

"Hmp!" they both huffed at the other and headed out to the car. Shyne spotted the creep in the creepy van.

"That man followed me the other day!" Shyne snitched knowingly. She'd read enough of her mom's diary to know she'd just sealed his fate. "Want me to go inside and..."

"Stay away from him!" Yolo demanded as she slammed on the brakes. The fire in her eyes warned Shyne from one of her smart comments.

"Okay, Mommy," she moaned like a ten-year-old. She leaned back into the plush leather seat and rode in silence. The vibrations of the car soon put her to sleep.

"Mommy, there go that man again!" Shyne's son whined, pointing at the same van.

"And I'm grown now so Yolo can't tell me nothing!" she cheered, cupping her breasts. They were a lot bigger than they would eventually be in real life, but this was her dream after all so they were what she said they were.

"Huh?" her baby asked, looking up at her. Her father came over to see what was going on.

"What's going on?" Asad asked.

Shyne lowered her head coyly and giggled at her handsome husband. She was as smitten in her dreams as she was in real life.

"There..." the child tried to repeat and point, but Shyne shut him down.

"Nothing. He's just tired. Ge the rest of the kids so we can go take a nap," she interrupted.

"Rest of what kids?" Asad asked, scratching his head and looking around. If she was talking about kidnapping one of these kids, he wanted no parts of it.

"Um... Okay. Yeah, let's go home," she said, realizing they only had one child in this dream. "You probably better drive."

"Um... Yeah," he said and took the keys. Shyne was relieved to see that they lived in the same house that they lived in now. That meant the van would be at the same place. She planned to go there first chance she got. It would have to wait, though, because first things first.

"Put him in his bed and meet me in ours!" she whispered urgently when they arrived at home with the baby sleeping in his car seat. She rushed upstairs humping the air as she went. "Un-un-uh!"

****

Shyne looked down at her sleeping husband before quietly rolling out of the bed. She then crept into the closet and got dressed to kill in a plastic sweat suit so she could hose off the blood. After peeping in on their sleeping child, she eased down to the basement. That's where she kept her deadly devices.

"Let's see here..." she mused as she ran through her assortment of guns, knives and flame throwers. The choice between brass knuckles and a mini flame thrower came down to eenie, meenie, minie, mo.

"Sucks to be you," she laughed as she collected the brass knuckles. "Looks like little Timmy is about to get beat to death.

Timmy was just Timmy until he stopped growing in the fourth grade. By sixth grade, he was officially Little Timmy because everyone outgrew him. Getting girls his age was out since he was so small. Even if he could get one, what could he do with a fourth grader's dick? That's why he turned to girls his own height. The only problem with that was they were eight-years-old.

Little Timmy scoured the residential areas and parks for kids to molest. By age forty, it didn't matter if they were male or female as long *as he could get them into his van. He'd gotten on Shyne's radar and now she was on his front porch.*

"Ugh!" Timmy fussed at the ringing doorbell. He was masturbating while watching cartoons and didn't appreciate the interruption. It wasn't the actual cartoons that excited him, it was the children in all the commercials that came on in between them. He was too close to the finish line to stop now so he threw it into overdrive. A little boy pushing a truck on the screen pushed him over the edge. He came with a loud grunt, spewing semen everywhere.

"I know you're in there," Shyne fussed and rang the bell again. She heard footsteps approaching and got ready. As soon as the door opened, she sprang into action.

"Hell..." Little Timmy began but a vicious blow knocked the 'o' and several of his teeth down his throat.

He staggered backwards, but Shyne was on his ass. She swung the door closed with her foot so she could beat him in private. And beat him she did. Timmy lifted a frail arm to block the blows but the blow broke his arm. Shyne then broke his nose, his jaw and his cheekbone. He turned to run but Shyne clipped him and sent him sliding across the hardwood floor.

"Okay, okay! No more, please!" he pleaded. He never once asked why she was there beating him. He knew his fuck shit would catch up to him one day and that day was obviously today.

"Okay, I won't hit you anymore," she smiled ominously. He would rather have been beaten than what she had in store for him. She retrieved a squirt bottle from her bag and sprayed him from head to toe.

"Okay, okay, beat me! Beat me! Please!" he pleaded when the gas soaked him. "It burns!"

"You think it burns now..." Shyne laughed and lit him up. "Now it burns, motherfucker! Burn, motherfucker, burn!"

Shyne cheered so hard at the burning pedophile that she woke herself up. She looked around and saw that they were parked at the mall with her mother looking down at her.

"Wanna get some Cinnabon?" Shyne asked nonchalantly and unbuckled her seatbelt.

"Sure," Yolo replied happily. "And on the way home, we'll stop and get you some help."

Chapter 18

"What are you so happy about?" Yolo demanded when she awoke to her happy husband. Not only was he smiling brightly, he also presented a tray of all her favorites. "Beef bacon, hash browns, cheese eggs... What did you do?"

"I didn't do nothing. Not yet, anyway. Look at the calendar!" he replied, pointing to the nightstand.

"Don't make no damn sense," Yolo mused, shaking her head. Today marked baby Malik's six week birthday. A special occasion because he could finally get some pussy. Mother and baby had a checkup for that morning and he planned to fuck by sundown.

"Makes perfect sense. Now eat up. I'll get the baby dressed," he said and went to do just that. The world's most prolific killer was also a doting dad.

He managed to keep a personal relationship with each child individually as well as with them collectively. Even Asad had become a member of the family. Killa also loved having his grandmother around no matter how much hell she raised.

"Good morning," Killa greeted and kissed Diedra on her cheek. The old lady blushed slightly from the show of affection. She saw a side of him the world didn't get to see.

"Good morning, baby. Just getting the baby ready for his checkup," she said while continuing to dress him. The child turned towards his father's voice and smiled. "I fed the rest of the tribe too since you only cooked enough for your wife."

"Well, it's a special occasion, so..." he laughed and scooped his son up from his crib.

"Mmhmm... Six weeks, I know. Guess I can take my grand babies to a movie," she said.

"Yeah, but a PG-rated movie. That last one was a bit much," he reminded.

"What? *Reverend Cash* was based on a true story! A preacher from right here in the ATL," she said with her eyes wide. Killa just smiled and walked away.

****

"Clean bill of health!" the lady doctor announced. Both mom and baby were in tiptop shape. "I do suggest some sort of birth control to space out any future pregnancies. Depo, the pill or even the withdrawal method."

"Withdrawal! Dude has thee worse pull out game!" Yolo shrieked.

"Seems like a lot of work for nothing. A waste," he shrugged.

"Well, hook me up with that shot!" Yolo said, tapping her vein like a heroin addict. "Give it to me! Give it to me!"

"Umm... Actually it goes in your buttocks," she said and prepared the dose. "You may experience some weight gain."

"Shyne would love that," Yolo said, shaking her head. The girl now insisted on calling her Big Mama.

The rest of the day drug on painfully slow for Killa. He cared nothing about dinner or board games. He wanted some pussy. The large, busy family kept him busy until it was well after midnight when he and Yolo were finally able to retreat to their bedroom.

"I'ma be—" Killa began, but was interrupted be a deep yawn, "beat that pussy up!"

"How romantic," Yolo quipped sarcastically. Crude as it may have sounded, that was exactly how she liked it. Nice and slow or hard and fast, it didn't matter as long as it was Killa inside of her. He was the only man on the planet who had been. Sure, she'd sucked a dick or two back in the day, but she'd bit them off so they didn't count.

The two stripped on opposite sides of the bed then climbed on and met in the middle. A kiss, a rub and it was on. Not on and popping, but on and snoring. Both husband and wife passed out from the long, busy day they'd had. So much for beating the pussy up when Killa slobbered on his pillow.

"Take that!" Killa said, dreaming about some pussy. He jumped and bolted awake. He frowned in confusion at the numbers on the clock. According to it, it was slightly after four AM. He couldn't remember if he'd gotten laid or not so he looked under the covers to check. He looked over at Yolo snoring and slobbering and let her be. Instead, he rolled out the bed and pulled on his pajama pants. He then set out for the kitchen in search of a snack.

Killa stopped halfway down the stairs upon hearing a soft, melodic tone reach his ears. His heart seemed to flutter as the words penetrated his soul. A soul that was once inclined towards evil, but now reproached itself. At that moment, his soul was at complete rest and satisfied.

Bismillahir Rahmanir Raheem, Alhamdulillahi Rabbil Alameen translated into in The name of God, The Most Gracious, The Most Merciful. All praise is for God, The Lord of everyone and everything in existence.

"Amen," he said since you didn't have to be Muslim to agree to that. There's nothing worthy of worship except God, and that is a fact shared by all people of all faiths.

Killa crept forward expecting to see Asad praying alone. He did a double take when he saw Shyne beside him praying. His heart fluttered once more before he continued on his mission.

****

"Mmmhp!" Yolo grumbled and frowned when she felt water splash on her face.

"My bad. Did I wake you?" Killa asked, ready to flick more water at her if need be.

"Give me that!" she fussed, taking the water from him. She gulped it down and passed the empty glass. She rolled out of bed and marched towards the ensuite. Her bare bouncing ass cheeks had an audience as she went.

"I'm gon' get some pussy! I'm gon' get some pussy!" Killa sang softly.

He was right, too, because Yolo marched straight back out and attacked. She climbed atop of him and wiggled his hardness inside of her wetness. She took a few preliminary rocks before finding her stroke.

"I..." Killa began but got shushed. Yolo was in no mood for any of his smart aleck comments. Not now, when she was in search of a nut.

"Oh yeah," Yolo moaned as she rode into Orgasmville. It was a welcoming town full of fireworks and fanfare. She rode even harder and invited Killa to join her. He did and went stiff as he exploded inside of her. Yolo let out a howl and shivered from the force of her own orgasm.

After a few more hours of sleep, the parents joined the rest of the family for breakfast. Diedra had showed out and cooked a meal worthy of the long dining room table. Killa and Yolo were greeted by snickers and subdued laughter.

"What?" Yolo finally demanded as the kids turned red from bottled up hysterics.

"Nothing, ki-ki-ki," Xavier, the spokesman, lied and laughed.

"Oooweeee!" Sun howled like a wolf, cracking everyone, including Grandma Diedra, up.

Yolo turned beet red in embarrassment realizing that was her cum call.

"You kids really need to close your door at night," Diedra comforted and giggled.

Chapter 19

"So, let me tell you about your daughter. The crazy one. We went to the mall and..." Yolo began and commenced to relay the dream Shyne had shared with her. It ended with the creep in the neighborhood in the creepy van. "Where are you going?"

"To go murder van man," he replied, frowning up as if the question was utterly ridiculous.

"Naked?" she shrieked, since that really was utterly ridiculous.

"Well, no. I probably should put some clothes on, huh?" he asked.

"Nope! Bring that thing back over here!" Yolo said, pointing at the dick dangling between his thighs. He did and they did and then took a nap.

They awoke mid-afternoon and showered together. Six weeks was a long time so they fucked once more in the shower. Summer was coming to an end so they tried to keep the children busy with different activities.

"Guess, I'll take the boys," Yolo said with an ominous sigh. The four of them together could be a lot of work. Xavier was a budding lady's man, just like his dad. He and Killa may not share the same DNA, but he was still his father's son all day. Rico and Sun were definitely going to break something. Asad was the only one with common sense and manners, but sometimes he followed his bad ass brothers-in-law straight into trouble.

"That means..." Killa said with stark terror in his eyes. "I got... The girls. Shyne...the baby and Grandma!"

"Have fun!" Yolo laughed and commenced to get cute. A pair of snug jeans showed off her round butt while an equally tight shirt did the same for her perky breasts.

Killa twisted his lips at how sexy she looked. He almost protested, but remembered the boys would be with her. She felt the same with him in his slipped into linen slacks, silk shirt and loafers. A woman wouldn't be able to get near him with wild child Shyne in the area.

"Everyone ready?" Killa asked, finding the entire family in the den.

"Yes!" they all called, fully dressed and ready to ride.

"Okay, girls with me, Boys with mom," he said, scooping the baby up. He was a boy, but Diedra didn't go anywhere without him.

"Yes!!!" the boys cheered and high-fived. "Let's go to the mall!"

"Let's!" Yolo agreed. She led the way out to Killa's truck, leaving him to use the mini-van full of car seats. He loaded little Diedra in her seat and then baby Malik.

"I want to go to the mall, too! Just not the same one as them," Shyne huffed, all indignant like he was just the driver and not her father.

"Okay, honey," he said because being the driver is part of being a father. That meant a much longer drive up 85 to the other mall while Yolo and the boys hit Lenox Mall.

The shorter drive got them there that much quicker. Xavier, Sun and Rico jumped out before Yolo could come to a complete stop.

"I'll escort you, Ma'am," Asad offered, being the gentleman that he was.

"Mmhmm," Yolo huffed, giving him a hard time as usual. Truth be told, she would love to have him as a son-in-law one day. She pulled to the valet and handed over the key.

"Need anything...else," the young valet said, pausing to lick his lips like LL Cool J, "Just hit me up."

"I'll hit you up alright," Asad growled and moved to do just that. That's the downside to learning karate. You're gonna want to try it out. Luckily for the attendant, Yolo stopped him from chopping him in his neck.

"Easy, tiger," she chuckled and turned him towards the mall. He grinned importantly as they walked hand in hand towards the entrance.

"What set y'all claim?" an older teen dared as Xavier, Rico and Sun entered the food court. He couldn't figure it out since all of them wore different colors. He and his friends all wore their gang colors from head to toe. All the good colors were already taken so the upstart had to use what was left, pink. The ten, fifteen and sixteen-year-olds scowled menacingly.

"What?" Rico shot back. He had his father's quick temper and was always ready to pop it off.

"Who y'all supposed to be, the My Little Ponies?" Sun cracked up. He had his dad's sense of humor. He liked to fight also, but waited on his older brother to give the green light.

"Nah, we the P-Boys! Straight out of Buckhead," the leader declared. Even kids from the upscale hood wanted to be hard. The P stood for 'prosperous' but P sounded cooler.

"Pussy? Pink? Powder Puff?" the trio of brothers took turns guessing at what the P stood for.

"What's going on here?" Yolo asked when she and Asad arrived on the scene just before it turned into a crime scene.

"Nothing!" Sun quickly replied unbelievably while his brothers nodded in agreement.

"Well, let's go eat something," she said, steering her tribe further into the food court. They were outnumbered two to one, and that wouldn't be fair; for the P-Boys, that is.

Yolo made the cheapskates use their own money to buy their lunch. Asad was generous enough to buy hers, too. They found a seat to eat and watched the P-Boys picking on smaller kids, girls and old people.

"Mom!" Rico fussed when they witnessed the bullies take an old lady's purse. They rifled through it, took the cash and then tossed it at the woman's feet. All Yolo heard was 'mom' instead of Miss Yolo like he and X generally called her.

"Asad and I are going to Game Stop," she said and stood. The boys took it as a green light and stood as well.

"I'm staying with my brothers. I'll catch up," Asad replied. Bless his heart, he wanted in on the rumble to come.

"Oh Lawd, I'm gonna have to explain to this child's mother why he got locked up in Georgia," Yolo mumbled as she walked away. She knew Killa would have a fit when he heard about this. At least she could say she didn't see it.

The boys were all trained in the art of war by the legendary Karate Joe. Even Asad had secondhand training via Sun and Shyne. They split into two groups like lions hunting their prey and moved forward. X and Asad arrived first and struck.

"Ha-ya!" Asad shouted and chopped one in his throat. He dropped, gasping for air, and Xavier kicked him. One tried to run, but Asad clipped him and sent him sliding.

Rico and Sun joined the fray and it was an all-out battle. What started as ten bullies reduced with each karate chop and kick. The ones still standing ran so they wouldn't end up stretched out like their friends. Security arrived and started snatching collars.

"No! They started it! That ones in the pink!" the crowd insisted. The guards were familiar with young thugs and carted them away. The food court erupted in applause for the heroes.

****

Killa had fewer kids but just as much trouble. He had the newborn strapped in a carrier against his chest while his toddler rode in a stroller. Shyne darted in and out of stores while Grandma ventured into Victoria's Secret. He frowned in confusion at what she could possibly be buying and why.

A couple of hours later, they ended up at the food court. Shyne stood in line for pizza while Killa kept an eye on her from the S&S Gourmet Burgers and Fries line. He also kept an eye on the man in front of him who was also watching Shyne.

"The one in blue is cute, no?" the man asked, seeing that both he and Killa shared the same view. Almost, since Killa was looking at her afro-puffs while he gawked at her little butt.

"Gorgeous," Killa agreed. The smile on his face contradicted the boiling rage within him. He glanced around at all the faces around him. Hundreds of witnesses saved him from being murdered on the spot.

"Yes, so precious at that age," he sighed a sick, love-struck sigh. "The budding breast nubs, tight little butts, mmm..."

"Grrr..." Killa rumbled. He looked around again and confirmed there were just too many people.

"Hold my spot. I have to relieve myself," he said and bolted for the men's room. Killa rushed over to his grandmother and dropped off the baby.

"Uh-oh," Diedra laughed at the mask of murder on his face. "Somebody about to get fucked up!"

"Sss...yes...*My Little Pony, Dora the Explorer*," the pedophile grunted as he jacked off in a stall. He was on the verge of busting a self-inflicted nut but didn't make it. Along came a killer who burst in and choked the shit out of him. Kinda fucked up getting choked out while choking your chicken. Once the life was out of the man, Killa removed his belt and put it around his neck. He attached it to the stall to make it appear to be a suicide. He skipped happily out of the men's room and rejoined his family.

Chapter 20

"So, how was the mall? Boys give you any trouble?" Killa asked when he and Yolo climbed into bed.

"Trouble? No. No trouble at all," she said and flicked on the TV to change the subject. Only problem was, they were the subject.

"A brawl at the mall was captured on several cell phones..." the news reporter said. Several clips of Killa's kids beating up the bullies played on the large screen. Yolo scrambled to change the channel.

"Un uh. Swear y'all can't go nowhere," he chided, shaking his head. His gloating was short lived when the next report played.

"Registered sex offender Amos Malory was found dead in a bathroom stall at the mall. The medical examiner ruled his death a suicide due to auto-erotic fixation..."

"You did that!" Yolo said, twisting her lips up daring him to deny it.

"You are so pretty," he said, flashing her one of his killer smiles and then kissing her cheek. It was meant to be a diversion and it worked. A few minutes later, they were fucking like there was no tomorrow. There was a tomorrow, though, and they had a DA to kill.

They awoke the next morning, fucked again, showered and then joined the family for breakfast.

"We have announcement," Shyne announced, getting everyone's attention. Killa braced himself, knowing anything could and usually did come out her mouth.

"Lord," Yolo prayed, bracing herself for the same reason. Shyne was eleven, so some things she didn't have to worry about, but still.

"Asad and I have decided to move up our wedding," she said with Asad nodding in agreement. He was an agreeable person and Shyne got what Shyne wanted. Now she wanted to prevent him from going to New York in a couple of weeks.

"How soon? After college, right?" Diedra asked since that was the plan.

"Next week," she replied and went back to eating as if that were the end of it.

"Um..." Killa said, looking to Yolo and his grandmother for help.

"Not," Yolo replied. "By law you, need our permission to get married if you're under sixteen and you do not have it."

"Fine!" Shyne pouted. She stood from the table and marched away. Once she cleared the room, she came right back with some last words. "At sixteen, I'm gonna be a wife or a baby mama. You decide!"

"Girl, I got yo' baby mama!" Yolo growled and tried to go after her. Luckily, Killa got her before she could get up.

"Chill, she's just talking," he reminded. They could only blame themselves for her being stubborn and spoiled.

All eyes fell on Asad, causing him to smile nervously.

****

The District Attorney had been abusing his authority for decades to abuse blacks and Hispanics. He wore a suit instead of a robe, but still lynched people. He routinely fabricated or suppressed evidence to falsely convict innocent men. Yet every time a crooked cop killed an unarmed black man, he turned a blind eye. Painting victims as villains, with his racist paint brush. He was about to get fucked up for it.

"That him?" Yolo asked when Bob Harper stepped from the courthouse. He wore a shit eating grin after railroading a black teen into ten-years in prison.

"Yup," Killa replied, ready to wipe that grin off his face. After he actually did eat some shit, that is. He pulled his phone out and called his friend Wali, the one who worked at the zoo.

They followed him with their eyes until he reached his car. Then they followed him in their car waiting for an opportunity to kidnap him. None came so they followed him home.

"Fuck this," Yolo said as he pulled into his garage. She jumped out and ran in behind him before the door could close.

"Who..." the DA asked until Yolo lit him up with a Taser. He dropped, slobbering and shaking on the ground.

"Me," Yolo laughed. She hit the switch allowing the door to open so Killa could enter.

"Aww man," Killa fussed when the man's bladder released. He let out a sigh and looked for some gloves.

Yolo went inside the house and found his computer. She logged in and confessed to railroading black me and boys for decades in his name. "Ready?" she asked, returning just as Killa shut the car trunk with him gagged and bound inside.

"Yup," he replied and got behind the wheel. Yolo followed in their disposable car. They drove across town and ended up at the zoo.

It had just closed for the day, but Wali granted them access through a side entrance.

"What's it gonna be? Lions? Tigers?" Wali asked with glee. It did his heart good seeing the demise of bad people.

"How about elephants?" Yolo suggested. It would have been kind of cool to see them stomp him like the piece of shit he was, but Killa had an even better idea.

"Where's the gorilla cage?" he asked, putting smiles on everyone's faces. Everyone except Bob, that is.

"Who are you people? What do you want with me? Do you know who I am?" he demanded. Only problem was the gag in his mouth made it impossible to understand.

"What? Huh?" Yolo teased, cocking her ear closer. "Stop whining."

"Well, save it for later cuz that gorilla is going to tear him apart!" Wali laughed.

Killa made sure by throwing rocks at the primate. It served a distraction as Wali opened the back door and wheeled him in.

"Showtime!" Killa announced. The ape was .38 hot, rattling the bars trying to get to Killa. Killa smiled and pointed behind him.

The gorilla frowned curiously and turned around. He couldn't believe the man was actually inside with him. He made his way over slowly to investigate.

"Mm-mph, mmph!" Bob grunted. It was obviously a dis in gorilla talk because the gorilla fought.

"Damn!" Killa laughed when the animal snatched his arm completely off. He beat the man with it a few times then tossed it aside. He picked the man and beat everything with him, the floor, the walls, the bars, and the trees. The life left his shell somewhere along the way.

"Show's over," Wali sighed and aimed the tranquilizer. The gorilla raised his arms like it was a stick up but still got shot. They waited until he was fast asleep to collect the corpse.

"You're welcome," Yolo laughed when Killa and Wali tossed the arm and body into the lion cage. "Now he's unarmed."

****

"Uh oh," Yolo said, seeing smoke in the direction they were heading. That was a big deal since they were heading home.

"Probably not even close to us," Killa said, even though it sure looked like where heading. They were still miles away but the closer they got to home, the closer they got to the fire.

Fire trucks were seen entering their subdivision, making it worse. They both breathed a sigh of relief when they saw it was a few blocks away from their house. Nosey Killa followed the smoke and saw it was the creepy van man's house on fire. He stood out on the street in his cartoon character robe lamenting over his home.

"Looks like the fire started in his van and spread to the house," Yolo surmised as they crept by.

Killa shrugged and swung around the corner and went home. "Hmp?" Killa wondered when they entered the quiet house. It was after midnight but that never meant anything. He checked the door and found all four boys stretched out sleep.

"Swimming," Yolo said, knowing it always wore them out. "I'll check on the girls. You go get ready."

"Ready?" he asked curiously.

She grabbed his package for reply.

"Oh, ready!"

Killa came up the stairs two at a time to get naked. Yolo kept her word and looked in on the rest of their brood. Little Killa and Diedra were sleeping soundly so she peeked in on Shyne. She opened the door and got hit right in her nose from the strong smell of gasoline.

"Oh, no you didn't!" she laughed as two and two came together. Shyne burned that man's van and inadvertently, his house. She wasn't mad, though, and backed out shaking her head.

"Oh, yes I did!" Shyne snickered when she closed the door. She pulled her mother's diary and began to read.

Chapter 21

"Oooh ooh! How about Sky from *Black Ink*?" Yolo suggested. "She be doing *the* most"

"Nah, how about them damn Atlanta *Housewives*? Or the whole *Bad Girls Club*? We gotta kill them," Killa replied. They were bored stiff and looking for their next kill.

Over the last few years, they had erased some of the most stubborn stains from the planet. They most recently found and eliminated a terrorist sleeper cell before they could harm innocent people along with the reputation of Islam.

They'd killed so many rappers and R & B divas that the industry got the message. Now the only thing on the radio was positive music instead of the destructive garbage of the past. Stay in school was now more popular than turning up and getting drunk, high and pregnant.

"Ummm..." Yolo hummed, racking her brain for someone to kill. Anything to take her mind of the twins' sixteenth birthday that was days away. She and Killa made a promise years ago and it was time to pay up.

They both assumed their daughter would grow out of it or change her mind but she was as determined and committed as ever. Most girls celebrate sweet sixteen with a big party and Shyne was no exception, except hers would be a wedding reception.

They agreed not to prevent her from marrying Asad once they turned sixteen. They managed to stay close despite the long distance during the school year. Asad still came down to spend summers and winter breaks. Even married, they would live in separate states until they graduated. Shyne was never boy crazy but she was always crazy about that boy. Killa knew it was the good example of husband and wife set by him and Yolo as well as Asad's parents that urged them to marry. There would be no boyfriend, girlfriend, baby mama or daddy. Just husband and wife in honor and dignity. Amen.

"Guess I'll go get Christi from the airport," Yolo sighed. Her beloved little sister had flown in from California for the special occasion.

"Guess I'll, um...what am I supposed to do again?" he asked in confusion.

"Relax, get some rest. You have to give your daughter away in a few hours," she replied. Killa enjoyed the ass cheeks hanging out of her panties as she walked to the bathroom. He entertained the thought of joining her in the shower but entertained it too long and she returned wrapped in a towel.

"I'm saying, though..." Killa said tracing her curves with his eyes. "You know what would really relax me?"

"Boy stop," Yolo giggled at the come on. After all this time, the couple still adored each other. "Maybe we can have our own honeymoon later tonight."

"Honeymoon!" Killa groaned at the thought of his daughter again. Neither expressed interest in sex but at least they would be married.

"Three girls in Shyne's class are pregnant right now. Even way up here in these exclusive suburbs. Let's not guess how many abortions!" Yolo reminded. She didn't have to remind him of how good a person Asad was. There was no one better on the planet to take care of their daughter.

"Yeah, yeah," he agreed since they'd had this talk ad nauseam. "Guess I'll go back to sleep,"

Killa went back to sleep until Yolo returned with Christi. After a brief reunion, the womenfolk left for the wedding chapel. He went down to hang out with his sons until it was time to go.

Asad sat alone meditating while his brothers played videos. His lips moved in conjunction with a counting motion of his fingers. Killa had seen him do this often over the years but finally asked what it was.

"Just remembering my Lord," Asad explained without stopping. "Glory to God, praise God and God is the greatest."

"Why you wanna marry my daughter?" he asked again. Same question he'd asked for almost ten years and always got the same answer. Men are the protectors and maintainers of women. It was sufficient but today, he had a different response.

"Because, she's my best friend," he said, making eye contact.

That was good in enough for Killa. Yolo was his best friend so he could relate. They bumped fists and got ready to leave.

****

"I can't believe you're getting married!" Bryonna gushed as she fussed over Shyne in her wedding dress. They'd managed to maintain their long distance friendship as well. Shyne was determined to maintain the life she dreamed about. Her parents being alive and well made it that much better.

"Believe it!" she shot back and humped the air. She and Bryonna cracked up while Yolo and Christi twisted their lips. "Just playing, mommy."

"Mmhm," she hummed. She and Killa raised her to be a lady and that's what she'd become. She couldn't be more proud of her and Asad. They would live with her and Killa while going to college until they got a home of their own. "Anyway, it's about time, isn't it?"

"Past time," Christi frowned down at her watch. The nuptials were set to begin at two and it was two past. She pulled her phone to inquire but someone knocked on the door.

"Sup with the bootleg preacher? The Imam is ready. Everyone is ready," Killa fussed. The bride and groom decided on using both a preacher and an Imam to officiate the wedding.

"Stuck in traffic," Christi answered, holding her phone. "Said twenty minutes"

"Twenty minutes is plenty of time," Yolo dared, raising her eyebrows.

Killa replied by snatching her hand and pulling her out of the dressing room. He dragged her down the hall and entered the bathroom.

"Just an ole freak," Killa laughed as they struggled to free enough body parts to fuck. He unzipped his suit pants while she lifted her dress and pulled her panties to the side.

"You like it!" she shot back and lifted her leg.

"Love it," he corrected and slid inside of her. They fumbled around in the cramped room. It took some doing but he finally found his stroke.

"Yo, where's pops?" Sun asked, looking around the chapel.

"With mom," Rico said, shaking his head and laughing.

"With mom where? The preacher's here. It's time to get the show on the road!" he shot back. Rico just pointed since he was laughing too hard for words. "The bathroom? Together?"

"He'll figure it out," Xavier laughed as Sun stormed off to retrieve his parents. He rolled up and knocked sharply on the door, then put his ear to it.

"Shit, I'm cumming," Killa grunted urgently.

Yolo was a few strokes behind and needed to catch up. "Wait, for...me! I'm cumming too!" she shouted.

"Good," Sun replied and turned to his laughing brothers. "It's cool, they both said they're coming." His brothers laughed even harder.

A moment later, Killa and Yolo stepped out. She looked guilty and he, sleepy. She took her seat next to Asad's parents and waited for the bride.

"Are you okay?" Asad's mom asked, looking concerned. "You're out of breath and your face is flushed."

"Just excited is all. My baby is getting married," she replied. She was saved from further questions when the wedding march began to play.

Asad looked like he was about to pass out and was visibly shaking. He settled down and smiled broadly when his bride-to-be stepped out escorted by her father. Killa looked sleepy despite the proud smile on his face. He knew some may frown on him marrying off his 16-year-old daughter. While most of their daughters had boyfriends and babies, this was more honorable than that, so fuck them.

"You okay, Baby?" Killa asked as he escorted his daughter down the aisle. "You're shaking."

"That's you daddy" she replied and squeezed his shaking hand. They shared a quick glance that put them both at ease. Their heads lifted in pride as they approached the altar.

Killa nodded at his soon-to-be son-in-law and handed her over. Sun stood next to Asad as his best friend and best man. All turned to the clergy and the show was underway. The Imam commenced in Arabic then translated into English. He and the preacher took turns until they were pronounced husband and wife.

"Tell me this is one her crazy dreams" Yolo said with tears of joy streaming down her face.

"Nope, it's real. Time for a happy ending and happily ever after," Killa replied, hugging her. They both heard the alert go off on his phone from the 1-800-Killa app.

They smiled at each other knowing the weather was about to change. Summer was about to be Killa Season once again.

Chapter 22

"That's the one I want!" Chico proclaimed greedily, rubbing his hands together like a housefly.

No one could tell the overweight lover he wasn't fly since he routinely bagged strippers out of the strip club. Truth be told, he was 350 pounds of shit who had to pay like he weighed for a woman to even look his way. However, being a drug distributor for the resurrected Black Mob gave him plenty of treats to trick with.

"That one, boss?" his right hand man, Steve, asked with a pained expression. Out of all the strippers in the club, he picked the only one that wasn't butt ass naked. Not that she didn't look good in the pink boy shorts with caramel ass cheeks hanging out the bottom. A halter top showed off her hard stomach while holding back plump softball sized breast. Still she looked shy, nervous even. "She ain't buss it open or nothing!"

"I know. She the wholesome type," Chico said, licking his lips. He'd been trying to wife one of the loose women for a while with no luck. Lucky for him though because even a magician can't turn a hoe into a housewife. A hoe can turn herself into one, but no man can.

"A'ight," Steve shrugged and went to collect her from the stage. Part of his duties were collecting hoes for the night and dropping them off in the morning. He let out a sigh when he reached the stage and ordered the woman down. "Come on. Boss wants to fuck you."

"Ha!" she huffed and turned her back on him. He paused for a second to watch her booty shake before coming around the other side. "Do you know who Chico is?"

"Girl, Chico pay like he weigh," a butt naked stripper cheered. She tricked with the trick herself and leaned in to add, "He got a little dick and come super quick!"

"I'm good," the stripper declined. She shot a glance over to Chico and scrunched her face up at him. The rejection reminded him of his youth, making him want her even more. He got zero pussy growing up in Detroit until he got his weight up in the dope game. Now he was the head of Black Mob's Detroit operations and had something to put his dick in daily. Except tonight because this one kept shaking her head 'no'.

"She said no boss," Steve announced when he returned empty handed. "How about her? Or her? Ooh! Or that one!"

"Fucked them all already," Chico said, trying not to pout. He rocked in his seat building momentum and lifted himself out of his seat. He had an attaché case full of mob money and grabbed it to use as bait. Bass like sardines, catfish bite on gizzards, but you need cold, hard cash when fishing for thots.

The stripper smiled as she watched the man waddle her way. She wasn't a very good dancer, but turned it up a notch to seal the deal.

"Girl, what you doing? You ain't gone get no tips like that!" a veteran stripper chided over the music. She was a pro hoe and knew enough to know how a stripper should at least take her clothes off. "These niggas wanna see curvy hips and pussy lips!"

"Un-uh!" the new girl said, grimacing and shaking her head. The veteran stripper shook her head, too, when the girl actually blushed. If the girl didn't want any money she would get it herself.

"Hey!" Chico called from the edge of the stage. It took two more 'heys' for the girl to turn her head. Chico opened the brief case and let the dead presidents speak for him. He only planned on parting with a small part of the cash, but used it all as bait. The girl turned her nose up then turned her back and shook her ass. "This is fifty thousand dollars!"

There was a small stampede of whores and hoes when they saw how much money was at stake. The new girl was the only one who wasn't interested and Chico was in love.

"I'm gonna marry you!" he declared, nodding to make it true. "I'm gonna suck your pussy inside out!"

"How romantic," she cringed at the notion. He probably meant well, but it sounded painful to her.

"I could use the money I guess for my mom. She's crazy. Not crazy like drooling and banging her head against the wall. She's more like a lunatic."

"And money would help her. Help me, help you, to help her," he said, extending his chubby fingers. The girl didn't take the hand, but she did step down off the stage to follow him and the cash.

"What's your name, lil' mama?" Chico asked since it's good etiquette to get a name before you put your dick in someone.

"Um, Tisha," she replied following him through the club. The veterans snarled jealously as he led her away. None particularly wanted to fuck him again, but would for a satchel full of cash.

"We out!" Chico barked to Steve, causing him to pop up like he had a spring-loaded ass. He fell in step behind her and watched her heart-shaped behind shift from side to side. It wasn't one of those big, ghetto booties, but still looked good hanging out the boy shorts. He had no problem with sloppy seconds and would be ready once Chico got off and went to sleep.

"Here you go, little mama," Steve said, holding the door for her to enter after his boss was seated. "What's your name?"

"Donna," she replied and scrunched her face, trying to recall the name she used before. She shrugged since it didn't matter anyway. She was pretty sure neither man would be talking about what happened tonight.

Chico had his dick out by the time the door closed behind her. Almost out that is because he didn't have enough dick to come all the way out of his pants.

"Come on and let a nigga get a little appetizer," he purred, reaching for her head for some head.

"You already have a little appetizer," she snickered shyly at the little penis. "Wait 'til we get to your place and I'm gonna rock your world!"

"And I'll rock yours!" he shot back as if he really could. He flirted and burped as they rode out to his secluded house. She had been there earlier today and already knew the way. She looked at the rental car she parked a block away from her earlier visit. Steve pulled into the driveway and came around to open the doors.

"Four, sixteen, eight, eight," the young woman giggled along to Steve entering the code to disable the alarm.

"How you know?" he challenged. This was a serious breach of security, but Chico didn't care. He was ready to fuck something.

"I was here earlier. Don't worry. I didn't steal nothing. I dropped some things off," she vowed honestly.

"Come on, Tisha," Chico fussed and took her by her hand towards his. "I want me some head!"

"I get head first though!" she insisted. Steve watched her tight booty as she walked away and waited on his next.

"Thought she said her name was Donna?" he asked, scratching his head. He shrugged it off and fixed a drink. Knowing Chico, it wouldn't be long before he would have her to himself. He talked all that shit and spent all that dough, but couldn't stay in the pussy more than a couple minutes.

"Get that shit off!" he demanded once they reached him room. The girl giggled and blushed when he stripped out of his clothes. He was wrinkled, hairy and fat with a tiny dick hidden behind his pubic hair.

"OK, chill. Lay back and let me dance for you. Then I want that head," she purred. The fat man followed directions and climbed on his bed. She stood over him on the bed and did some whack moves since she wasn't really a very good dancer.

"You're not really a dancer are you?" he asked since she was jerking around like a chicken.

"No," she pouted and reached behind his pillow. She removed a shiny metal ring and slipped it over his head.

"What's this?" he wondered and cocked his head. She reached down and lifted his head straight again.

"DC 2000. You did say I could get some head right?" she asked, flashing her mother's smile. She was a lot like her mother in a lot of ways.

"What does it do?" he asked just before she hit the switch. He wouldn't hear the answer since his head popped off and rolled away. She followed it off the bed and leaned down to explain.

"DC 2000. Short for decapitator, not sure about the 2000," she said, scratching her head. "Anyway, it's my moms. She lets me use it, but I really need to get something of my own. My own signature-killing device. The Shyne-nator or something. Well, I'm going to go kill Steve now, so I can go home to my family."

"There she is. That was quick?" Steve teased when Shyne emerged from the room with her hands behind her back. "Ready for the main event?"

"I am," she said with a smile that contradicted the baseball bat she produced.

"What's that for?" he asked with a smile, but didn't like the answer since he didn't have a smile anymore.

"Ugh!" Shyne grunted and swung the bat. It erased his front teeth and knocked them down his throat. He gagged and choked on his fronts while she went to work.

"Yeeoow!" he screamed when she broke his chin with the next swing.

"Batter up!" the goofy girl yelled when he went down on one knee. It put his head in position for the speeding bat. The resulting crunch of brains and bone spread that pretty smile on her face once more. He was about as dead as one can get, but she still beat his head in then broke every limb on his body. Bones protruded through skin like tree limbs after a bad storm. The gory scene would have made most girls lose their lunch, but Shyne isn't like most girls. No, she's her mother's daughter.

Chapter 23

"Welcome home, baby," Asad greeted when his wife returned from her latest business trip.

"That's not how you welcome your wife home after being gone for a week!" Shyne fussed as she marched towards the bedroom. Her clothes flew off with every step she took. Asad cracked his sideways, smiled and followed her into their room. An hour later, he was sweating profusely and struggling for air. She was balled up in a fetal position sucking her thumb.

"You good?" he asked hopefully. He was spent, but would go another round if she wanted. After all, Shyne gets whatever Shyne wants as far as her husband was concerned.

"Water, water!" she pleaded and gasped. He rolled off the bed and went to retrieve a glass of water. She got up, too, and wobbled on rubbery legs on her way to the bathroom. She got herself together and went to turn on the shower.

"Here you go, baby," he said, returning with her water. She downed it in one long gulp and pulled him into the shower. After round two, they got cleaned so they could get dressed.

"Let's go see my parents," Shyne suggested once she was properly welcomed home. As expected, he agreed and they set off to the suburbs.

"So, how was your trip? You handle your business?" Asad asked as he drove.

"It was great! I did handle my business. The virus is destroyed," she said cheerfully. Her husband didn't understand how his goofy wife became a cyber security expert. Companies from all over the country were requesting her services to get rid of viruses.

That's exactly what the resurgent Black Mob was; a virus in need of dead. Her parents destroyed them once before she was born, but they grew back like weeds. Shyne was a weed killer just like her parents.

"Shyne!" the two youngest siblings shouted when they saw their beloved big sister pull up. They dropped what they were doing and rushed to the car before she could open her door.

"Hey, guys!" she sang and got out. They wrestled on the front lawn for a few minutes before heading to the house. "What's mom and dad doing?"

"In the room. They made us go outside to play," Diedra snitched with a pout. If Shyne were to be jealous of anyone, it would her pretty, little sister. Shyne got their mother's good looks, but her sister favored their grandmother. She looked like a little Indian girl with long dark hair pulled into Pocahontas braids.

"Well, you guys need to get out the house sometimes," she advised. These digital children of this digital age rarely saw the sun. They entered the well-appointed house and Shyne yelled up the stairs for her parents. "Mom! Dad! I'm home!"

"Shit!" Killa fussed when his daughter's voice reached them.

"Un uh! Don't stop!" Yolo said, throwing it back to meet his back shots. She arched her back and sealed the deal. The house could have caught on fire now and he wouldn't have pulled out of his wife. Instead, he plunged to the bottom and out to the hilt. Down to the bottom and out to the hilt. It paid off when she came and coated his thick dick in that good cream that only good pussy produces.

"Shit!" he grunted and let go. The couple shivered and shook from the spasms of a mutual orgasm. Everything is better when you can share it with someone you love. Especially busting a good nut.

"Ma! You in there!" Shyne called and wiggled the knob to the bedroom door. She covered her mouth with a hand to stifle a giggle and knocked some more. "Ma!"

"Cock blocking ass," Killa grumbled and pulled out of his wife. He wobbled towards the bathroom while she went for her robe. "Your daughter."

"Can't stand this girl!" Yolo lied as she went to open the door. She would never admit it aloud, but Shyne was and always would be her favorite. "What, little girl!"

"Hey, mommy! What's wrong? You're sweating? You look flushed," she said and tried to put the back of her hand to her forehead to take her temperature.

"Girl, boo! Get out of here. We'll be down in a few!" Yolo said, knocking her hand away. She stepped back and closed the door in her daughter's face.

"Round two?" Killa asked with a waiting erection when Yolo reached the shower.

"You can't even count." she said, shaking her head as she climbed in the shower. She turned her back to him, bent over and said behind her, "This is round 4."

Once Killa and Yolo wrapped up round 5, they stepped out of the shower and wrapped in plush towels to dry off. Yolo watched her husband apply lotion to his legs and got turned on again. That led to round 6 and another shower. It's a good thing her tubes were tied, twisted and burned because they went at it almost daily. After all these years, they were both absolutely crazy about each other. They were both absolutely crazy, too. Poor Asad was leaned over sleep on the sofa when the host finally came down stairs.

"Daddy!" Shyne lost it and cheered like she does whenever she sees her celebrity father. Superman had nothing on Killa in her book.

"Hey, baby," the doting dad greeted and hugged his daughter. Asad awoke from the commotion and stood to shake his father in law's hand.

"As salaamu alaykum, Asad."

"Wa alaykum as salaam," he greeted with a firm handshake and eye contact just like Killa had taught him. Killa practically raised him and raised him to maintain and protect his daughter. Meanwhile, Shyne and her mother excused themselves to the kitchen just like any normal mother and daughter would. Why wouldn't they since they are a normal mother and daughter? Well, except they kill people and set stuff on fire.

"So, am I getting another brother or sister soon?" Shyne teased since she knew what her parents were doing. It wasn't hard to tell since they were always doing it.

"Better question is when am I getting some grandkids?" Yolo shot back quickly. "You guys have been married for what, five years now?"

"Yup, cuz I'm twenty one now. Anyway, I don't know. The way we get it in I would have thought we would have had six by now! Just this morning we—"

"I'm sure I don't want to know. I do want to hear about your trip though?" the mother said, lowering her voice not to be heard by the men in the next room.

"Detroit was great," Shyne whispered through her smile. "Chico gave me some head."

"I hope you cleaned my DC 2000? It was filthy when you came back from Tempe," Yolo grimaced. "You need your own thing. Like a flamethrower or something since you like fire so much."

"I love fire, but a flamethrower is kinda bulky, no?" she asked, scratching her curly head and twisting her lips thoughtfully.

"We'll come back to it when you come back from Tulsa. They got a virus that needs killing," Yolo snarled. Her vendetta with the Black Mob was the stuff of legends. She often wondered what her life could or would have been if she hadn't been raised by the notorious crime syndicate. She shook the thought away realizing that her life was perfect. Every event, good or bad, led her to this here and now.

"What's happening in Tulsa?" Shyne asked eagerly. She knew her mother's hatred of the Mob ran deep from reading the diary. Yolo wasn't able to do it herself, but her crazy daughter gladly took her place.

She took it upon herself to murder a Black Mob member who moved into their condo building. The man kept flirting with Shyne every time her husband blinked. She took him up on his offer to "Netflix and Chill" but got he "Netflixed and Killed" instead. The murder had shed light on the resurrection of the Mob. They came from all over the country in a show of force and showed their hand. Yolo almost came out of retirement to blow the funeral up. Heavy police presence couldn't stop her, but her husband did.

"Torrey Flowers. Age 35. Married, two kids at home and two more with the side chick. He controls sex, drugs and hip hop in the city," she explained to her daughter.

"I hope they have insurance and fond memories of their dad," Shyne growled.

"Huh?" Killa asked hearing the word 'dad' as he entered the kitchen to grab drinks for him and his son-in-law. Asad wasn't thirsty, but Killa was nosey, so he made an excuse to check on the ladies.

"Shyne was just telling me how we should be grandparents soon cuz she and Asad get it in like crazy. This morning they—where you going?" she laughed as Killa snatched two sodas from the fridge and ran. "He won't be back."

"Does your husband know? What we're doing?" Shyne asked in a whisper.

"Does yours?" she shot back since she wasn't the only one keeping secrets.

"Nah, I tell him I'm doing I.T. work. I hate lying to my husband though," she pouted. Her bottom lip began to quiver as if she were about to cry.

"Girl, don't be no punk. You're doing what needs to be done. God's work! Like an apostle or something. Too much?" she wondered as her daughter's lips twisted into a 'yeah right'. "Well, they still need dead."

"And that's exactly what they're gonna get. Dead, all of them, everywhere!"

"I wish I could come with you," Yolo sighed. She hadn't killed anything in years except a fly here or there and it was killing her.

"Yo! That would be so dope!" Shyne cheered way too loud. Her nosey ass father lifted his head in the next room to hear what he could hear, but she brought it back down.

"Can you imagine? Yolo and Shyne, getting it in! You should come."

"I'm not leaving my babies home alone with that dude!" she reeled at the idea.

"You mean my father?" Shyne frowned in shock. "Yo, you left me and my brother alone with him how many times? And look how we turned out!"

"And you think that helps your case?" Yolo cracked up. Tears streamed down her face and her yellow face turned red as she guffawed loudly. "Yo, you're a fire bug. Sun is a damn weirdo. Rico is a hoe. X is a goon. Asad is the only one who turned out OK."

"Well..." Shyne said and stopped when she couldn't think of a reply. Her mother was right. Sun was a weirdo and Rico was a hoe. Xavier was the only one who moved back to New York. He was an aspiring rapper posing as a goon, but most rappers do so it's cool. "Can grandma watch them?"

"Sure! That's exactly what she's going to do. Watch them do whatever the hell they want to do," Yolo chuckled. "Let's not forget she is who raised your father!"

"Ah..." Shyne nodded in agreement. "Well, one day you and I will have to take a girls trip. It's gonna be epic!"

"We're going to really fuck some shit completely up when we do!

Chapter 24

"Harpo, who these hoes?" Harpo's girl, Tammy, demanded as she scanned his phone's photo gallery. It took a few tries, but she managed to get by his security codes once again.

"Bitch, how you get in my shit again?" he fussed and snatched it from her hand. "You know what I do and you ain't got no problem spending the bread!"

"But, they so...young!" she said with mixed emotions stuck in her throat. Yeah they were young, but she did like spending the dough her porn producing husband produced, but the girls were getting younger and younger. These latest were just children doing grown up stuff.

"I don't like it either, but what choice do I have?" he asked and actually waited for an answer. He hoped she did have a way for him to get out of this situation he'd gotten himself into. He heard Black Mob on a record and started using the brand. That invited the real Black Mob to step to him with an offer he couldn't refuse. It was either get down or lay down. Down in a box that is and what kinda choice is that?

"Let's just go! Fuck Tulsa! Let's go somewhere, anywhere!" she pleaded so they could escape.

"I ain't leaving my city," he said, sticking his chest out defiantly. "A hurricane couldn't get me out my city!"

It sounded good, but little did he know a huge storm was headed his way. Hurricane Shyne was meaner than Katrina and much more destructive.

"Boy, stop! You let some voice on the phone scare you into giving up half yo' money and run your business! With yo' bitch ass!" Tammy fussed, which was what she did most and the best. Harpo drifted into one of those pleasant daydreams of choking the life out of her. Little did he know, he was about to get his wish. Not exactly how he dreamed it, but same result.

****

"Have a nice trip, babe," Asad said, trying his luck when Shyne finished packing.

"That is not how you send you wife away on a trip!" she fussed. Shyne gets what Shyne wants, so her husband gave her the business. An hour later they set off for the airport.

"Where, um, this time?" Asad asked as he drove to Atlanta's busy airport.

"Tulsa, Oklahoma," she replied and thought about her dream where her brother got to knock the mob off. Now she was going for real. She would have rode her bike out there to kill the child porn producer. The fact that he was Black Mob was gravy on her potatoes.

"I wish you could come."

"But I can't. Not yet anyway until things settle down at the store," Asad replied. They had recently opened a bookstore and business was booming. He had to manage the joint and had no time for trips.

"Yeah, I know," she pouted. She would love to take him and just sneak out to murder the mob while he slept. He had no problem sleeping from all the sex. They arrived an hour early and went to an upper parking deck and got it in once more. Shyne gets want Shyne wants.

Shyne landed a few hours later and took a rental to her hotel. The last goodbye made her sleepy, too, so she took a nap. She had already done her homework, so she knew where Harpo would be that night.

*****

"Quit playing and throw that dick, wit yo' bitch ass!" Tammy yelled behind her to Harpo. He was throwing it just fine, but always threw it a little harder when she made him mad. That's why she chumped him off while he was delivering back shots. "Do I need to grow a dick and bend you over!? With yo bitch ass!"

"Stupid ass bitch," he mumbled under his breath and threw his hips into overdrive. He gripped her wide hips and threw that dick with everything he had and some he borrowed.

"Oh, yo' bitch ass tryna make me cum! That's what you, mmm, want? Ok, ok! I'll cum!" Tammy moaned and came all over his dick. He kept on pounding until it got the best of him, too. Harpo snatched out of that good snatch and bust a nut on her back.

"That was a good one," a voice said in the darkness and clapped. The lovers froze when they realized they weren't alone. Most guys can appreciate an audience when they know they really laid it down, but Harpo knew he was in trouble.

"Did they send you?" he asked, meaning the mob. His erection deflated and fell out of his woman.

"Told yo' bitch ass this would happen! Told you we should have left town!" Tammy snapped. Shyne cocked her head curiously as she listened to her berate her man. She read him the entire riot act calling him so many different kinds of bitches that it made Shyne blush.

"Bruh, is she always like this?" Shyne asked while Tammy continued to verbally abuse the man. She would never dream of speaking to Asad like that. Her husband was mild mannered, but would choke a chick if he had to.

"Pretty much. She don't got any respect for me," Harpo admitted and lowered his head in utter defeat. "I'on know what to do?"

"Beat her," Shyne suggested and sat back to watch.

"Beat who? I wish this nig—ugh!" Tammy started to say as Harpo started to get on her ass. He snuck her with a sucker punch that she ate like cake. Tammy wasn't no punk though and fought back. Shyne pulled her phone and sat back to record the fight. And what a fight it was. Tammy obviously watched footage of Muhammad Ali's famous rope-a-dope and executed it perfectly. She used her meaty arms to cover and deflect his wild punches. Soon he started to slow down when he got tired.

"Had enough?" he asked with his last bit of energy.

"Mm-mm," she said, shaking her head. Now it was her turn and she demonstrated how to whoop an ass properly. She threw a combination of punches, kicks and elbows that folded him up like a cheap lawn chair.

"OK, OK!" Harpo pleaded when his woman beat him into a fetal position. Shyne just shook her head at the lopsided fight. "OK, you got it!"

"I know I got it. With yo' bitch ass!" she said with a few parting stomps and kicks. She stood and turned to Shyne with her fist balled and barked, "You told Harpo to beat me!"

"Yup!" Shyne giggled and raised her gun. The long silencer muffled the two shots that shut her up forever. "I'm not tryna fight you, Sophia!"

"Good for your big ass!" Harpo cheered and hopped to his feet. He used one of them to give the big bully a kick in her head.

"Really, bruh? She dead," Shyne said, twisting her lips into a 'yeah right'. "You know why I'm here, don't you?"

"Cuz I shorted the last payment? It was her idea," he said, hooking his thumb at the dead woman. "Now that she's gone..."

"I can just let you go? That's not why I'm here. You shoot videos of kids doing grown up shit," Shyne growled.

"They made me! I'm a movie producer, but they made me film kids! They said they would kill me!" he whined. Shyne saw why his woman didn't respect his whiny bitch ass in an instant.

"Ironic, huh, since I'm going to kill you for doing it. Damned if you didn't and damned cuz you did. I'm gonna kill them, too, though. Who runs the show? Where is the head?" Shyne asked so she could decapitate it.

"I don't know. All we get is phone calls. Me, Roscoe and Marcus never seen a soul. We just pay them," he said, dry-snitching on his friends.

"Well, if you wanna live a little longer, I wanna know how you pay," she demanded and pointed the pistol. She took note of the names Roscoe and Marcus so she could visit them next.

"Here," he said and passed her his phone. It contained banking information about his monthly payments. Shyne couldn't decipher it, but knew her mother could.

"Thanks," she said and looked down at her watch. She watched a few seconds tick off then raised her gun.

"Wait! You said I could live a little longer?" he pleaded and pointed.

"Five seconds is a little longer," she shrugged and shot. A silent round to his forehead dropped him on top of his girl just like she found them. "Now it's time to visit Roscoe and Marcus."

*****

"Nigga still ain't answering," Marcus said when Harpo's voice mail came on again. He was supposed to meet them to hang out for the night, but was a no show. What they didn't know was that his next appearance would be at his wake. They didn't know either they would be joining him shortly.

The big ballers of the city kept a condo to trick off in with the city's strippers and thots. Harpo made it when he could if he didn't have a black eye or busted lip. That's why it was no surprise when he didn't show or answer his phone.

"That big bitch prolly got him sucking her dick," Roscoe quipped. "Wish I would let some bitch run me. Picture some bitch telling me what to do!"

"Shit, she prolly making the nigga suck his own dick. Got him stripping 'n-shit. Speaking of strippers, where Nita 'n-dem?" he asked just before a knock on the door. "OK then!"

"Harpo sent me," Shyne greeted when Rosco snatched the door open. He poked his lip out at the strange girl staring up at him. She was cute and all, but not the big booty strippers he was waiting on.

"He did? Where Chocolate and Pineapple?" he said, looking in the hall behind her. For some reason strippers always name themselves after flavors. It's understandable, but deceptive. They should use flavors like mold, yeast and fungi.

"Yeah, well Chocolate had a really bad yeast infection and Pineapple got crabs and lobsters. Shits bad, yo!" she said, walking in the apartment. He shrugged at her round little ass and ignored the Louisville slugga in her hand.

"You the scripper?" Marcus asked for the same reason. Shyne looked far too tame for their taste. They were seconds away from finding out just how wild she was.

"Yeah, I'm the scripper," she mocked. "Except y'all gotta strip, too. I ain't fixin' or finna be the only one naked!"

Both men shrugged since they planned to screw her like they screw all the other strippers. Shyne waited until they both had their pants down and sprang into action. She swung for the fences and nearly knocked Rosco's head off. He was the lucky one who died instantly.

Marcus, well he wasn't so lucky.

"What the fuck!" he screamed and lifted his arm to deflect the blow. The blow turned his forearm into two when she broke it. He lifted the other one and got it broken, too. Then his leg, collarbone, next leg and neck. Shyne literally broke every bone in his body.

"Would you go on and die already?" she whined when he just kept hanging on. She winded up one last blow and knocked his soul over center field. "Thank you! Now I can go home to my husband."

Chapter 25

"Can we go out to eat?" Shyne begged playfully as she dressed.

"Yup," Asad eagerly agreed since his wife wasn't a very good cook. She was smart, funny and sexy, but sucked in the kitchen. Odd, since her mother could cook anything from burgers to babies, tacos to toddlers. She did teach her how to break a body down into quarters like a chicken.

"Um, you was just a little too happy about that! You really don't like my cooking?" she asked with a pout.

"You are so pretty," Asad replied, squinting from her blinding prettiness.

"I am?" she gushed, blushed and giggled. It worked every time and changed the subject. "You, sir, have just earned yourself a coochie coupon! Redeemable anytime you want."

"Yay, thanks," Asad said, shaking his head. He certainly didn't need a coupon or reason. Shyne wanted a baby, so he was on call 24/7.

The couple made a striking appearance anywhere they went. She was a pretty, curly-head woman like her mother and he was a 6'4", chestnut-colored hunk. He cut his braids and now wore his hair cropped close to his head. They grew up together and knew each other so well they could communicate without saying a word.

"Can we get chicken and waffles?" Shyne asked since it was her husband's favorite food. She barely beat him to the punch by suggesting they swing by her favorite burger joint.

"Sure," he replied and pressed for the elevator. It came a moment later and let them board.

"Hey, whatever happened to that guy? The one with the gold teeth and lady shirts. Who used to wink and blow kisses at you when he thought I wasn't looking."

"Who? I don't, I don't remember who?" Shyne feigned, scrunching her face and scratching her head.

"Mmhm," he laughed at the phony display. "I was waiting to catch him by myself."

"Yeah, well I haven't seen him since..." Shyne said and recalled the fond memory of sending him to that big ghetto in the sky.

"There she is! I been waiting to catch you alone!" Aaron cheered, rubbing his hands together like a housefly.

"Is that right? Well, I've been waiting to catch you alone, too," she assured him, but for a different reason. He was thinking "Netflix and Chill" while she had "Netflix and Kill" on her mind.

"Well, come on then," he invited her when the elevator door stopped on his floor. Shyne knew she shouldn't, but couldn't resist and wouldn't let him keep disrespecting her husband.

Shyne followed him down the hall, trying not to laugh at his funny walk. He adopted a ditty bop trying to be cool, but it looked more like he was switching when he walked. The lines between femininity and masculinity has blurred in recent years. Dudes could now twerk, wear dresses, suck dick and no one would raise an eyebrow. The old school rules still rule because this new school was gay.

"Un huh," Aaron nodded as he swung his door open expecting Shyne to be impressed by his gaudy decorations. The moron had a hot tub and stripper pole right in his living room. A hundred-inch TV dominated the wall while a leather sectional monopolized the rest of the room.

"What do you do? Rap?" she assumed since it was obvious he had more money than class like someone who came into a lot of money quickly.

"Nah, I'm a trapper. Black Mob shit!" he bragged. Shyne squinted at the name she recalled from her mother's diary. Her blood boiled at the name of the organization that tried to destroy her parents.

"What's that?" she dared. She was here to beat him up for being disrespectful to her husband, but if he was what he claimed, he would be her first kill. But if there were more, then he wouldn't be her last.

"Black Mob? We the biggest, baddest crew in the country! We err where! Atlanta. New Yawk. Detroit," he bragged as her blood began to boil.

"Ugh!" Shyne grunted and surprised them both when she attacked. She swung a vicious elbow that removed two of those gold teeth he loved to flash. He slammed back against his door, but Shyne didn't let up. She shot a nasty knee into his groin that doubled him over. He wanted to bust a nut, but that wasn't quite what he had in mind. The next knee straightened him back upright where another elbow awaited. He finally fell face down, sound asleep. Shyne pulled his blouse around his neck and began to squeeze. She squeezed until his bladder released in death.

"Oh, now you wanna pee on yourself, huh?" Shyne mocked the corpse. She got a quick giggle until the reality of what she did settled on her shoulders. "Uh oh."

Shyne felt a rush of satisfaction as she looked down at the dead man and smiled. She shrugged and dragged him into his well-appointed kitchen. Aaron had a steady diet of takeout, but he still had all the bells and whistles. She found a high-end knife set and got ready to get down to business.

"Not messing up my stuff," Shyne huffed and stripped out of her clothing. Aaron wanted to get her naked in his house and got his wish. He probably should have wished he was alive because he was too dead to enjoy it. Shyne flashed back to her mother teaching her how to cut up a chicken. It suddenly dawned on her why she would refer to wings as arms as she removed his tattooed arms.

Shyne tried to ignore his dick as she worked his legs off. The head was last. She stuffed the body parts into trash bags and got to work searching his condo.

"You can't spend this where you're going," she mumbled as she collected the cash. She turned her nose up at the slum jewels on the dresser and kept searching. She grabbed all papers and info on the Black Mob and threw them in a bag. The body parts went into the condo's dumpster, *but she dropped the head off at the address listed as 'Boss Man' from the papers. He would have been next until she told her mother who told her to save him for last. Boss Man was on borrowed time and didn't even know it...*

"Um, Shyne?" Asad said, snapping his wife from her pleasant daydream when the elevator reached the lobby.

"Uh? Nope, haven't seen him. Un uh," she said, shaking her head and walked off the elevator.

"Not again?" Shyne said when they pulled up to her parent's house and found her younger siblings outside again. "Those two go at it all day, everyday!"

Asad snapped his head at the pot that just called her parents freaks. The poor fellow was forced to perform on demand like a cable box. She saw him looking and laughed, "So!"

"Shyne!" Diedra and little Killa shouted and rushed her when she stepped out.

"You got us food? Mom won't feed us," her sister pouted while her brother nodded.

"No, little con man and woman. This is for your mom," Shyne said, lifting the takeout bag out of Killa's reach. The kids turned on Asad as she marched to the house.

"What you got?" Diedra demanded while her little brother patted his pockets.

"Break yourself, big bruh!" the pint-sized jacker insisted. They got what they wanted when he tackled them both and wrestled with them while Shyne went inside to disturb her parents' groove. She started up the stairs until she heard her mother's laughter from the rear.

"What!" Shyne reeled when she found her parents in the den watching TV instead of locked behind their bedroom door. She went straight to her daddy and plopped down on him. "Here, mommy. We got you chicken and waffles."

"Thanks!" Yolo said and tore into the bag. She was halfway through before she asked her husband if he wanted some. "Have some?"

"Uh... no," he laughed and turned to his daughter. "How's my baby girl?"

"I'm your baby girl!" Diedra shouted when she walked in and heard him using her title. She rushed over and dived between her sister and father.

"Sellout," Shyne mused and stood. "Guess I'll just take my mom then. Come on, mom."

"Hole up!" Yolo said as she scarfed down the last of the food. She stood and followed her daughter out to the backyard. "Nice work out there. Three for one, huh?"

"Yeah, Harpo gave up his buddies," she laughed. She was always amazed how these thugs snitched each other out as soon as the heat comes down.

"They always do. No one wants to die alone," Yolo nodded. She would know since she put the Mob out of business once.

"So can I get Boss Man now?" Shyne pleaded, bouncing like she was asking for a slice of cake and not permission to murder.

"Not just yet. If he's really running the show, then let him wait on it. Let him watch and wait as his whole network gets knock off. One by one, city by city," Yolo snarled. Her daughter could see how personal this was for her and knew she would take care of Boss Man personally.

"Where to next then?" she asked, ready to go anywhere and murder anybody.

"New York City! You need to pay your big brother a visit. He's having problems with the Mob but I don't want your father to find out," Yolo said casually while knowing how protective the woman was about her brothers. She smiled internally when she reacted just like she expected.

"Grrrrrr."

Chapter 26

"You crazy, Fuck-Shit!" Bougie-Boy laughed and slapped his knee like a good hype man should. A real hype man will guffaw at the lamest lines and whackest jokes.

"I'm serious! That bitch pussy looked like some roast beef. I told her the only way I was eating that was in a sandwich!" the rapper insisted. He was right since his latest conquest from the club had way too many miles on her vagina. "Still fucked her though."

Fuck-Shit got his name honestly by age five. He was a horrible little boy who peed in his grandmother's iced tea and stole from the collection plate at church. Pastor told his grandmother not to bring that little bastard around no more and he got worse. When he stole her dentures all she could say was, "That's that fuck shit" and the name stuck. He's been on the fuck shit ever since.

"I hate a big beat up box!" Bougie said, shaking his head, mourning the vagina walls. Vaginal walls are a terrible thing to waste.

"Who opening up for me tonight?" the rapper asked. His shows were the biggest in town, so it was an honor. With the Black Mob behind him, he managed to top the charts and rule the airways.

"That dude X from High Bridge is dope! We should—" his assistant suggested, but got cut off.

"No can do. He ain't Mob and don't wanna pay homage," Fuck-Shit declined with a frown. The Black Mob ran the club scene and as in anything else, you had to get down or lay down. "Matter fact, he need to start paying!"

"I'on know?" Bougie said, scratching his head. He wasn't quite sure why Xavier Forrest garnered so much respect, but knew he was not to be fucked with.

"What?" Fuck-Shit reeled at being questioned. Sidekicks usually don't question anything. They're obedient and do what they are told to do.

"OK, I'll tell him what you said," Bougie Boy sighed. He got up and headed over to the studio where X was recording.

*****

"Yeah, that's some real bullshit," Jay said as he stopped the track and waved Xavier out of the booth.

"What?" X asked and sat down next to him to listen to his vocals. The answer would have to wait when he checked his phone. "My sister is here!"

"Word!" the engineer cheered a little too cheerfully for the protective big brother. A dangerous glare wiped the eager smile from his face and he tried again. "Oh word, that's cool."

"Yeah, now what was you saying?" he asked again. Again he would have to wait when the door opened and in walked Bougie Boy. Both men's eyes went wide at his skinny jeans and big red sneakers. His jewelry clinked on his neck and wrist.

"Sup, fellas," Bougie greeted, extending his hand to be shook or slapped five. It was neither as the two men frowned at his painted fingernails.

"What?" X wanted to know so he could get back to work. He had just laid his vocals and was eager to hear the playback.

"Tell him. Tell him what you just texted me," Jay dared. He was glad not to be the bearer of bad news. He just hoped X didn't kill the messenger.

"Oh yeah. Well, Fuck-Shit said you can't open up cuz you won't get down with the team. He want you on Fuck-Shit's records! He'll give you a whole ten percent and split your publishing with you!"

"I'm gonna whoop his ass," X said to Jay as if Bougie wasn't there and still talking.

"Whip or whoop? There's a difference you know," Jay asked, seeking clarity. Bougie Boy was still touting the benefits of signing with the Black Mobs record imprint while the two debated what kind of beating he should get.

"Like a parent does a child," Xavier explained. He would know since he got plenty of them back in his day.

"Like, put him over your knee?" Jay chuckled while the man kept talking.

"Yeah. If he wants to act like a boy, I'm gonna treat him like one," X said. His mind was made up, so he stood and removed his belt.

"Don't whoop me, bruh," Bougie demanded putting a little more bass in his voice. His plea fell on deaf ears as X moved in. His lifted him by the arm and turned him like a mother does her three year old.

"Didn't. I. Tell. You. Not. To. Come. Around. Here. With. That. Fuck. Shit. From Fuck-Shit!" Xavier asked and beat his butt. The man reached his hand down to deflect the blows.

"What the—" Shyne laughed in disbelief as she walked in on the whooping. Asad blinked and rubbed his eyes to make sure he was seeing what he was seeing.

"Oh! Hey, sis. Give me one second," X said still whooping that ass. "Now! Run. Tell. Yo'. Daddy. That!"

"That's messed up!" Bougie Boy cried with tears streaming down his face. X was smart enough to beat the man without leaving visible marks, unless Fuck-Shit saw his ass on a regular basis.

"OK, bye-bye," Shyne told the man as he stormed out pouting. She turned to her oldest brother and rushed into his arms. "Xavier!"

Asad smiled at the loving reunion then frowned at the engineer staring at his wife's ass. Shyne didn't wear tight clothes, so he had to work to see her shape under the long shirt covering her backside. Jay felt his eyes and turned away before he got in trouble.

"As salaamu alaykum, Asad," X greeted and hugged him next. "What brings you guys to town?"

"She got a contract up here. We decided to make a vacation out of it," Asad explained.

"Good, you guys can catch my show tomorrow night!" X cheered while Jay glared.

"Bruh, he said we can't get on the showcase," he whined. He was pretty sure negotiations had broken down when X gave the messenger a spanking.

"Bruh, I'm gonna be in that show. Trust me!" X assured him even though he was unsure himself.

As much as he hated to admit it, he may just have to sign with Fuck-Shit records just to get out and that's that fuck shit.

*****

"Are you sure you don't want to come?" Shyne asked since she already knew the answer. Her autistic husband was plenty social around friends and family, but she was pretty sure he had no desire to hang out in a loud club full of strangers. She was also pretty sure she just put it on him and knew he was ready to go to sleep.

"Nah, you and Xavier have fun," he said between yawns. They had a busy day ahead visiting friends and family in New York, so he rolled over and went to sleep.

Shyne took advantage of the opportunity to rush out to Long Island to her childhood home. Her mother granted her access to the basement arsenal and a thousand ways to kill. She entered the code and stepped inside.

"Oh my!" she gushed and felt her knees buckle when she saw all the guns, knives and other deadly devices. Shyne could pick out an outfit in under a minute. Picking the proper punishment for Fuck-Shit took an hour. Then she saw it. "Perfect!"

Shyne drove back out to the city and headed to the venue where Fuck-Shit was performing. His 'That's That Fuck Shit" tour was doing big numbers in it's nightly shows. It was the ticket to the big leagues and that's why X wanted in.

"Where's my brother?" X asked meaning her husband when he saw Shyne in the club. He frowned at her skimpy outfit and knew Asad couldn't be anywhere around. "I'm telling."

"Snitch," she dared, but he shrugged his shoulders. "Dude, I'm tryna help you get on the tour."

"I may have fucked that up," he admitted when he saw Bougie Boy glaring at him from the VIP section. He was standing next to a seated Fuck-Shit like a bodyguard even though they had two large ones nearby.

"Sit yo'ass down!" Fuck-Shit insisted once again. The man hadn't sat down since he returned from his whooping. Of course he couldn't, wouldn't tell his daddy another man whooped him.

"I'm good, yo. Tryna spot you a bitch to take home. Not unless you want some more roast beef!" he laughed, then winced when the movement in his skinny pants hurt his freshly whooped ass. It throbbed again when he saw X begin to approach.

"I come in peace," Xavier said as he raised his arms so security could pat him down.

"He cool. He don't want these problems," Fuck-Shit arrogantly called out. Security backed away and let him by. He like a lot of people began to believe his own hype.

"Sup, bruh. Sis," X nodded to Fuck-Shit and then his sidekick. Bougie Boy didn't appreciate being called sis and sucked his teeth like a sis.

"Chilling. I heard yo' lil' mix tape. You a'ight," he said, twisting his lips at his own statement. X was a beast and he knew it. He was 'next' and the Mob wanted in.

"Word," X laughed since he knew he was better than just a'ight. He was the bomb.com and everyone knew it. "I was thinking about your offer. We may need to talk about points, but we can do something."

"Say word!" Fuck-Shit shouted. "Let's get up tomorrow and chop it up. I'ma put you in the next showcase!"

"That's what's up. I'll hit your secretary tomorrow," he said nodding towards Bougie Boy once more. Bougie Boy sucked his teeth once more as he walked away. They both watched as he walked up on his cutie pie sister.

"Come on, let's bounce." he insisted and took her arm. "I made peace. I'm in."

"OK, but I'm still hanging out. I don't get out much you know," Shyne pouted. Her big brother was immune to her bullshit and shook his head.

"Not," he laughed and began to steer her towards the door.

"Hey, X," a pretty young thing sang and stole the attention from his sister. "'Member me?"

"Yes," he said even though he didn't. He wouldn't mind making memories with her though. Along with a couple of puddles on his comforter. She was the type you fuck on top of the sheets, with the lights on and camera rolling.

"OK, bye-bye," Shyne giggled and waved as the woman escorted her brother out of the club.

"I'da took the cute one," Fuck-Shit said discriminately as he watched the transaction. Luckily for Shyne, Bougie Boy was too embarrassed to get a good look at her when he got his ass whooped and didn't recognize her from the studio.

"Me, too," he lied. He would have taken the same one X picked or the dude behind her.

"Go get her," Fuck-Shit said instead of 'fetch' but with the same result. His hype man took off like a dog after a stick.

"Excuse me. My dad... I mean boss wanna meet you," he barked at Shyne and turned around and led her back to the VIP section. He was as proud as a golden retriever returning with a stick. He almost expected a pat on his head, but almost got a kick in his ass.

"Bruh?" Fuck-Shit laughed when he returned alone. He couldn't hear what he told Shyne, but saw her react by twisting her face, crossing her arms and staying put. Hard to get always works better than easy to fuck. "Want something done right, do it yourself,"

"So," Bougie Boy whispered and sucked his teeth once again. One of the security men who just returned from prison gave him a wink. His effeminate ways were turning him on.

"You enjoying yourself?" Fuck-Shit asked as he pulled up on Shyne.

"No. I'm ready to go," she said, looking bored.

"Let's go then," he invited and offered his elbow. She looked at it, him, then put her arm in his. "My name is Fuck-Shit."

"Shyne," she admitted since he'd never get to repeat it. He waved his security off when they attempted to join.

"I don't need no security for a girl," he joked. Shyne genuinely cracked up since she'd heard those same last words before. She honesty admired the brand new Bentley as he hopped in the driver side.

"Punk," she mumbled and opened the door for herself. A quick drive later, they pulled up to his Westchester condo unit and got out. Fuck-Shit was neither gentle nor a man as he led her up to his abode. She had to open her own doors because he was on the fuck shit as usual.

"Take your clothes off!" he demanded as soon as they crossed his threshold. He was eager to see what was under the form fitting dress live and direct.

"You first," she dared while digging in her purse. He shrugged and dropped his jeans and drawers in one tug. She only glanced at his meat to get a good shot. She aimed the modified taser and fired.

"Huh?" Fuck-Shit asked in confusion when the steel barbs dug into his dick. A second later she pulled the trigger again sending way too much juice into his body.

"Dang!" Shyne giggled as he did his dance. It was a cross between the Harlem shake and electric boogaloo. His poor dick shriveled into a strip of bacon as it cooked. Death came as a relief when the strong current stopped his heart. "Mind if I take a look around? Collect any cash and valuables? K, thanks."

Shyne took a few minutes in the condo to find whatever she could on the Mob. She added a satchel full of cash to her collection and left.

She drove the Bentley back into the city and parked near their hotel. Asad was still sleeping soundly when she slid into bed next to him. She cuddled up and fell fast asleep.

Chapter 27

"Hello?" Sun questioned as he took the unknown call. He'd been getting the weirdest calls the last few days and it was getting old. The callers seemed to know him, but he didn't know them. He gave his number to so many women on a daily basis it wasn't unusual to have a disgruntled boyfriend call every now and again, but this was beyond that. This was down right strange.

"Sun?" a male caller said, smiling through the line. The tone was baritone, yet had a slight timbre of bitch-ass just below the surface just like the others.

"Yeah, who this?" he barked, ready to bite. He was really sick of whiny boyfriends mad because their girl got some side dick. That's all he was since he was still single. He was desperately in love with his sister's friend, Bryonna, but she wouldn't give him the time of day as of late.

"My name is Calvin. I saw your profile and wanted to get to know you," he said hopefully.

"What profile? Where?" Sun said, knowing he had him mixed up since he didn't do social media. He certainly didn't do dating sites since he was a walking dating site. Six foot one, handsome and driving a nice car was all he needed to bag a woman. Sun got his barbers license and opened several popular spots around his adopted city of Atlanta.

"On D.L.B.," Calvin said, lowering his voice just above a whisper.

"D.L what?" Sun barked as he typed D.L. and waited for the rest of the site.

"B. D.L.B.," he repeated. Sun pressed the last letter, hit search and gasped.

"Down low brothers!" he screeched. "The fuck this got to do with me? How did you get my number?"

"From your profile. You're a real cutie pie, Sun Jackson," Calvin gushed and fluttered his eyes.

"Sun Jackson?" Sun asked while searching for the profile. He found it with his smiling face and dropped the phone in shock. "How? Who? What..."

"Hey!" he cheered. "So, we gonna hook up? Wanna come by my place? We can Netflix and Chill or Firestick and Dick"

"No, you bit—you know what? Yeah, where you stay?" he asked while putting his shoes on. He mentally wrote down the address and tore out of his bachelor's pad.

A few 'blinded by rage' filled minutes later, his GPS announced his arrival. Calvin was peeping out the cracked doorway while hiding behind the door.

Uh oh, Calvin thought to himself when he registered the look on Sun's face. It was a mask of malice, but it was too late.

"Who made that damn profile? What's the password? How do I log in?" he demanded. Calvin couldn't answer even if he knew since Sun lifted him on his feet by his throat. He choke slammed him to the ground and put his foot in his neck. "What's the password!"

"I, don't, argh, know!" he managed to get out passed the size 12 on his throat.

"Try, the customer service num... ber."

Sun used Calvin's phone and angrily dialed the 1-800 number. A male with another effeminate voice came on the line and asked how he could help.

"By taking my damn picture off this site!" Sun growled.

"You lost your password?" he gushed with a girly giggle. "What's your user name? I'll reset it."

"I don't have a user name. It's not me. Just my picture!" Sun replied. "Sun Jackson. It's my picture and phone number, but I didn't open it."

"Don't duck back in the closet, honey. Come to the light," he sang. Luckily he was states away in a call center or he would have a foot on his neck, as well.

"If you don't take my picture off this site, I'll—" he demanded. The operator got the hint and pulled up the profile.

"OK, OK. No need to get testy with your testicles," he giggled as he deleted the account. They deleted several a day from scorned girlfriends and college prankers.

"Somebody got you real good!"

"And this is funny to you?" Sun asked, still ready to take a trip to wherever he was.

"Un uh!" he said, shaking his head vigorously as he worked. He made a grand display of his last two keystrokes and declared, "Deleted!"

"Now you," Sun said down to the man underfoot. Calvin began to cry and Sun felt bad for him. He reached down and helped him up since it wasn't his fault.

"Who did you make mad? Scorned girlfriend?" he asked, trying to be helpful.

"Bryonna, but she wouldn't... that damn Shyne. Shyne!"

*****

"What's next?" Shyne asked eagerly as she and her mother made side items ready since Killa and his sons worked the grill. Asad and Rico stood proudly by as dad did his thing to the jerk chicken.

"Cali. They have an infestation that needs dead. You bringing your husband again?" Yolo asked.

"Hope so. I can't go too long without his... smile," she smiled wickedly. The smile didn't last long before her name was called.

"SHYNE!" Sun screeched as he rushed into the house. "I see her car! I know she here! Shyne!"

"Uh oh," Shyne said and slid behind her mother.

"Girl, what did you do?" Yolo asked to be sure if she wanted to protect her or not. She often wondered how she got away with some of the stunts she pulled on her brothers.

"Nothing," she lied to her as Sun barged into the kitchen with his fist balled up.

"Hey, Sun. Nice haircut!"

"Thanks, I... Never mind my haircut! You made a profile on a gay website with my face and phone number!" he shouted.

"Yeah, sis. You on your own with that one," Yolo advised and slid out the way. She didn't want to be a witness, so she left the twins alone in the kitchen.

"Me?" Shyne reeled and pointed at herself in mock shock. Sun twisted up his lips in disbelief, so she came clean. "It's time you came out of the closet. I been knew you was...ugh!"

"Hey, what the hell is going on?" Killa demanded when he walked in on his son choking his daughter. "Get off her boy!"

"Dad, she made a fake profile on a gay website!" Sun whined.

"Oh, Ok then. Carry on," he said, lifting Sun's hands back to Shyne's neck.

"Daddy!" Shyne whined and got some help. Killa let out a sigh and intervened once more.

"Ok, but why would you do that to your brother? He'll come out when he's good and ready. You can't rush..."

"Pops! I'm not gay! What's wrong with you people!" Sun insisted

"Well, you do wear skinny jeans. Oh and that romper that one time?" Killa said, trying to keep a straight face. The lines of femininity and masculinity had blurred. Fashion trends had dudes walking around like some bad bitches.

"Bruh, I didn't wear no romper! If I did I would have put up a profile my damn self!" he said, getting a laugh out of all of them. The levity lighted the mood as well as the grip on her neck.

He calmly turned to his twin for explanation. "Why? Huh? Why I gotta be a D.L.B? Now I gotta changed my damn number, again!"

"Cuz, man. I ain't like the way you did my friend! Bryonna loves your punk ass and you keep treating her wrong," Shyne said with a genuine pout.

"Mann, I love her too, but..." Sun said as if that answered the question. It didn't so she pushed on.

"Man, what? That's not an answer, bruh."

"I know. It's just she's, she don't, won't, I'm saying though," he stammered and tap-danced around his answer.

"Won't put out? Has morals? Saving herself for marriage?" Shyne fussed. "But how many chicks from back home got kids? HIV?"

"Yeah but—" he attempted, but got shut down again.

"But nothing! That's all you care about is butt! Booty, Butt, Ass! You should be ashamed of yourself! Got a good woman who loves you and... I just can't with you!" Shyne fussed and walked off.

"I'm sorry, sis. My bad, I...wait a minute?" Sun frowned when he realized he fell for her shit. Once again he'd been Shyned.

*****

The Forrest family cookout was in full swing by the time Xavier arrived from the airport via ride service. He would have arrived earlier, but a late night show delayed him in New York until this morning.

"Look what the cat dragged in!" grandmother Diedra cheered when X appeared. She rocked out her rocker and stood for a hug. As expected, he made a beeline straight to the old lady.

"Hey, grandma!" he said, giving her a tender squeeze. He let out a grunt when she hit him with a grandma hug. "Still got it, I see."

"Sup, yo," Killa greeted when his oldest finally made it to him. Being a dad sometimes means being last, but never least. "I hear you the man now."

"Yeah, the whole scene opened up when Fuck-Shit had his accident," he relayed. He had no idea his sister rigged the scene to look like he peed on a live current and fried 'til he died.

"Yeah, that's... crazy?" Killa said, scratching his head curiously. It reminded him of a hit he and Yolo did twenty years earlier. He squinted at his wife tending to little Killa and twisted his lips. If he hadn't been sure she was with him last night, he would have sworn it was her.

"What, pops?" X asked of the perplexed look on his face.

"Nothing." he said, now squinting at his daughter. She saw him and smiled. She had her mother's smile, which was good, but she also had the same look in her eyes. That faraway gaze of a lunatic. He couldn't help but wonder if she wasn't a lovely little lunatic just like her mother.

Chapter 28

"Killer Cali," Shyne sang, as she got off the plane at LAX. She felt mixed emotions that her husband couldn't make it. But business was booming, so he couldn't just leave the store. Not to mention Shyne kept running off his female employees if they even smiled in the same room as Asad.

"Dang, mama! Whew wee, that ass is fat!" a man catcalled as Shyne made her way to baggage pick up. She ignored him since she was use to dudes trying to pick her up. It was the price of being cute in this day and age. She tried to ignore it, that is until dude grabbed her hand. "Hole up, lil' mama."

"How old are you?" was the first thing that came to mind when she turned to see who had her by the wrist. The caramel colored man had cornrows and the latest fashions, but looked at least fifty in the face. Specs of grey in his hair and crow's feet around the eyes gave him away.

"Twenty nine," he lied and cracked a greyish smile. "I work in the music biz. I can make you a star."

"Can you now?" Shyne asked and finally pulled herself free. She had plenty of work to do and wanted to spare grandpa until she tried to walk away and he grabbed her booty. That was punishable by death, so she invited him to die. "Wanna take me some where to eat?"

"Shoot, we can go to my house? It ain't far," he said and led the way. He often played the airports and bus station for young women travelling alone. His music biz pitch was still working after twenty years.

"I'll have to follow you since I have a rental," she explained. George pumped his fist realizing he scored one with a little money. Most of the young girls he bagged were broke. That made his job of turning them out and selling them to porn producers and pimps that much easier.

"OK, just follow me." he said and waited in the parking garage. A few minutes later she pulled up and blew her horn. "Oh, you like to blow, huh?"

"Mmhm, and I'm gonna blow your mind when we get to your place," she replied, matching his dry chuckle. He proved he wasn't in any business when they pulled up to a rundown Watts apartment. Shyne smiled upon hearing all the hooping and hollering of the neighborhood. It meant no one would pay attention to his screams.

"Welcome to my humble abode," George said and stepped aside so she could enter. He assumed he got away with grabbing her ass the first time and grabbed it again. This time she whirled and slapped his chewing gum out of his mouth. "Feisty! You like getting your pussy ate?"

"I'on know," Shyne admitted and frowned curiously at the notion. She was married, but there were still a lot of things she had yet to indulge in. That was one of them. She saw a baseball bat leaned behind the door and became more interested in that. "What's this for?"

"Case one of these young niggas run up in here again, I mean if they did. I'll beat they as to death!" he bragged. Shyne smiled at the good idea and gave it a try.

"Like this!" she asked and swung the wood at his leg. The shin snapped almost as loud as the howl he let loose. "Or this?"

The next blow broke his face and prevented him from answering. His shoulder blade was next to go. It connected to chest bone, which was connected to his hip bone. His hip bone was connected to his, well to make a long story short, she broke every bone in his body and left.

*****

The southern California chapter of the Black Mob ran Mexican black tar heroin to school kids. A rash of recent overdose deaths caught Yolo's attention, so she sent her representative. Who better than her own dangerous daughter? Shyne was like her mother in more ways than one.

"Oh wee!" Shyne cooed after a good bout of phone sex with her husband. Actually she had self-sex while he listened. "That was good, baby!"

"Straight now?" he asked so he could get to bed. The time difference kept him up way past his bedtime in the week she had been gone.

"No, but I will be soon," she replied since her surveillance was done. She was able to track a distributor named Kris to his supplier named Jamie to the connect named Jorge. They were all about to die tonight.

"When are you coming home?" Asad asked with a pout she could hear through the line. He missed his wife even, if she was a horny little monster.

"Tomorrow. I'm wrapping up out here tonight," she said. She assured him she loved him more to his 'I love you' and they disconnected. After washing her hands, she got dressed to kill.

Shyne left her hotel and headed over to Long Beach. She followed Kris enough to know he would be making a pick up. As expected, he was still inside which allowed her to place the magnetic device under his car. Jamie's car was next to be outfitted with the latest in designer explosives.

Kris came out with a fresh load of dope to ruin more lives and pulled out. Jamie was right behind him, so Shyne made sure to keep a safe distance. She pulled the two burnout cell phones and used one to get both men on a three-way call.

"Hello?" Jamie asked at the unknown number. It could have been business, so he quickly took it.

"Jamie?" Kris asked when he heard his voice. They both were surprised when Shyne joined the call.

"Hey, guys. It's me, Shyne," she said as if they knew who she was. "Anyways, I'm here to kill you guys for selling drugs to kids. So bye-bye!"

Shyne used the second phone to detonate the devices under their cars. Kris's was the first to blow and his car did a complete back flip. It landed back on its wheels, but he was scrambled like an egg.

"Shit!" Jamie shouted when he saw the explosion. He rushed to get out of his own vehicle before it blew up, too. He almost made it, but almost doesn't count. He got one foot on the ground when the bomb went off. The blast sent him flying in the air directly into a building. He made out a little better than Kris, but was still going to the morgue and that's all that matters.

"OK, Jorge. You're up," Shyne said and turned around. She followed the GPS turn by turn until she reached his house.

Shyne sat and watched for movement for a moment before moving on. The place was eerily quiet compared to the busy happenings earlier. She was on high alert as she crept forward disguised as a girl scout. She looked too old, but she looked quite sexy in the uniform, so she was invited.

"Huh?" she asked when she reached the ajar front door. She eased in and raised the gun prepared for battle, but quickly saw someone beat her to it. Jorge was in several pieces all over the den. Two security men sat at the table with their heads down in pools of blood. The bullet holes in their temples told the rest of the story. It saved Shyne some time, but she was still disappointed at not getting to put him down herself. That begged the question, "Who did?"

*****

"Hey, ma. What you been up to? Go anywhere this weekend?" Shyne asked, squinting at her mother doing her sister's hair.

"Somewhere like where?" Yolo asked without looking up from the braid she was working on.

"Mmhm," she repeated then stared at her father as he walked through the family room and sat down.

"And where you been this weekend? Huh? Don't know what I'm talking about either, huh? Huh!" Shyne demanded. Killa frowned got up and walked out mumbling something under his breath. "Oh, I got your crazy little girl, playa."

"Shyne, what the hell is wrong with you?" Yolo asked for probably the millionth time in her life.

"Pregnant if you ask me," Diedra said, coming in on the tail end of the question. That got Yolo to look up at her daughter.

"No, I'm not!" Shyne shrieked as if she was in trouble and touched her stomach.

"Wait, I'm married! But I ain't pregnant."

"Look pregnant to me," the old lady said, commandeering the remote and changing to rap videos. She hated the music, but loved to talk about the rappers. "Where's my favorite one with the nasty name and girl shirts?"

"Dead," Shyne giggled. "Said he peed on an electric current and fried to death.'

"Get rich or fry trying!" Yolo cracked and cracked herself up. Little Diedra looked up at her and shook her head.

"Anyway, mommy. I was in California doing that job, but when I got there it was already installed?" Shyne said and again tried to gauge her mother's response. All she got was a parental...

"Oh, that's nice," she said, finishing up. "Your dad booked a family trip to Disney."

"What family? Our family? All of us? Together?" Shyne rambled for clarification.

"What's wrong with that girl? Besides being pregnant?" her grandmother wanted to know.

"I am not pregnant!" Shyne insisted and stormed out just like she stormed in.

Chapter 29

"What have we here?" Craig sang as the door to a semi truck was pulled open. It contained a fresh shipment from Mexico and he always liked to pluck one or two for his personal stash.

"Got some from Honduras!" the driver said as he swung the door open. The smell of death wafted out and assaulted them both. "Not again!"

"Man, you guys are costing me a ton of money in shrinkage," Craig griped as if the human cargo were broken eggs instead of broken people. "Sort them out so I can see what's left."

The driver and his assistant got busy, pulling dead bodies from the living.

"Agua, por favor," a little girl pleaded. Craig looked her up and down nodding. He settled in on her little breast nubs and pulled her aside. He plucked a similar brown twelve-year for himself.

"What do we do with these?" the driver asked of the twenty dead teens and girls. Craig just shrugged and put his newest additions in his car.

"Shut up!" Craig barked to the sniveling kids in his back seat. They huddled together for protection as he pulled away. He pulled through a drive through for happy meals, which the starving girls happily scarfed down.

The little girls may have lived in squalor in their home countries of Honduras and Guatemala, but somehow knew the mansion they pulled up to wasn't going to be much better. They looked around the grand foyer with marble flooring with muted awe. This was an expensive place to live and neither had any money.

"Rosa, get them ready!" Craig barked to his housekeeper. Lately, the old lady had become more like a zookeeper who took care of his pets.

"Si, senor," she replied with a bow and whisked the girls away. She took them each to a separate bathroom and into the tub. Once the dirt and grime of the long journey was washed away, she dressed them in totally inappropriate clothing and styled their hair. Rosa led the girls up to the master suite and crossed herself for forgiveness before knocking on the door.

"Come in!" Craig barked. The door opened and his eyes went wide at the sight of his newest additions. The 12 year olds looked like 13 year olds and that was just perfect.

Rosa scooted them inside and gave them a longing glance at their lost innocence. She crossed herself once more for forgiveness she didn't deserve. She was a party to his crimes and deserved the same thing he had coming.

"Up here!" he demanded and patted the large bed. The girls looked at each other for guidance. Rosa's warning to do whatever senor said urged them forward.

Craig felt an erection growing as he scanned their scrawny legs and knobby knees. The type of things that drive a pedophile crazy. He used a space-aged looking remote control and turned on the tv. He split the screen to let the girls chose their future. One side showed Craig sodomizing a girl their age. The other was a snuff film with him strangling a girl their age.

"Which one?" he asked in Spanish, pointing between the two options. Both girls chose life over death, even if it came with abuse.

Craig smiled and poured drinks for all to numb their little bodies for what was to come. He was so eager to enjoy his latest additions he didn't even register the doorbell.

"Who is it?" Rosa sang and pulled the large ornate door open. She didn't bother to check first since there weren't any burglars in this neighborhood. She should have checked first since a killer was in town.

"Hola!" a cheerful voice greeted from behind a large silencer. Rosa cocked her head curiously for an explanation and got one.

'Psst' the silent pistol whispered and sent a bullet into her forehead. She took two steps back to welcome him and dropped dead. The killer smiled down at the woman as they stepped over it. Nothing satisfies like killing someone who really needs dead.

They eased up the stairs and let their ears guide them down the hall. The sounds of sex behind a door further infuriated the killer. A solid kick opened the French doors as they rushed in. They felt only slight relief that the sex was on TV, but the girls were still half naked and half drunk.

"Who the fuck are you! What the fuck are you doing in my house!" Craig demanded and stood.

"Killing you," the killer said and demonstrated by putting a bullet in his forehead. The girls were immune to blood shed from the violence of their homelands. They clapped and rushed over to hug their savior. "OK, OK. Let's go."

*****

"Bad girls move in silence and violence," Shyne rapped in a whisper as she slipped over the back fence to Craig's house. This was the point of no return, so she quietly cocked her weapon and eased forward.

An open slider granted access to the plush den. She upped her gun and rushed in, ready to shoot. Shyne twisted her lips ruefully at the empty room and moved forward. A curious frown distorted her pretty face when she found the dead housekeeper in the foyer.

Now she was on high alert as she moved on. She did her homework and had the layout of house and knew exactly where the master suite was.

"Aaah!" she shouted and rushed in pointing the gun and getting disappointed once again when she found Craig staring off into the afterlife. "Aww, man!"

Shyne scratched her head and frowned trying to figure out who beat her to the punch. She touched Craig's dead hand and saw he was still warm. She raised the gun again just in case his killer was still around. A search came up empty until she reached the basement.

"What the—" Shyne said as the voices of young girls reached her. Each was kept in a small cell of their own. This was where Craig kept his personal stash of underaged concubines. She took a minute and let them all out and led them outside.

"Sit here," Shyne told the ten kids and sat them on the curb. It was too many to move, so she placed an anonymous call to 911 to report the rescued girls.

"Que es tu nombre?" a fearless little girl stood and asked before Shyne could leave.

"I'm...Wonder Woman," she said and struck a pose. She giggled at the look on her face and took off back through the backyard.

Asad was still sleeping soundly when she returned to the room. She slid in next to him, but couldn't sleep. The nagging question of who beat her to the kill kept her up all night. The whole family was here, so it could have been any one of them.

*****

"Good morning," Shyne and Asad said as they arrived to the dining room the next morning. Most of the family had already gathered except two of her brothers.

"Where's Sun and Rico?"

"Sun and Rico had company from the club," Xavier snitched. He met a girl, too, but sent her home already.

"Mmhm," she dared and looked at her parents. They nonchalantly ate breakfast, but someone beat her to yet another kill and she wanted to know who and why. She squinted as she analyzed and scrutinized her family. Sun and Rico arrived and got the same. "Mmhm."

"What's wrong with her?" Rico asked, looking around to see who would answer.

"She's Shyne," Sun said, causing heads to nod including her husband.

"Oh, that's funny, huh?" she snapped at Asad who quickly changed his tune. Shyne didn't run him, but she would run her mouth for days and he could do without all of that.

"She pregnant is what she is," grandma said, tossing in her two cents.

"She is?" Killa cheered. He was ready to be a paw-paw rocking in a rocking chair.

"Am not! Why you keep saying that, grandma? I just had my... um?" Shyne paused and twisted her lips as she tried to recall just when she did have her last cycle. "Well, I'm not."

"Mmhm," Yolo said knowingly. Meanwhile Shyne went back to trying to figure out which one of her killer family beat her to another kill.

Chapter 30

"Oh shit, I am pregnant!" Shyne acknowledged when the pregnancy test confirmed her grandmother's prediction. Now her dilemma was whether she should tell her mother or not.

Shyne remembered the diary and how her mother made plenty of kills after conceiving her and her brother. She nodded her head in agreement that she would kill until she started showing and her mother pulled the plug on her. In the meanwhile, she had a plane to catch.

"Hey, big daddy," Shyne sang as she stepped from the bathroom.

"Oh, OK," Asad huffed and began to undress. Shyne gets what Shyne wants and he knew what she wanted whenever she called him big daddy.

"OK. First, that's not what I wanted. Well, I do, but not right this second. And two," she said and paused to thrust the test strip in his face. "You're going to be a father!"

"Allahu Akbar!" he shouted because God is the greatest and all the glory is for Him alone. He rushed over and hugged his wife off her feet and twirled her around.

"Thank you!"

"That's not how you thank me," she said with a few humps on his leg. Shyne gets what Shyne wants, so he carried her over to the bed and gave it to her. She missed her plane, which allowed Chip to live a few more hours.

*****

Chip ran the drugs and gangs in Newark, New Jersey for the Black Mob. A recent drive by on rivals killed a little girl and got him put on Yolo's radar. He had to die, so she sent her representative.

Shyne landed in Newark and picked up her rental car to explore the city. Her heart ached at all the lost souls she saw. Kids forced to get it how they lived because of how their parents decided to live.

The lines of family and community had blurred until they were no longer recognizable.

Teen girls realized they could have a baby and the state would take care of them and it. That made a baby daddy more desirable than a husband. A dope boy baby daddy was even better, so they could get free weed until he died, went to prison or both. Boys selling crack to their crack head dads and getting blowjobs by crack head aunts. They shared forty-ounce beers, blunts and baby mamas. Everyone living for the moment knowing they could die at any moment. It wasn't all Chip's fault, but he was still about to get fucked up for it.

*****

"Thanks, Chip," Juanita said as she rose from her knees. She provided excellent customer service by tucking the freshly sucked dick back in his pants. It was extras like that, that made her number one.

"Shit. Thank you, Auntie," he said and thanked her again with a couple bags of crack. He knew it was fucked up getting head from his aunt, but she had the best head in the city. Everyone wants the best.

After the good blowjob, he got on his task of supplying the city's traps with dope. In exchange he collected cash from his dealers. The ones who didn't sell for him still had to pay a tax to operate in his city. Little did he know, he had to pay, too. He returned home with a hundred grand and found a cutie pie in his kitchen.

"Who the fuck is you? How you get in my shit?" Chip demanded when he found Shyne at his table eating a sandwich. She held up a finger signaling him to wait while she chewed.

"Sorry, pregnant girls gotta eat," she explained. Chip took a step towards her, but she raised a pistol that froze him like a statue.

"Whoa!" he said and raised his hands. "What you got going on, lil' mama?"

"Oh, just a little experiment." she said and motioned for him to sit with the gun. He complied and cocked his head curiously at his nebulizer. She had taken it completely apart and modified it before putting it back together.

"What did you do with my shit? What if I have an asthma attack?" he itched.

"I modified it a lil' bit. You're about to have a crack attack!" Shyne giggled as she cuffed his hands behind his back and secured him to the chair. Chip watched her ass when she left only to return with a batch of freshly cooked crack.

"So, what is this? A robbery? Who sent you? Sa'id? He back on that shit, huh?" he moaned. He alternated between itching and moaning while she hooked up her invention.

"No, my mom sent me, but she gave me free reign to kill you however I like," she explained. He began to shake his head vigorously and clamped his lips tight when she tried to put the mouthpiece in his mouth. "OK, see if I shoot you, you'll open up!"

"Chill!" he fussed when she pressed the gun into his crotch. That trick did the trick and he opened his mouth. She stuck the mouthpiece in and taped it shut.

"OK, now..." she said putting a large chunk of crack on the modified nebulizer and lit it. It began to billow fresh crack smoke directly into his life. His eyes went wide and he thrashed around trying to prevent inhalation of the dangerous drug. He had no choice but to breathe and breathed in the noxious smoke. Shyne sat down across from him and watched as his eyes went wide, wide and wider. Smoke exited his nostrils as he breathed 100% pure crack.

"Oh snap!" Shyne cheered when she heard his heart pop inside his chest. His head dropped onto his chest when his soul came out his nose with the crack exhaust. She scooped up his bag of money and headed for the door. "Just be glad I didn't set you on fire."

*****

Shyne arrived back in Atlanta and headed straight home to her husband. He welcomed her home properly and put her to bed. She needed the rest since her mother had another mission for her. Someone in Pittsburgh made her radar and needed dead.

"Who?" was all Shyne asked since the why didn't matter.

"A ras clot, bumba clot Jamaican bati boy named Sherman," Yolo growled with venom dripping from her mouth. She was right to angry about the child-molesting monster. He wasn't actually Black Mob, but her daughter didn't need to know that. Sherman's stepdaughter made a desperate complaint on the old 1-800-Killa website. Officially it was out of business, but unofficially it was still monitored.

"Well, I'm gonna give him the light," Shyne vowed sharing her mother's anger.

"Speaking of fire. I got you something. Come on," Yolo said in a conspiratorial tone. Shyne knew whatever it was, it was going to be good when her mother led her down to the basement. It got even better when she told her to "Grab the fire extinguisher!"

Shyne complied and followed her down the stairs after locking the door behind them.

"What is it?" she asked when her mother produced what looked like a flare gun.

"This..." Yolo said with a dramatic pause and aimed at a mannequin. She pulled the trigger and the gun spit fire, laterally and engulfed the figure. "The Shyne-inerator 2000."

"Cool! Whack name, but cool device," Shyne said and reached for it. She held it up and twisted it as she inspected.

"Well, we'll work on the name," Yolo said, taking the fire extinguisher and putting out the flames. "It's lightweight, rechargeable and sustainable."

"It's great! I can't wait to use it." Shyne cheered and danced around.

"Well you don't have to wait. Your plane leaves in an hour." her mother advised.

"OK, I have to go say goodbye to my husband first," she said and rushed back upstairs with her new toy. She sped back downtown to the condo to say her goodbyes.

*****

"Oh shoot!" Shyne fussed when she awoke hours later. Her goodbyes ended up putting them both to sleep.

"What?" Asad asked when her outburst awoke him. He sat up and looked around for the problem.

"My flight! My mom's going to kill me!" she grumbled and rolled out of bed.

"Your mom?" Asad chuckled. "She wouldn't hurt a fly!"

For all Shyne's hurry, she still took her time in the shower and getting dressed. She packed a bag for the trip and Asad drove her to the airport.

"Aww, man!" she moaned when the next direct flight didn't leave for six hours. Even a series of connection flights couldn't get her there any quicker. She bit the bullet, bought her ticket and sat down to wait. She decided to kill time the best way she knew and grabbed her phone.

"Hello?" Bryonna answered hopefully. Hopefully Shyne was calling with news that Sun had finally come to his senses and decided to marry her. They had dated for years, but ultimately Sun got tired of her not putting out. Especially when women threw themselves at him every day all day.

"Hey, girl. What you doing? And you better not say waiting on my brother!" she demanded.

"Huh? Who? Me? Nope, un uh. Not waiting on Sun to marry me at all. Why, he said he ready?" she asked and held her breath.

"Anyway, guess what? I'm pregnant, is what!" Shyne gushed. She had to pull the phone away from her ear when her friend screamed for joy. She waited for the screams to subside before putting it back. "Thanks, girl. I guess the secret is doing it five times a day?"

"Yeah, cuz four wasn't working for you. Anyway, where you headed now?" she asked when the sounds of the airport came through the line.

"Pittsburgh. A company needs me to install some stuff. Network and stuff," she mumbled. Shyne couldn't really run the I.T. story to her since she was one herself.

"Mmhm. Girl, what are you really up to? All these trips? Extra money? I hope you're not cheating on Asad! He's the sweetest guy in the world! You—"

"Chill, chica! I would never even look at another man. I've been in love with him since first grade!" Shyne said with enough indignation for her friend to believe her.

"Well, you're still doing something and I want to know what!" Bryonna demanded. She pressed and pressed until Shyne's flight number was finally called.

"What! I'm not letting you off this phone until you tell me what you're doing!"

"OK, OK. I'll tell you, but you can't tell anyone. Not even my brother!" Shyne insisted. "Swear!"

"I swear I won't tell a soul," she said, crossing her heart as if Shyne could see her. Ironically she knew her so well she could see it since she always did.

"OK, my plane is boarding, but I'll tell you. I have to go city to city to fight crime. I'm... Wonder Woman."

"Shyne! Hello? Shyne!" Bryonna yelled into the dead line. She tried again but it went straight to voicemail since she turned it off for her flight.

Shyne arrived it Pittsburgh several hours later and hopped in her rental. She didn't even bother booking a hotel because she wasn't staying. The plan was to set the dred on fire and catch the next thing smoking while he was still smoking.

"Aww, man," she moaned when she reached the address and found a crime scene. She parked up the street and walked back to mingle with the other spectators. "What happened?"

"Sherman got fucked up is what happened," a woman said with a pleasant smile. "Piece of shit got cut to pieces."

"Pieces? Like a hot machete?" Shyne asked, twisting her lips. The woman twisted her head to get a look at whoever asked the odd question. Of course the woman never read Yolo's diary to know about the hot machete her dad was fond of.

"I guess," she shrugged. "I wouldn't care if they used a butter knife. As long as that bastard got dead."

"Hmp," Shyne wondered and headed back to the airport to go home. Curiosity got the best of her and forced her to call her mother.

"Done? How'd the Shyne-inerator 2000 work in the field?" Yolo asked eagerly.

"Um, fine? Where are you?" Shyne asked and squinted. "Better yet, where's my daddy?"

"Downstairs, why? What's wrong?" Yolo asked ready to handle whatever it was.

"Nothing," Shyne said, twisting her lips again. Someone beat her to yet another kill and she needed to find out who.

Chapter 31

"Bae, we need to double up on some of our investments. I wanna make sure we leave something for the kids," Yolo sighed.

"Man, fuck them kids!" he said and meant it. They had provided the best upbringing they possibly could, including having both parents together in the same house.

"Yeah, you right. Fuck them kids," Yolo laughed and high-fived him. She turned to the nightly news for her news junky husband and laid her head on his chest.

"Another child went missing today and police are no calling these recent kidnappings related," the reporter reported.

There had been a rash of kidnappings in the city of Atlanta. The police wanted to pin them all on Wayne Williams again just like they did with the missing and murdered children in the eighties, but he was still safely tucked away in prison.

"I could have told you that," Yolo said as she and Killa watched the news from their bed.

"Hmp?" Killa replied as the wheels began to turn. For some reason black children and teens were going missing every other day. He tried to find a connection to something, but Yolo distracted him by purring and rubbing his leg like a cat in need of attention. Only because she had a cat in need of some attention. "What are you doing?"

"Asks the man with like nine kids," she quipped and reached for his crotch. It reached for her back when she reached it and grew stiff in her hand.

"Melts in your mouth, not in your hand," he suggested and got what he was after. Instead of melting, it only grew harder which was exactly what she wanted.

"All aboard!" Yolo called out as she mounted her husband. She wriggled him inside of her and slowly sank down to her bottom. She found her stroke and began to stroke. Killa gripped handfuls of ass cheeks and guided her up and down. Yolo rocked herself to a nut and rolled off onto her back.

"My turn," Killa growled and took position between her legs. He slid back inside her slippery lips and found a stroke of his own. A smooth up, down, side to side, circle stroke that made her cum again. She squeezed her vagina tightly and shoved him over the edge.

"Mmm," Yolo moaned as her husband climaxed deep inside of her. She rubbed his back while he spasmed and thrashed. It was real comforting until she spoke again and fucked it up. "You know I'm pregnant again."

"Huh?" Killa whined and went limp in an instant. "But how? I, you, your tubes?"

"I'm just kidding, but I'm pretty sure Shyne is. She hasn't said anything because she, I mean we, um..." Yolo said and stopped before she said too much. His good dick often made her ramble and say more than she should.

She played it off with a deep yawn and batted her eyes. She cuddled up next to him and pretended to fall asleep. Killa laid there for a few minutes then eased out of bed. He slipped down to his basement man cave and got on his computer to see what he could find out about these missing kids. Yolo waited a few minutes herself then got on her tablet and did the same.

*****

"What's good, good people?" Sun greeted as he entered his downtown barber shop. All the long faces quickly wiped the jovial smile from his face. "What's wrong?"

"Jacobi," one of the barbers said, shooting a glance over to his empty chair. He was one of the best barbers in the city as well as well liked among his peers.

"What about him?" Sun asked and braced himself for what had to be bad news.

"He died. Opiate overdose," Heather said and broke down once more. The lady barber dropped her clippers and rushed into the office.

"Wow," was all Sun could say. He lost track of how many people he knew or knew of had recently died from overdose. Instead of sorrow, he felt a wave on anger sweep over him. It was quickly followed by helplessness. If the government couldn't stop it then how could he? His fingers snapped when he recalled the one weapon he had that they didn't: Shyne.

"What?" Shyne spat when she took her brother's call. She gave him a hard time, but loved her twin just as much as she loved herself.

"Jacobi died," he said and knocked away a tear. He could literally feel his sister getting angry through the line.

"I'm on my way," she said and rolled off the sofa. Asad heard the distress in her voice and got dressed, too. They hopped in their car and headed downtown to meet their brother.

*****

"You need a cut, baby," Shyne suggested, looking at her husband's hairline while he drove.

"OK," he agreed to both the cut and her wanting to speak to her brother alone. He greeted Sun warmly with a pound and hug.

"I'll take you," Heather offered with a smile. Shyne erased it with a dirty look as she and her brother went to the rear.

"So, what we gonna do? What can we do?" she asked once they settled in his office.

"I'on know, but we can start by getting rid of some of these pill mills. It's beyond me how the authorities allow legalized heroin?" Sun moaned.

"How we gonna get rid of the pill mills when they legal? Pass a law? Protest? Have a rally?" Shyne huffed since all those things proved to be ineffective. There was so much money to be made selling drugs that the powers that be legalized opiates so they could get rich.

"No, we're going to burn them down." he said getting a devious smile out of her twin.

"Somebody gonna be pissed when all their spots go up in flames!" she replied.

"Yup, and they gonna reveal themselves in the process. And I'm going to kill them." Sun growled.

"OK, bruh." Shyne nodded. She didn't really believe her brother could kill a fly, but she could. Once the owners of the pill mills came forward she would murder them for him. He wouldn't bust a grape but she certainly would.

*****

"Business is booming!" Shyne said as Sun pulled up to a midtown pill mill. It was nothing more than a legal dope trap with a steady flow of upscale junkies.

"Business is gonna be burning soon," he growled sounding just like their father.

"Yeah, well hold that thought until I come out," Shyne said and hopped out of his car. She sashayed her ass inside while her brother waited.

"Welcome to Marietta Pain Management. How can I help you?" a cute white girl asked from behind her desk.

Can I get pills?" Shyne dared and cocked her head. Surely it couldn't be that easy to get the highly addictive drugs.

"Sure! What kind would you like? We have Oxy, Perc..." she sang a laundry list of drugs. "Do you have a prescription?"

"No. So, I can't get any?" she asked and almost breathed a sigh of relief.

"Sure! Our in-house doctor will write one up. Just step over to the next window," she said, pointing to her left.

"Here?" she asked, stepping a few feet. Her answer was answered by a middle-aged doctor.

"What kind of pills would you like?" the man asked with his pen poised over his prescription pad.

"Um?" Shyne asked in disbelief. "I don't know, but I am pregnant."

"Well I guess we'll start you off with some oxy," he decided and scribbled the script.

"Just take this to window three."

"Three?" she asked and headed to the window. She passed the prescription forward and was able to purchase the deadly addictive drugs. She left in a daze and headed back to the car.

"What?" Sun barked and hopped out ready to bite when he saw the distress on his sister's face. She let out a sigh and got back in the car. He got back in and asked again.

"What?"

"Yo, I told them I was pregnant and they still gave me pills! Just wrote me a prescription on the spot," she said in shock. Sun was in shock too but for a different reason.

"Pregnant! You're pregnant?" he turned and asked.

"Huh? Stay focused, dang it! These people are contributing to the opioid epidemic. They probably killed Prince!"

"Man I loved Prince!" Sun fussed and got angry. He didn't realize his sister just changed the subject on him. Once again he'd been Shyned.

*****

"You need to let me do it. I heard what you said earlier. Does mom and dad know? What Asad say? Is it a girl or a boy?" Sun rambled as they drove back over to the mill pill.

"Bruh, chill," she said to calm him down. "We can do it together. We both place the charges and you can press the detonator.

"Bet!" he agreed with a fist bump. They both hopped out and set off in different directions around the building. They placed Shyne's homemade incendiary devices as they went until they met around back.

"Pull off so we don't get hit," she advised once they were back in the car. Sun replied and put the car in gear. They made it about half a block before Shyne hit the button and detonated the devices.

"Hey!" Sun whined when the night lit up in an orange glow. "Man!"

"Sorry," Shyne said, but she wasn't sorry. "Well, we still have to see the doctor who writes prescriptions for pregnant women."

"Bet he won't be writing shit for anyone anytime soon," he vowed and headed in the direction to his house. The GPS announced their arrival a short time later and Sun hopped out. He marched up the walkway and through the doctor's front door.

"Who the hell are you?" the man demanded and stood. Sun replied with a straight right hand to his mouth that sat him back down.

"I'm, the, man, who doesn't, appreciate, you, making junkies out, of pregnant women," he explained in between punches. Now it was the doctor who needed pain management when Sun broke his face and both arms.

Sun and Shyne burned down pill mills and beat up the phony doctors who wrote the phony prescriptions. After Atlanta, they moved on to Alabama and Carolina. Now they got the attention of the people at the top of the food chain.

Chapter 32

"Another one of our investments has been destroyed by fire. This time in Charleston, South Carolina," Herbert reported hesitantly. No one liked to be the bearer of bad news, especially when it was millions of dollars in losses. "B.M.C has a loss over two million dollars this month as a result of these arsons."

B.M.C was a publicly traded company as Baker Management Company. But those in the know, knew this was the new Black Mob. It was now ran by the Baker family. The blue blooded white clan was able to harness the inner city drug and pussy trade to fund their legitimate ventures. They funded the late rapper Fuck-Shit who started a movement. Brand conscious niggas from all over the country claimed to be down and gladly paid a fee to join the franchise.

"I don't believe in coincidence," Mrs. Baker announced from the head of the table. She was losing money in every city Shyne visited and it was beginning to add up. "I want to get to the bottom of this. Now!"

"Yes, ma'am," Herbert said with a bow and backed out of the room.

"What do you think, mom?" Chase asked as soon as the room cleared.

"I think someone is deliberately sabotaging our operations. I want them found and eliminated," she replied. The hunters were about to become the hunted.

*****

"This makes no sense," Yolo whined as she analyzed financial records and reports. She made sure Shyne collected as much paperwork as she could find from her hits. Lately, most had gotten burned up by the Shyne-inerator 2000. Yolo was able to trace payments made from several mob factions to an investment company who shuttled the funds to B.M.C.

"What doesn't make sense?" Killa asked as he came into the room.

"Nothing!" she snapped and snapped her laptop closed and spread her legs. Her husband zoomed in on her crotch like she knew he would.

"OK," he said when the plump vagina changed the subject. He moved closer to indulge without knowing he had just been Yolo-ed. He twisted her into her favorite position and gave her the business. After he rocked her to sleep, he slid out of bed and picked her laptop. He gently used her finger to bypass the fingerprint scanner to open her computer.

"They don't call me Killa for nothing," he chuckled at her curled up in a ball with her thumb in her mouth. Her attempt to Yolo him had backfired. His eyes went wide when he got a glimpse of what she and Shyne had been up to. He copied her files, closed the laptop and grabbed his phone.

"Hell... lo?" Sun asked when he took the late night call. "Is, every... thing, mmm, OK?"

"Busy son?" the observant father asked as he picked up on whimpers and moans in the background.

"Um, a little," he admitted, watching the young woman riding him backwards. A call from his dad trumped everything and he would have pushed her off and rushed to his side in an instant.

"I see. Meet me for breakfast," Killa said and clicked off. He slid back into the bed and spooned with his wife.

A few hours later, the father and son were seated across from each other enjoying S and S chicken and waffles. The good food paused the conversation until they ate half their plates.

"You look tired, Sun," Killa remarked when his son let out deep yawn. Yawns are contagious so he followed suit.

"I am. Was up all night all up in this little red bone cutie," Sun bragged. "Back shots, side shots, Cowgirl, reverse Cowgirl..."

"Yeah, me too," Killa laughed. "I had your mom bent—"

"Chill, dad!" Sun grimaced and thrust his fingers into to his ears. The last thing he wanted to hear was about his parents having sex. Killa wasn't all that interested in hearing about his son having sex so they were even.

"OK then," he laughed and got down to business. "Your mom is at it again."

"Is that what happened in Tulsa?" he asked. He arrived to handle Harpo, but found someone had beat him to the kill. "New York, too! Man I wanted to get that fuck boy Fuck-Shit."

"Yeah and these pill mill fires got your crazy sister written all over it!" Killa reasoned.

"Um..." Sun said since he was down. "I doubt it. She's pregnant, so I can't see her burning down clinics and beating up doctors."

"I bet you can't since you did it with her," his observant father said, twisting his lips dubiously.

"No, I, we...How you know we did it?" Sun confessed like he always did when confronted.

"Cuz you just admitted it, buster!" Killa laughed. Little did he know he had the same tells his son did when not telling the truth. That's why Yolo always knew when he wasn't telling the truth. "And she's pregnant?"

"Yeah, but she made me promise not to tell mom," Sun explained.

"Because she knows your mom would have shut her down," Killa nodded.

"So, what you gonna do?" he asked wide eyed with excitement.

"I'm gonna shut her down. Then we're gonna have to step it up and finish getting rid of the Black Mob!"

*****

"Where you been?" Yolo asked and squinted at her husband when he returned. She paid attention to his pretty lips that tend to quiver when he's not telling the truth. His light brown eyes would bat and look away when he made shit up.

"Sun and I had breakfast. He was telling me about how he twisted up some little cutie he met, so I told him I was doing the same..."

"No you didn't!" she blushed and gave him a playful pop. She was satisfied that he was telling the truth even though she was quite sure he was in her computer last night since he left his favorite porn sites in the browser. She hoped he hadn't seen her files on the mob, but he did. Now they were in a race to get to them first. It was mother and daughter verses father and Sun. Killa had an ace in the hole and planned to play it first chance he got.

"Anyway, I'm gonna fire the grill up later. Call the kids over."

"Is Xavier still in town?" she asked and reached for her phone.

"Yes, call him, too," Killa said. The more the merrier even though Shyne would be the guest of honor. "Make sure Shyne comes."

"OK," she agreed, but knew he was up to something. She shrugged her shoulders knowing she would soon find out.

"Hey, mommy," Shyne greeted, sounding guilty since she had just starting dancing naked on the table when her phone rang.

"Hey, baby. You busy?" she asked, hearing distress in her voice and trap music playing in the background.

"Um, no," she said, but didn't come down from the table. "What's up?"

"Yo, daddy wants to cook out, so you and my good son come over. You know your bad ass brothers will all be there," she explained.

"As long as he making some jerk chicken!" Shyne insisted needlessly. First of all, Killa knew his daughter loved his famous jerk chicken and two, she was the guest of honor.

"Where were we?" Asad clapped once she hung up. He leaned back as she continued her striptease. It started on the kitchen table and ended up on the kitchen floor. Somehow the refrigerator door came open, but that didn't stop their second session of the day. A nap and shower later and they were late to the cookout. That was just enough time for her father to plan his surprise.

*****

"What are you up to?" Yolo asked. Killa was doing a lot more than normal when he decorated the backyard like a party.

"It's a party!" he explained and getting another squint from his wife. He recognized the human lie detector test and rushed off. Luckily, he was saved by the bell when Asad pulled in the driveway.

"As salaamu alaykum!" Asad greeted as he led Shyne into the house.

"Sup, yo," X replied with a pound and hug. "They in the backyard."

"Hey, lil' mama," Shyne cheered and scooped her little sister up and patted her brother on his head.

"I'm not a puppy!" little Killa grumbled and wiped her touch away.

"Yes you are," she laughed over her shoulder and went out into the back door. "Hey, big mama!"

"I got your big mama," Yolo replied. "Hey, Asad. How are you doing, baby?"

"Fine," he said and blushed from her kiss on his cheek. "Where's pop?"

"Your father-in-law is up to something. Can I borrow your wife?" she said and steered Shyne away.

"I got one for you. You ever been to Charleston, South Carolina?"

"Um, no," she lied. Her mother squinted when she saw her husband's 'tells' in her face. Shyne had no intention on telling her that she and Sun were just there burning down another pill mill. "What's going on up there?"

"Better yet, what's going on here?" Yolo asked when Killa produced a huge bouquet of pink and blue balloons bearing 'Congratulations'.

"Tonight, we are celebrating Shyne and Asad's first child! Congratulations, baby girl!" he sang and produced the bouquet to his stunned daughter.

"Told you," Diedra boasted and pumped her fist. "I knew it, I knew it!"

"Shyne?" Yolo asked and cocked her head curiously. "You're pregnant? And didn't tell me?"

"Damn snitch," she snarled at Sun. He was the source of the leak, but he looked just as shocked as she did. Shyne turned back to her mother to explain, "Cuz, you would try to shut me down. I got some killing to do."

"Had! Cuz, you right. You're shut down," Yolo said and stormed off with her feelings.

"I'm changing my number," Sun said, knowing she would get him back. He tried to hide behind Bryonna when Killa pulled Shyne to his side.

"Sorry to put you on blast but..." he said and shrugged since he really wasn't sorry. "Oh and I know what you and your mother have been up to. No more. It stops now. Let me and your brothers handle it."

"No offense, daddy, but I can handle myself. You forget I'm a grown woman and—" Shyne fussed until her dad shut her down with one word.

"Asad!" he called and waved his son in law over.

"OK, OK. You're a snitch just like your damn son!" she fussed and stomped off.

"Come on, Bryonna," Shyne said, pulling her friend away from her brother. "Don't talk to him. I seen him on a gay website!"

"Mom!" Sun shouted like they were ten again. Yolo sat back and enjoyed the organized chaos that is family.

Chapter 33

"Come on, let me cum. It'll be, just like, old times," Yolo pleaded while working her lips, tongue and neck in perfect harmony.

"Um..." Killa said. He didn't want her to cum, but he wanted to cum, so he kept his mouth shut and she kept her mouth full. It did the trick and the blowjob concluded as a good blowjob should.

"Whew! I'm full," Yolo giggled after her midnight snack. "Thanks for inviting me!"

"I um, OK," he relented when she snuggled up next to him. He let out a sigh then cracked a smile. It would be just like old times. Killa and Yolo, killing again. The next morning, Yolo sealed the deal with his favorite breakfast and filled the family in on the trip.

"That means I'm in charge!" six-year-old little Killa announced when his parents announced their trip. "You have to listen to me cuz I'm the man!"

"In charge of peeing in the bed!" little Diedra huffed and big Diedra cracked up.

"Or crying," his great grandmother tossed in and high-fived her namesake. Killa felt bad for his baby boy, but not enough to help him out. He shrugged and left him on his own.

"Don't worry, baby. Mommy loves you, even if you do pee the bed. And cry a lot," Yolo comforted himYolo style. Killa cocked his and squinted at his mother wondering how that was supposed to help. Finally he got up and stormed off, too.

"Chicks over di—"

"Diedra!" grandma Diedra shrieked in disbelief, but Yolo twisted her lips.

"Like you didn't teach her that," Yolo said knowingly. "You right tho. We run this!"

*****

"So, what you got on Charleston?" Killa inquired as he drove towards the airport.

"Whoever this Black Mob is moved into the space your son created when he burned down the pill mill," she replied and got cut off.

"Your daughter, you mean. Chick comes in smelling like premium unleaded and you blame Sun," he said, shaking his head. He wasn't there when it was planned, but he was pretty sure it was Shyne's idea.

"Anyway, it seems like they were in the right place at the right time because heroin sales spiked immediately! I didn't want to tell the twins, but they actually made it worse," Yolo said with a frustrated sigh. The kind of sigh she sighs when someone is about to get fucked up.

"Well, no need to tell Sun and Shyne. We'll just do what parents do and clean up their mess," he comforted.

"And make a mess of these dope boys in the process!" she cheered. As usual, Killa had resources on the ground in Charleston and had the goods on the whole operation.

Charleston mob was ran by a short dark-skinned man called Geechi. He heard about the mob on a mix tape and proclaimed to be down. Word reached the real mob who put the press on him and charged for the use of their brand. Just like no one can throw some big ass M's on a burger joint and call it McDonalds. In exchange they supplied him with the east coast finest heroin.

"Let's check into the room and regroup before we do the do," Killa suggested when they reached the historic city.

"Can we stop by that church?" Yolo asked. Only the pleading in her voice made Killa agree because it still pissed him off. He clenched his jaws tight and set the GPS for the new destination. Minutes later they arrived at the scene of the mass shooting.

"Dang..." she moaned at the overwhelming feeling of death. The feel of so many innocent lives lost at one time. Sure she'd kill two and three times that amount in one day, but they were fucked up people who needed dead. Killa couldn't even look at the historic building.

"You good?" he asked as he pulled from the curb. She didn't bother to answer since he already pulled away. Instead she turned her head so he wouldn't see the tear that escaped.

*****

"I'm gonna need my fix," Yolo demanded when they reached their room. Killa wasn't in the mood for love, but he told his wife she could have whatever she wanted so he got undressed to give her what she wanted.

Yolo folded her arms over the pillow and laid her head down with her ass up. Killa owed her one, so he came in and ate her out from the back. He licked her to a mild orgasm then gave her the dick. The dick did the trick and distracted them both from the depression from the massacre. After a mutual orgasm, they huddled up and drifted off to sleep.

"Shit!" Killa fussed when he woke up hours later. They had overslept for their date with death. "Get up, babes!"

"Shit!" Yolo echoed when she hopped up. Luckily she didn't need to get cute to kill. She dipped in and out the shower and dressed in all black. "Ready?"

"Let's ride," he replied and led the way out of the room. First stop was to his connect for guns and knives. Geechi's family could claim his body when they were done but Yolo was keeping his head. The rash of overdoses combined with the church created a dangerous silence in the car as they rode over to Geechi's house.

Killa got a sinking feeling when he heard sirens in the distance. They got less distant the closer they got to their destination. He tried to pretend not to smell smoke until a fire truck sped by and turned on Geechi's block. There was no ignoring when it pulled in front of Geechi's burning house.

"Yo damn daughter!" Yolo said shaking her head.

"And your son," he said when he spotted the twins in the gathering crowd. Sun saw them and gave a quick wink and salute. Yolo reached across her husband and flipped them off.

"Aww, man," she groaned in disappointment. She was so hurt at losing the outlet for her anger. If she had any idea of how badly Geechi was killed before Shyne set the fire she may have felt better.

"I know," he said wistfully since he felt her pain. They were both too wired up to return to the room, so he just kept driving. They drove by a rowdy biker bar just on the outskirts of town. Both looked at the name on bar, then at each other. Sun and Shyne weren't the only ones to communicate through telepathy. They both smiled and nodded as Killa made a u-turn. "White Lives Matter, huh?"

"No guns," Yolo dared as Killa found a place to park for a quick getaway. "Just knives and whatever we find inside?"

"You ain't said nothing," he agreed. They both pulled knives and brass knuckles from their bag. They shared a quick kiss and hopped out. The point of no return came when they reached the door.

"Thank you," Yolo greeted with a curtsy when Killa held the door for her. The bouncer cocked his head curiously when the African Americans entered the whites only bar.

"You niggers lost?" he asked with a chuckle, but didn't find the answer so funny.

"But now we're found," Yolo sang like an old negro spiritual and stabbed him in his throat. That wiped the smile off his fat face when the blade came out the back of his red neck. Killa sprang into action and grabbed his club when he fell. It wasn't stealing since he didn't need it any more.

He did and clubbed the occupants of the first table as Yolo stabbed the next table. The Killer couple swept through the rowdy bar, slashing and bashing as they went. It was exactly the same brutal death Geechi met at the hands of their children. Sun beat that man so bad he begged for death. Shyne gave him a taste of his own medicine when she shot him full of heroin. Geechi beat himself up even more when he flopped around on the floor as he overdosed.

By the end of the rampage, thirty rednecks lay dead or dying. Yolo slipped into the back to make sure no one would survive. Killa helped by smashing the bottles of alcohol while she cut the gas line in the kitchen.

"Let's go!" Yolo shouted as she ran passed at full speed. The gas came out a lot quicker than she expected and the place was set to blow.

"Uh oh," Killa blurted when he realized something was wrong. He didn't need to be told twice and fell in step behind her. They just reached the front door when the bar exploded. The blast picked them up and dropped them off across the street.

"That was dope!" Yolo cheered like she just like she did on a rollercoaster. "Can we go again?"

"Probably not," Killa said as he picked them both up. They were singed and scraped, but otherwise okay. Killa looked down at the 'White Lives Matter' sign as they drove and delivered one last message. "All lives matter!"

*****

"Well, good morning," Yolo snarled when she and Killa met their kids for breakfast the next morning. Killa held her by her hand just in case one of his children said something slick. He had no doubt she would climb across the table and choke one of them. Both of them probably.

"My bad, mom," Sun said sincerely and batted his brown eyes at his mother. Killa felt her soften and knew she bought his bullshit. "It's just... OK, we burned down the clinic, but then the people got on the heroin."

"We had to fix it, mommy," Shyne added and batted her eyes, as well. "We had to make it right."

Oh boy, Killa thought inwardly when Yolo sank into her seat. They just pulled one of his moves and it worked.

"Well, I get it," she admitted and nodded. "Except I told you to fall back until you have my grandchild, young lady!"

"OK, mommy. I won't do it noooooo more!" Shyne vowed and crossed her heart. It was a good look since they couldn't see her fingers crossed under the table. Shyne gets what Shyne wants and she wanted the Black Mob dead.

Chapter 34

"It's time!" Shyne yelled when her mother answered her call. Her water had just broken and it was time to have baby number one.

"We're on our way!" Yolo said and rolled out of bed like a fireman. "Get up, yo. Your daughter is about to give birth!"

"OK, let me know what she had," Killa said and flipped over to go back to sleep. He heard his wife suck her teeth and stormed into the bathroom. He thought he was in the clear when he heard the water running.

"Bruh, you can get up the easy way or the hard way, but you getting up!"

"Chill, yo," he barked when she stood over him with a pitcher full of water.

"I got your chill!" she dared. "Now get up!"

"A'ight, Yolo. You know I choke chicks," he warned and flipped his back to her.

"Yeah and I douse dudes with water." He didn't move, so Yolo shrugged and let him have it.

"Oh no you don't!" Killa growled and grabbed her ankle as she tried to flee. "Un uh, come here."

"Quit playing!" Yolo squealed in delight. They wrestled on the wet bed until somehow he ended up inside of her. "We gotta.... go!"

"I know," Killa grunted and kept stroking. He rolled them over and let her ride him to a mutual orgasm. They jumped up and took a mutual shower and hit the road. He sped the whole way downtown to the hospital. Yolo hopped out before he could even come to a complete stop and ran inside.

"My daughter is having a baby," she told the woman at the reception desk.

"Elevator, third floor," she said, pointing at the bank of elevators. Yolo rushed over and took one up. She turned left and right and saw her son-in-law in the waiting room. "Where is she? Did she have it? What you doing out here? Is everything OK?"

"Um..." Asad said, trying to process what she just said after what he just saw. English was his first language, but he couldn't remember any of it at the moment. It was easier to point, so he pointed at the delivery room he just ran from. Yolo took off and burst through the door startling the doctor and nurses.

"Where's my daughter? Is everything OK? Is that..." she paused seeing the newborn being tended to by the nurse.

"Hey, mommy! I had a baby!" Shyne cheesed, sounding worn out from the delivery.

"I see!" she said, coming to her daughter's side, but watching the baby. "Is she OK?"

"He is fine. His name is Muhammad!" she said happily. "Where's my daddy?"

"Right here," Killa said as he entered the room. He went straight over to Shyne as the nurse brought the clean baby back to his mother. "What is it?"

"It is your grandson." Shyne said, smiling down at her baby. "Can my husband come back in now?"

"Yeah, cuz I'm leaving!" the doctor said in a huff and stormed off.

"Girl, what happened?" Yolo asked since it was obvious something happened.

"Chile, that doctor tried to see how far I was dilated and Asad snatched his hand out and picked him up by his neck!" Shyne laughed. The nurse shook her head and tried not to laugh. "Not his fault. I did always tell him it's his pu—"

"I'll be outside with my son," Killa said and fled the room. His wife and daughter along with the nurse cracked up. Sun and Bryonna both arrived at the same time when he got back out.

"You can go in," Killa told Asad and shook his hand. "Congratulations!"

"Shukran," he said in Arabic since his English hadn't returned yet.

"Sup, pops. What she have?" Sun asked, trying to pretend he didn't see Bryonna.

"Mmhm," Killa laughed and left the two alone. He understood his son wanting to sow his wild oats, but hoped he'd settle down with the smart, ambitious and pretty girl.

"Oh hey! I didn't see you," he greeted since she stared in his face with her lips twisted into a 'yeah right'.

"Bruh, I rode the elevator with you," she shot back.

"I thought that was you! You look different. Did you dye your hair or..."

"Shut up!" she barked and pulled him into the delivery room. They both smiled seeing Asad holding his child. The room was silent except for the father gently reciting the call to prayer in the child's ear. He said it Arabic, but by now they all knew the words and nodded in agreement because God is the greatest in any language.

"You two are next," Shyne gushed to her friend and brother.

"Who! With her, him!" they both grimaced and shook their heads. No one including the nurse who didn't even know them bought the phony denial.

*****

"Well, I guess we can get back to work, huh?" Killa said as he navigated back home from the hospital. They had taken a break from breaking off the Mob until their daughter gave birth. Neither wanted to be across the country when the call came.

"Yes, sir. We need to go back to Birmingham and do it all over again! Remember last time we were there?" Yolo smiled fondly.

"No," Killa shrugged and got popped for being a man. "Anyway, what's happening down there?"

"More overdoses. Kids this time," she said of the still spreading opioid epidemic. It was spreading like a bad rash throughout the country. It was getting so bad even Killa couldn't kill it.

"Grrr," Killa replied and changed course. Birmingham was a quick two hours west which meant the mob had two hours more to breathe. It was deja vu when they ended up at the same pool hall once operated by the Black Mob decades earlier.

"Wow!" Yolo said as history repeated itself. She was the only one feeling nostalgic because Killa didn't remember any of it.

"So, how you wanna do this?" Killa asked as they staked out the gangs hangout.

"Run in and murder everything moving?"

"Why don't you chain the doors, then start a fire and I get up on the roof and gun down any one who gets out?" she suggested, reminding him of how they eliminated this same threat in this same place. It had been rebuilt nicely and that's too bad because it was about to get burned down once again.

"That's whack! It'll never work," he rejected. They went back and forth for a few minutes until Yolo got her way. She always did since Killa knew a happy wife meant a happy life. And nothing made Yolo happier than gunning down bad guys.

Killa did the honors and poured gas around the building. He spared no expense and got the premium grade gasoline. Meanwhile, Yolo watched from across the street on a rooftop.

"So silly," she said, seeing Killa dance to the music emanating from inside while he worked. He did his same little two step all around the building pouring gas and then put chains on the doors. She waited until he gave the thumbs up and backed a safe distance from the back door. Yolo shot the building causing a spark that lit up the dark. The building burned for a couple of minutes before the people inside realized what was going on.

"I smell smoke," the local leader named Bamboo asked, scrunching his face.

"Me, too," his sidekick announced. That's when they saw the flames licking at the windows. There was a mad dash for the doors and things went from bad to worse.

"The fuck!" Bamboo moaned when he realized they were trapped. He led the rush to the back door and found the same. By now, smoke began to fill the building and all lungs inside. Desperation finally propelled him out a side window.

"Let the games begin!' Yolo said and took aim at his fitted cap. It didn't fit anymore when she knocked the top of his head clean off. His sidekick decided to try his luck with a back window, but Killa sent him right back in with a bullet in his forehead. The mob got to choose between smoke inhalation or gun shot. In the end, they all got dead and that's all that mattered.

Two hours later, they were back in their bed sleeping like their newborn grandson.

Chapter 35

"I still can't believe you have a baby!" Bryonna gushed as she rocked baby Muhammad in her arms. The weather was nice, so they dined outside on the restaurant's patio.

"I can't believe it took so long the way we be getting it in! I'm surprised we don't have nine!" Shyne laughed. A group of men caught their attention as they entered the popular spot. The only thing louder than their clothes and jewelry was their voices.

"Black Mob in this bitch!" an obvious sidekick announced as they came out on the patio. No one cared, so everyone went back to their tacos. Everyone but Shyne who locked in on the leader. The medallion read 'Boss Man' in cloudy diamond baguettes.

"Shyne?" Bryonna reeled when her friend stared at the men. "Stop staring!"

"I'm not!" she fussed and grabbed her phone to call in the calvary. A one-man army. "Yo, I'm at S and S Tacos. Get down here now!"

"I know them shits is good, but you having a taco emergency?" Sun laughed. Laughter or not, he went for his shoes so he could leave.

"Shut up stupid and get down here!" she fussed and clicked off.

"Where you going?" Sun's female companion of the day asked.

"Duty calls, ma. Let yourself out," he said over his shoulder. When family calls Sun comes running.

"Who was that?" Bryonna fussed as if she didn't know. She knew exactly who is was and peeped in the glass to check her reflection.

"Yeah right. When you two gonna quit playing and get together?" she asked, but didn't pay attention to the reply. She was too busy watching Boss Man. She swore to her parents she wouldn't go anywhere and kill, but this kill fell right in her lap. She wouldn't have to leave Atlanta.

"Cuz he's a jerk!" she fussed and kept on fussing. Kept on fussing until Sun arrived at the restaurant. He didn't bother going inside and just walked up to the patio gate.

"Excuse me," Shyne said and went over to meet her brother. Sun winked at Bryonna and got the finger.

"Sup, sis?" he asked as his eyes followed his ears over to the loud mouths.

"That's them," Shyne nodded. "He's the Boss Man dude in my building that I was talking about. Let's get him."

"Now?" he asked then shook his head no. He was strapped now and had no qualms about putting one in his head in front of all these people, but not in front of Bryonna. "Probably not."

"Nah, probably not. I need you to follow them cuz I'm with your wife," she said daring him to deny her. He shot a lovesick glance her way and proved her point.

"Look at my nephew! He's so tiny. Like a little da-warf," he said, looking at Bryonna holding the sleeping child.

"A what?" Shyne asked of the new word. "What's a da-warf?"

"A little person. You know, bigger than a midget, da-warf," he explained. "You never heard of a da-warf? Remember we had the book? Snow White and the seven da-warfs?" Shyne sat there staring and blinking in disbelief when she realized he meant dwarf.

"Bruh... Just don't do nothing to them until I get there," she said and walked away shaking her head. "A da-warf."

"I'm on it," he assured her and turned to leave. He blew Bryonna another kiss and got flipped off once again. He went back to his car and waited for Boss Man and company to leave. He watched Bryonna's booty when she left with his sister and nephew after their meal then tuned back in on the targets.

Two hours of tacos and Margaritas later, they left and got into a brand new Range Rover.

"Oh, you getting robbed!" Sun cheered as Boss Man went store to store spending big money. He purchased clothes and jewelry like a kid does candy. The proverbial fool parting with his money.

Sun wasn't even mad when his tail led him to a strip club called Heads or Tails. Especially since he had gotten both head and tail out the joint in previous visits.

"Hey, Sun," a voluptuous stripper cheered and pressed her big stripper titties in his face. He basked in the big titties for a moment, but kept his eyes on his prize.

"Hey, yourself, Chocolate." he greeted when she released him from her bosom.

"Mocha," she corrected with a giggle that jiggled the titties.

"My bad. Knew it was a flavor," he said and ordered a beer and a table dance. He alternated between her oiled ass cheeks and watching his man. He felt some kind of way seeing him make it rain in the VIP. It was money out his pocket since he planned to rob the man. Luckily for Sun, dude had plenty of bread. She stole his attention when she made her ass cheeks clap.

"You ain't even paying attention to me," she pouted as if she didn't get paid per view, not pay per song.

"Sure I am," he assured her a vagina a rub as he inserted a bill in her garter. The heat from her box reminded him of the morning they spent together a few weeks back. It had the opposite effect and turned him off instead of on. He spent his time and money with the thot while ignoring a good woman like Bryonna. "I'm tripping!"

"What's wrong, baby? You miss this wet-wet?" she moaned and wiggled her as.

"Mmhm," he said. He did, but didn't want it again. Boss Man stood and headed towards the door with two strippers in tow.

"I'ma call you!" Sun lied and tossed her a tip. He hopped up and rushed to catch up with them. He needed to find out where he laid his head, so they could chop it off.

"You gone have call a cab, shawty," Boss Man advised to his hype man. His face dropped at getting dropped from the after party.

"Yeah, hell yeah. Mob in this bitch!" he cheered with his voice cracking in disappointment. He continued the hype as Boss Man loaded the women in his truck and pulled away. "Mob shit!"

"Sup, yo. You Mob?" Sun asked jovially like a groupie.

"Hell yeah!" he nodded boastfully even though he didn't have a ride home.

"You dudes run this city! I been wanting to get down with you guys! You know Boss Man?" he asked.

"Hell yeah! That's my partner! We like this!" he said, crossing his index in middle finger like he didn't just get left.

"Nuh uh!" Sun dared, twisting his lips in disbelief. "You don't know Boss Man?"

"Bet? I'll show you where he stay right now!" he said, plotting on a ride home.

He would pass by Boss Man's house and get dropped off at his own house.

"Let's ride!" Sun cheered and led the way to his car. He fought the urge not to shoot the loud mouth the entire ride. 'If this nigga say 'mob shit' one, more, time...

"Turn right. Yeah, we getting all the money. All the bitches," the hype man hyped like a hype man does.

"Boss Man run the whole shit?" Sun asked since he wanted him to tell everything he knew. He asked strategic questions so he could.

"Hell yeah! He run the city. I ain't sure who he report to though?" Mitch said since he often wondered. "He send some bread up the ladder err month. Corporate shit, banks and shit. Turn left, right there!"

"That shit is nice!" Sun honestly admitted and slowed to get a good look. He mentally recorded the house number and street name as they went on to their next stop.

"Yeah, we run this shit," Mitch said again and picked up where he left off. "Mob shit!"

"Open that door!" Sun ordered and pulled his pistol. Mitch looked at his choices of getting shot or jumping out of the moving car and decided.

"Argh!" he grunted as he rolled and bounced on the asphalt. He was scraped and bruised, but alive for a moment. Sun saw him pop up in his rearview and turned around. "Uh oh!"

"Un uh," Sun said, shaking his head. When he saw he survived the fall he made a u-turn to go gun him down. His plans changed when he saw the dummy limping away in the middle of the street. He shrugged his shoulders and mashed the gas. He ran him over and drove back home to call his sister.

"Yo?" Shyne huffed out of breath. She just had her six-week check up and checked out just fine.

"Bruh..." Sun said shaking his head. "Anyway, I found his address. Let's get his ass!"

"Tomorrow, cuz I'm busy getting busy!" she said and hung up.

*****

"His ass is getting robbed!" Shyne insisted when Sun showed her Boss Man's big house.

"No doubt, but how we gonna get in?" he asked. A cable van drove by no sooner than the words left his mouth.

"Just like that," she said, watching the van pull into a driveway. They laid on the driver to make his stop and get back on his way. "Got duct tape?"

"Of course!" Sun reeled as if it were a silly question. He followed the van until the driver stopped to check his route. "Get him, girl."

"I got him, boy," Shyne said and hopped out. She switched her hips as she approached the driver's side window. Sun simply could not understand how guys sweated his sister the way they did. She'd been turning heads since she blossomed at 15, but to him she was just Shyne.

"Excuse me?" Shyne sang and tapped on his window. The driver ran his eyes from her head to her toes and back again.

"Hey there," he sang as his window came down. "What can I do for you?"

"I need to borrow your van. Oh and your uniform, please," she asked nicely and smiled.

"My van?" he asked in reply to the odd request.

"And uniform," Sun added as he opened the passenger door and slid in.

"Oh! My van and my uniform!" the driver repeated since the pistol pointed at his midsection explained things more clearly. He climbed into the back as directed and stripped down to his under-clothes.

Shyne got behind the wheel while Sun duct taped his hands and mouth. He dressed in his uniform and joined her up front. She doubled back and headed back to Boss Man's house.

"These your kids?" Sun asked as he leafed through the pictures in his wallet. What he was looking for was a way to keep the man alive.

"And wife?" Shyne tossed in as she stole a peek from behind the wheel.

"Mmhm," he nodded vigorously since the tape on his mouth prevented him from speaking.

"And this is your address?" Sun asked and read off the address on his license.

Again he grunted and nodded. "Well, keep your mouth shut about this or both your kids and wife will be calling me daddy."

Another grunt and nod saved his life just before they reached their destination. Shyne parked next to a spanking new Benz. Sun traded the cable tools for the tools of his trade to put in some work.

"Take this in, too," Shyne said, handing him her specialty device.

"What the heck is this? A flare gun? You lost at sea or some shit?" he giggled.

"It's the Shyne-inerator 2000. Don't be no hater," she huffed indignantly.

"Word! Mom got you your own thing?" he whined. "Why I ain't got my own thing? Like a Sun-minator or a um, Sun-ray beam... um device!"

"Cuz you whack," she explained. Sun twisted his lips ruefully and hopped out. He was genuinely in his feelings when he approached the door and rang the bell.

"Who?" a male voice asked and snatched the door open. The sudden movement almost got him shot in his face. But Sun held his composure since he wasn't Boss Man.

"Cable," Sun explained and pointed at the patch on his uniform shirt and then the van. "We got a service call, upgrade um, thing."

"Word? It was working just fine," he said skeptically.

"Yeah, but um, premium customers get a free upgrade. All the porn channels are now included," he said since even he would have let a stranger in for that.

"Blondes and Blacks?" he asked as he stepped aside to let Sun enter.

"Uh... yeah," he agreed since whatever it was made his eyes twinkle in delight. Also made him forget to lock the door behind them as he escorted him into the den. Now it was Sun's turn to be amazed when he the 100 inch TV. "Damn!"

"Rich nigga shit," Boss Man bragged from behind a cloud of weed smoke. "What's wrong with the cable?"

"Free upgrade. We getting Blondes and Blacks!" his partner cheered and cheesed.

"You and your white girls," Boss Man chuckled and took another pull from his weed. Sun texted his sister and pretended to service the cable box. He unhooked the TV and waited for her to enter the house.

"Hey, y'all!" Shyne sang so cheerfully as she entered that the men weren't even concerned by her sudden appearance.

"Hey!" Boss Man sang in reply and took another toke. "Thought you drove the hoes home this morning?"

"I did," he replied and squinted at her since he didn't remember her from the night before.

"That's Shyne and Shyne is no hoe," Sun said in defense of his twin sister. Every female was a hoe, let Boss Man tell it. He opened his mouth to tell it until he saw the gun in Sun's hand.

"Bruh, you let damn jackers in the crib. This shit coming out your salary!" he grumbled. He assumed correctly that this was a robbery not knowing it was so much more.

"Yeah, that's fucked up," Shyne instigated. "It's his fault. He let us in. Told us where you keep your bread, too."

"You should fuck him up! I know I would," Sun instigated and removed a hammer from the toolbox.

"I would, too. You may as well, cuz we 'bout to wipe your ass out!" Shyne teased. Boss Man frowned, nodded and took the hammer.

"Bruh!" Boss Man's sidekick pleaded and got knocked in his mouth. Sun watched over the beating while Shyne spread out in search of valuables.

"Dang!" Sun giggled as Boss Man beat the man damn near to death. It was an indication of how much money Shyne was gathering up stairs. So much money Boss Man had to try his luck to keep it.

"Aaaah!" he screamed and made a charge towards Sun. He caught a slug for every step he took as Sun gunned him down.

"I ain't even mad at ya," Sun told him as he blinked death into view. His eyes went blank when his soul seeped out the bullet holes.

"What happened!" Shyne fussed as she rushed to respond to the gun shots. She pouted when she saw him stretched out on the floor with his life leaked out. "Aww, man! I was supposed to use my Shyne-inerator!"

"Bruh, are you crying about this shit? Well, do him then, sheesh," Sun said pointing at the beaten man.

"Do me what? What's that?" he reeled when she pulled her device from the borrowed toolbox.

"Shyne-inerator 2000, patent pending, so don't try to bite. Well, you won't be able to since, well..." Shyne explained and pulled the trigger. Now it was Sun's turn to whine when he saw the thing in action.

"Aww, man! I want my own thing, too!" he complained when the ball of fire completely engulfed the man. The fire quickly spread throughout the room. "Uh oh, where's the bread?"

"Upstairs! Come on!" the race against the flames was on when they raced upstairs. They shoved all the cash and jewelry they could in bags and pillowcases and hit the stairs again.

"Shit!" Sun said when the fire spread to the stairs. He turned and led the way into a back bedroom. "We gotta jump!"

"I'm not jumping out no window!" Shyne fussed when he opened the window. His looked down to gauge the distance to the bushes below.

"OK," he said and pushed her out. She landed in the bushes and rolled out just before he tossed out their spoils and jumped himself.

"Can't stand you!" Shyne said as she limped behind him back to the van. She was scraped, shirt torn and dirty, but a hundred thousand dollars richer from the lick.

"I know, right," he laughed and got back behind the wheel. "You OK back there?"

"Mmhm," the driver mumbled and nodded. Shyne counted out ten grand and showed it to him.

"You want this or your wife and kids calling him daddy? And he's a dummy who pushes people out of windows!" she fussed.

"Mmhm," the driver said shaking his head vigorously. They didn't understand, but they got it. Once they reached their car they released him and gave him the money. They drove to Sun's condo to split their proceeds.

"Just don't tell mommy!" Shyne insisted since she promised not to kill anyone else.

"Like I would tell on myself! I just want my own thing!" he pouted once again.

Chapter 36

"OK, what part of don't kill anyone didn't you get? Huh, crazy woman," Yolo scolded. She cocked her head daring her daughter to ask 'huh?' like she didn't know what she was talking about. Boss Man's murder made the news and the ensuing fire had Shyne written all over it.

"OK, what happen was Sun did it," she snitched and nodded. It wasn't technically a lie since Sun did gun the man down.

"Remind me never to do anything with you," her mother said. "Anyway, there's sure to be a big turnout at his funeral. I can finish this!"

"He already got cremated," she snickered until a look from her mother shut her down. "I mean, I see..."

"Well, your father and I will be in attendance. Just for surveillance, so don't come unless I call for you. Once we cut the head off—"

"The body will die," Shyne finished as her twin brother came in. "Uh oh."

"Sup, yo. Hey, ma," Sun greeted and leaned in to kiss her cheek.

"Hello, son," she greeted and accepted the kiss then popped him in the back of his head. Killa came out just in time to see the smack. He wisely turned around again and left without saying a word.

"Ma! What you hit me for?" he reeled and rubbed his head.

"Wait for me, daddy!" Shyne called out and ran behind her father.

"Oooh! She said I did it huh? Well, I did, but it was her idea," he confessed.

"Yeah, remind me never to do anything with you either," Yolo said, shaking her head. "Damn snitches..."

"Your kids," Killa chided when Yolo came into the den complaining about their children. Meanwhile Sun and Shyne fussed on who snitched on who first.

"Never mind them. We need to make sure we're at this funeral," she said.

"We can't be there. There will be a bunch of cops and cameras," he reminded. "As much as I hate to say it, we gotta send them two."

"Can't we send Rico? Xavier maybe?" she pleaded. "The baby?"

"Xavier is on tour and the only thing Rico gonna get on film is booty. Lots and of big, round, firm—"

"A'ight, playa. I get the gist," Yolo said, twisting her lips. He was right though because this was definitely a job for Sun and Shyne. "So, you don't like my booty?"

"Huh? Yeah, it's OK. I mean fine. I mean I probably should take another look at it," he suggested.

"Like this?" she said, turning sideways and tooting her butt out a little.

"Eh, can't really tell. Let's go upstairs so I can get a good look at it."

"You so nasty," Yolo said wickedly and led the way upstairs. She took the stairs two by two with him close on her heels. The sprint up the stairs served as foreplay and they got straight to it.

"You the one threw me under the bus first!" Sun fussed. Their back and forth was interrupted by the squeaking and creaking above them since the home office was directly below their parents bedroom.

"Just like that, huh? Those two are ridiculous with it!" Shyne fussed like she wasn't a freak herself. Her parents may be killers, but they raised her right so she was only a freak for her husband.

*****

"You guys still here? I was about to call you two back over here," Killa said when he came back downstairs to get water for him and his wife. They both lost a lot of fluid during their lunchtime romp.

"Yeah, cuz we need to talk to you guys," Sun demanded with a little extra bass in his voice. He then leaned back and let Shyne take over since she was their official spokesperson. Killa knew it and turned to her to expound.

"Yo, we going to that funeral. We need to be in there to see who's who. Then, if the chance presents itself, we're going to take them out. All of them at one time," she said like she meant it.

"Is that right?" Killa asked and pursed his lips. It was followed by a shoulder shrug and an 'OK'.

"Nah, bruh. We ain't taking OK for an answer! We're grown and we proved we can—"

"Chill, Sun. He said OK. We in!" his sister explained as their father went back upstairs to fuck their mother again. A minute later the squeaking and creaking resumed above.

"Come on. We have a funeral to get ready for," Sun said and stood to leave.

"Yup, and we gone be dressed to kill!"

Sun and Shyne went their separate ways to get ready for the big funeral the following day. There was plenty of radio coverage when it was announced that a wake would be held at Boss Man's favorite strip club. Sun decided to go see what he could see since it happened to be his favorite strip club, as well.

*****

"Hey, Roscoe!" a woman sang and rushed to hug Sun's neck when he entered the club. The alias meant she was a one-night stand.

"Oh, hey girl!" he cheered back as if happy to see her even if he couldn't remember her name. He thought about extending the one night stand to two when she pressed her big titties on him.

"Messed up what happened to Boss Man. I just sexed him two nights before," she explained and cancelled the second night stand. The good thing about thots is they're easy to fuck. The bad thing about thots is they're easy to fuck. The thought suddenly turned him off and turned his thoughts to Bryonna. While these girls were busy shaking their asses for money, she was no doubt at home doing some nerdy shit all by herself. Both her dignity and hymen were firmly intact.

"Yeah, it was," Sun said, stifling a smile at the memory of gunning the boss man's big ass down. To add insult to injury he was burned almost beyond identification from the fire. The memory of the fire twisted Sun's lips at not having his own custom made thing.

"You wanna do something after I get off?" she asked even though there was only one thing they could go do.

"Not tonight, ma. I gotta work tomorrow," he declined.

"You not going to the funeral? I wanted to but it's a closed affair," she whined. The information made the trip worthwhile so he and Shyne didn't show up and not be able to get inside.

"Probably not. Got work..." he repeated and scanned the club. He shook his head at seeing strippers dancing on top of an empty casket. Thugs poured out little liquor and blew weed smoke in the air for their fallen soldier even though he wasn't in the box. Meanwhile, Shyne was busy with her own dilemma across town.

"Technically, it's not a church," she told herself as she rigged the gas lines in the funeral home. It was good she decided to break in because she was able to swipe a few guest passes and put herself and Sun's alias on the guest list. It meant staying up later making fake IDs to match their disguises. She made a copy of the guest list and had every head of the Black mob in every city. The beef would end tomorrow.

*****

"Hello?" Bryonna asked as she took Sun's call. She only took the late night call out of curiosity since they both knew no booty calls would be going down.

"What you doing?" he asked, picturing her with book on her lap and shower cap keeping moisture in her natural hair.

"Just came in from the club. I um, have company. So I um, have to talk to you tomorrow," she said and hung up on him. She wanted to call him right back and apologize for the lie and being rude. Playing hard to get can be hard sometimes.

"OK, that's what's up," he said into the empty line and smiled to himself. He put his car in drive and pulled from in front of her house. He made his next call to the first person on his contact list.

"Sup, yo. Guess what?" Shyne said, eager to share what she knew.

"The funeral is invite only. Closed to the public," he said knowing he scooped her news story.

"Aww, man! How you know?" she whined but didn't wait for an answer. "Anyway, I got us in. The whole gang will be there. It ends tomorrow!"

"Let's end it then!" he said and clicked off. Sun went to his condo and spent a rare night alone with his thoughts. He knew he wanted to be with Bryonna, but had more pressing matters to deal with. His mom and dad had their D.C. 2000 and now Shyne had her Shyne-inerator. He needed and wanted his own thing.

"Oh! I know a hammer! A big ass mallet and I can say, 'It's hammer time'!'"he thought aloud. It sounded good to him so he called his sister to let her now. "Yo, Shyne! I got it! I'm getting me a hammer! As my thing! A big ass hammer!"

"A what! Who you 'sposed to be, Thor?" she cackled. "Go to bed, mallet man!"

"Yeah, OK. I'll go to sleep, but in the morning I'll be woke again!" he moaned and went to sleep.

The next morning Sun awoke and got dressed to kill. He still felt some kind of way about his hammer idea getting laughed at, but in the end he wasn't Thor, so it was back to the drawing board. *Back to the drawing board*, he thought and called Bryonna again.

"Hello... shoot!" she answered and fussed realizing she took his call too soon. She told herself to let it ring a few times next time he called, but lost it when she saw his name and snatched it on the first ring.

"Get dressed. I'm coming to get you for breakfast," he demanded and hung up before she had a chance to say no.

"Well, I'ma wear what I want," she said defiantly to no one since he didn't give her an option. She rushed into her room to change and fluff her puffy afro. A few minutes later he was ringing her door. Sun would never admit to moving so close to keep a watchful eye on her.

"You ready?" Sun asked when she opened her door despite her being fully dressed. He slid past her into her apartment and looked around for signs of a male and found none.

"Yeah, I'm ready, dang! You searching my house and whatnot," she happily complained.

"Come on," he said and extended his hand.

"Yeah right!" she frowned up at his hand and locked her door behind them. They rode over to her favorite breakfast spot in silence, save a meaningful glance here and there. Once they were seated, Sun took the liberty of ordering for the both of them.

"I'll have the jerk chicken with whole wheat waffle and the lady will have the Nashville Hot with red velvet waffle. Two milks," he said without using the menu. Bryonna giggled inside but kept her composure.

"What are you up to? What do you want? Well, I know what you want and you can't have it, so what do you want?" she asked and cut to the chase.

"Getting my life in order. Getting my woman back," he said causing her to have a giggle fit.

"Sun, you full of games. You want to run around with these girls and—"

"And nothing. I wouldn't be here if I wanted anyone else but you. I want what Asad and Shyne have with you," he explained. "A family, a da-warf of our own."

"A da-warf?" she asked and cocked her head curiously. "What's a da-warf?"

"Never mind, eat your food. We'll talk about it later," he said. They laughed and joked like old times over the rest of their meal.

"So, what's next?" she asked as he drove her home. He had to steer with one hand since she finally took the other.

"Well, I have a funeral to go to now," he replied unsure if that was what she meant.

"No, us. What do we do next about us?" she pleaded.

"I guess we get married next. Hook it up and I'm there," he nodded.

"How romantic," she laughed, but hooked it up as soon as she got inside. She gladly made all the arrangements for a Vegas wedding AS-AP. She finally got her man.

Chapter 37

"You ready?" Shyne asked when Sun came to pick her up from her condo. She was dolled up in a blonde wig and large glasses to obscure her face.

"No, I'm not," he answered sarcastically since he was wearing a fake moustache and beard. "We'll just go down here and wing it."

"First of all, that's not what I'm talking about," she shot back, matching his tone.

"Second of all, I just got off the phone with Bryonna. I hope you not playing with her. Bruh, I will fuck you up about my girl. Burn your house down, set your car on fire—"

"Chill with the threats, yo. I'm good. I'm gonna marry her," he assured her and drove towards the funeral home. Shyne squinted as she stared at his profile trying to determine if he was sincere.

"You probably should park on the next block. This whole building is going up in flames," Shyne sang. Sun complied and drove the extra block. He didn't want to get boxed in by fire trucks or any scratches or soot on his shit. It meant he had to carry the extra heavy bag that much further. But he did like his car. Shyne locked eyes with Mrs. Baker in the back seat of her limo as they passed. She seemed so out of place, Shyne took note of the plates.

The twins walked back over to the funeral home with several sets of eyes on them. Sun dipped around back and chained the back doors so no one could escape. Shyne waited in front and deflected crass come-ons from Black Mob members from across the country.

"Sup, lil' mama? What you doing after we put this nigga in the ground?" The man from Miami asked. The leader of Houston tried to holla as did dude from Dallas. She sucked her teeth and turned her face dismissively at their advances.

"These dudes still tryna holla," she griped when her brother returned.

"At you?" Sun frowned curiously. He still didn't get the hype over his sister.

"Come on, da-warf man," she said, shaking her head as she led them inside.

"Stinks in here," Sun grumbled as they walked in. He scrunched his face up looking around for the source of the stink.

"Well, there are dead people in here," Shyne shot back until the familiar smell got to her. It wasn't embalming fluid or decay, but chemical compounds she knew all too well. "Yo, let's go!"

"What!" Sun called after her as she turned and rushed back towards the door. He wasn't sure what was wrong, but followed her lead and left the funeral home. A moment later, a huge explosion rocked the building.

Sun and Shyne were knocked to the ground by the blast and the limo pulled away. The gas lines Shyne rigged the night before caused a second explosion that knocked them down once again.

"Come on, yo!" Sun said, helping his sister to her feet. They rushed down the block and into his car. "Mom's gonna be hot!"

"That wasn't me! That smell was plastique. Someone put a bomb in there!"

*****

"Yeah right!" Yolo fussed when they relayed the events that made the news.

"They lying. Let's fuck 'em, up," Killa instigated from her side.

"Pops, I swear by Allah it wasn't us," Sun vowed. His parents twisted their lips, but knew that was his strongest adjuration and had to believe him. He might put something on 'err thing he love' and lie, but never if he swore by God.

"I was going to blow the building," Shyne lowered her head and admitted. "I was, but I didn't. I could smell Symtex when we walked in."

"That's military grade! No way a bunch of goons know how to get it or how to use it," Yolo said scratching her head. "Is history repeating itself and the Black Mob run by a white man?"

Now it was Killa's turn to frown at the unpleasant memory of the original Black Mob run by White Casper. Sun opened his mouth to report the white lady in the limo, but his twin sister read his mind and shook her head.

"And if it was the puppet master, why kill all the puppets?" Killa wondered aloud.

"Well, whoever it was did us a favor. Our work is done. Come on Sun, let's ride," Shyne said and rushed her brother from the house.

"They're up to something, you know," Yolo tossed out nonchalantly.

"No doubt. That's why I put a tracking device on his car," Killa said just as easily.

"Wanna go make love?"

"Nope. I wanna go fuck!" Yolo corrected and led the way up to their room.

*****

"Why didn't you let me tell them about the white lady?" Sun asked as they drove away from their parent's house.

"Cuz! Why let them have all the fun? Let's find this broad and knock her whole head off!" Shyne explained. Sun nodded in agreement since it made good sense. But only because they didn't know who they were dealing with.

"I know a lady who can track the plates. She works for—"

"Thots R Us? Another strip club? Sun don't hurt my friend! I swear I'll—" Shyne vowed and shook her head.

"Stop threatening me, yo. The lady works for DMV, bruh," he sighed and made the call. He relayed the tag number from Shyne and thanked his friend. "She said give her a couple of hours."

"Well, take me home," Shyne said and dialed her phone. "Hey, B. Mmhm, I'm with him now. Mmhm."

"What? What she saying?" Sun asked when his sister kept cutting her eyes at him and saying 'mmhm'. All he got out of her was more side eyes and another 'mmhm'. Sun called Bryonna the second Shyne got out his car.

"Mmhm.," Bryonna hummed when she took Sun's call. She intended to play hard, but let out a giggle.

"So, what you and my sister were talking 'bout?" he asked as he watched Shyne enter her building. He called the second she got out of his car.

"The wedding! It's gonna cost a million dollars and have lions, tigers, a giraffe..." Bryonna rambled in one breath. She could picture the stunned look on Sun's face and cracked up again. "Just kidding! I don't need all that. I'm more concerned with the marriage than the wedding."

"Oh, OK. Cuz I didn't mind spending a mil... yes I did! Who I look like, Gucci Mane?" he laughed.

"Boy, if you did look like him you would not be marrying me!" she laughed. They laughed and joked until he got home. "Anyway, we're going to Vegas!"

*****

"Bruh!" Yolo exclaimed when she got to the end of the financial trail. She retraced her steps and ended up with the same results. "Bruh!"

"Sup?" Killa asked and came around behind her to view the screen. His own sources came back with unbelievable results.

"All roads lead to Baker Management Company. A publicly traded company. This makes no sense," she said scratching her head.

"Ran by Marguerite Baker, age 62. Hampton Beach, New York," Killa said, coming up with the same information." Another example of greedy people taking advantage of the inner cities!"

"As they should! Why not if niggas wanna destroy their own people and neighborhoods? All they were going to do was take the money out of the community anyway!" Yolo shot back. They went back and forth for a while, but ended up with the same results. Killa and Yolo were heading to New York.

"Well, since that's settled..." Killa said once they agreed to disagree. They both learned when to let an argument go without declaring a clear winner since that required a loser. Who wants to overcome their loved one for the sake of winning an argument?

"Yup, look at this. Baker Management's biggest competition," Yolo said, pointing at another public company.

"Are you thinking what I'm thinking?" he asked since he was thinking about investing in the smaller company since the larger one was about to lose its head, literally.

"If you're thinking we're about to be rich then I'm thinking about what you're thinking about!" she cheered. The family had plenty of money, but stood to make millions more when they put Baker Management out of business.

*****

"Mom and dad swear they sooooo smart," Shyne laughed as she and her brother sped towards New York.

"I know, right!" Sun chuckled. "We gonna go up here and kill this broad and get back before they know we're even gone!"

"And I invested what we took from Boss Man into their competition. Once we put them out of business, we'll have millions!"

The twins got a good laugh as they raced towards New York to put the Baker family out of business forever.

Chapter 38

"Suckers!" Killa laughed as he and Yolo flew to New York. The GPS tracker showed the exact moment they passed over their children driving in North Carolina.

"My baby is making good time though," Yolo said proudly. Sun was her firstborn and very dear to her heart. He only preceded his sister by minutes but the impact was instant. Seeing his little face transformed her from monster to mother. Lunatic to lady.

"We should wait on them?"

"Did he tell you about his hammer?" Killa laughed. Yolo laughed too when he explained.

"Who he think he is, Thor?" she laughed. "My poor baby."

"Well, my sources tell me Mrs. Baker is having a thing Sunday and a board meeting Monday morning."

"Too bad she gonna be dead Sunday night," Yolo corrected. She let out a wicked little snicker until she was wracked by a sharp pain. "Owww."

"Is she OK?" asked the stewardess who just happened to be passing by when the pain hit.

"It's her whatchamacallit acting up again. I need to get her into a bathroom," Killa said, looking around urgently. "I have to give her her medicine."

"Follow me. You can use the staff restroom. It's bigger," she said and led them towards the front of the cabin. People looked sympathetically as they walked by with Yolo bent at her waist.

"Thank you," Killa said as he helped his wife inside. A miracle happened and Yolo perked up immediately.

"Come on with it!" she said, hiking her dress up and hopping on the counter. She often went commando for occasions just like this.

"Mmm," he marveled as she soaked his fingers when he fondled her as he removed his manhood. They both moaned when he slid inside of her.

Yolo and Killa made eye contact in between soft kisses and slow strokes. Quickies are supposed to be quick, but the couple made love from North Carolina to midway through Virginia. Yolo clamped her teeth on his shoulder to stifle her screams when overcome by an intense orgasm. Killa just let out a grunt when he exploded.

"Good thing I did bring panties!" she said, removing a pair and panty liner from her purse. "They gonna charge us extra if I leak cum all over their seats."

"Thank you. She's feeling a lot better," Killa informed the concerned stewardess as they exited the bathroom. He escorted the smiling woman back to her seat where she fell asleep instantly.

"Did she take something to help her sleep?" the woman whispered to Killa since Yolo's eyes fluttered trying to stay open.

"She took it like a pro," he assured her and joined her nap. They both were awakened when they reached New York.

*****

"Home sweet home," Yolo sang with nostalgia as they rode along the Long Island Expressway. She let out a sigh when she saw her exit up ahead.

"Yeah," Killa agreed even though his own sweet home was the Bronx. It was their first stop when they arrived. They had to swing by the house in Wyandanch since that's where they kept their arsenal. Plus, it was on the way to the Hamptons.

"We really do need to get my baby his own thing. It's not fair to him that Shyne has one and he don't," Yolo said in that motherly tone the father knew not to challenge.

"Oh, OK. We'll figure something out for him," he relented. "An exploding boomerang or something?"

"That's so whack!" she cracked up. Yolo laughed all the way to the house and around to the backyard. She became deadly serious when they entered the basement armory. "This place always turns me on!"

"Me, too!" he admitted feeling a stiffy coming on. He braced himself against a table and waited for the moment to pass.

"You are so silly," Yolo said, shaking her head. She moved on to the task of finding the perfect apparatus to murder the Baker clan. "Security?"

"Nope. They think they're untouchable. Think they're so smart no one would figure them out. Just an old lady and her sissified son, Herbert."

"Well, how 'bout dis?" Yolo suggested, holding up a set of matching brass knuckles.

"Eh..." Killa replied. "It would be nice to beat that old bitch. What about the son?"

"D.C 2000. What else?" she fussed with her hand on her hip.

"Well, it is your signature thing," he nodded in agreement. They packed a few pistols for the inevitable intangibles and hit the door. "Wish we still had pigs. That's my shit right there!"

"Mama will buy some pigs," she vowed, rubbing his wavy hair. They bantered back and forth all the way out to Hampton Beach where the Baker family was holding a white party. It was about to turn red.

*****

"Nice turn out, Gregory," Herbert nodded to their help. The caterers served surf & turf and champagne to the snobbish white folks all dressed in the white. The staff was the only off white faces in the place.

"Thank you, sir," the butler said with a nod in return. He braced himself when he turned to leave for what he knew what was coming.

"Did you see that?" Killa laughed when he saw Herbert pat him on his ass when he turned to leave.

"That's an unwanted sexual advance!" Yolo fussed. The real bartender and waitress were safety tied up in the basement so the killer couple stepped in. "He can be sued for that!"

"Or... we did come to kill him so..." he reminded. They served drinks and listened to rich white people's problems until the end of the party.

"I made a thousand dollars in tips!" Yolo said shocked by the total. "Guess I'll buy something for the baby."

"What baby!" Killa shrieked and went pale.

"Your grandson, stupid. I am not pregnant," Yolo said shaking her head. It was time to make their move so they dipped inside the house once the guest had vacated the premises.

"I knew that," he said now that he could breathe again since it wasn't her who was pregnant once again.

"Can I help you?" Gregory asked when he saw Killa and Yolo enter the kitchen.

"No, but we can help you," Yolo said. She decided to spare him since he was being sexually harassed.

"Walk this way," he said and turned to escort them into the study.

"So silly," Yolo giggled as Killa imitated his stiff walk like he had a stiff stick up his butt.

"He said walk this way," he snickered. Fun and games were over once they reached the Baker family.

"Gregory?" Herbert frowned curiously when he led the uninvited guest into the room. "What's the meaning of this? Who are these people?"

"I'm Yolo. This is my husband, Killa. We came to kill you," Yolo explained so friendly that Mrs. Baker thought she misunderstood her.

"Excuse me?" she asked with polite smile until Yolo socked her in the mouth that is.

"Mother!" Herbert shouted and hopped to his feet as Gregory took his seat to watch the show.

"Sit your bitch as down!" Killa shouted and he sank down and sat Indian style on the floor.

"Mother," he whimpered as Yolo had a conversation with his mother while she beat the woman.

"You, thought, it was, cute, to hide, behind black people?" She asked in between blows. Yolo could hit a lot harder, but she wanted to make it last. She wanted to punish the woman.

"Those stupid niggers deserved to be used!" she laughed despite losing blood and teeth with each punch. "I charged them to poison their own communities! Dumb niggas wanted to be down with something so bad they paid to be down with something that didn't exist!"

"And you're going to die for it!" Yolo said and turned up. The brass knuckles broke and crushed everything they hit.

"Now would be a good time to say goodbye," Killa leaned and suggested to Herbert as they beating intensified.

"Bye, mommy," he whimpered and waved just before Yolo knocked her soul loose from her frame.

"Mrs. Baker has left the building!" Gregory laughed when her eyes glassed over and the rattle of death escaped her throat. The sound of the doorbell quickly wiped the smile of his face. "Uh oh! It's the cops!"

"Oh, that's just our kids," Yolo advised as she stood up from the beating.

"Your... kids?" he asked in confusion.

"Yeah, we stopped in the Bronx so they could catch up. You mind?" Killa explained.

"Uh, sure," he said and went to open the door. He could see the resemblance when he looked out the peephole and pulled the door open. When he pulled, Sun pulled, too.

"Do what I say and you might be able to live through this!" Sun barked and shoved his pistol in the man's face.

"Where are the Bakers?" Shyne demanded in a whisper. He pointed to the rear and led the way.

"Walk this way," he said matching her whisper. Meanwhile Sun matched his walk just like his father did. Shyne just shook her head and her silly brother.

"What? He said..." he repeated just like his dad when they entered the den and saw his dad.

"Aww, man!" Shyne moaned when she saw her parents. Especially her bloody mother standing over the dead woman.

"Are you really crying?" Yolo asked her distraught daughter. "Don't be no punk."

"I'm not, but we drove all night and we wanted to kill them for you, but they already dead and..." Shyne rambled on in one breath. Yolo didn't buy it, but as usual her father did.

"Come here, baby," he said reaching for her. Shyne rushed over into his embrace while her brother twisted his lips and shook his head. "I saved him for you."

"Thank you, daddy!" she bounced and kissed his cheek. He slipped the D.C 2000 over the shivering man's head.

"Sucka," Yolo chided and chuckled as their daughter's crocodile tears went away instantly.

"What is th—" Herbert wanted to know, but Shyne hit the switch before he could finish his question. His head did a somersault and rolled away. Now it was Sun's turn to lose his head.

"It's not cool how you two kiss her ass!" Sun fussed, pointing at his sister. "You had twins, you know! I was born first, you know!"

"I know, baby," Yolo said sympathetically and stretched her arms wide. Her first-born rushed over to collect his hug and got popped in her head. "Boy, we like her better than you!"

"We do," Killa nodded. He tried to keep a straight face, but the look on his son's face cracked him up. "Don't worry, son. We'll get you your own 'thing'. Not a hammer though."

"OK. What about him?" he asked, hooking his thumb at the butler. Gregory held his breath hoping he would get to keep breathing.

"What happened here?" Killa asked the man. He must have known his life depended on his answer and gave the answer of his life.

"Herbert Baker was involved with some shady biker types who came and..."

"He's cool," Yolo said and turned to leave. Killa threw his arm around her shoulder to escort her out.

"So, what's next?" Shyne requested from the rear. Her parents looked her then each other. They both knew her story didn't end here. In fact, it was just the beginning. A smile spread on their faces when the same answer came to mind.

"Time to resurrect 1-800-Killa," Killa nodded. "Cuz there are plenty people in the world who desperately need dead!"

"And that's exactly what they're gonna get!" she vowed.

THE END

BAD COP
A Novel By
Sa'id Salaam

I hate funerals. Any funeral but especially cop funerals, they are the worse. A bunch of phony motherfuckers rejoicing that it was you instead of them laying in that box. Then, what's up with the kilts and bag pipes? Like all cops are Irish or some shit. Then your so-called brothers all misty eyed even though racism is alive and kicking in the force. Department preacher singing your praises no matter if you were straight as an arrow or crooked as a fish hook. Most of these guys and gals need to be in jail themselves. That vice detective in the front row got the biggest child porn collection in the Tristate area. The lady cop next to him sell more pussy than the law allows. The so-called drug taskforce got more dope in the street than the cartel but, who am I to talk huh? Just look at the position I got myself into. Laid out with my academy picture beside a closed casket. You know it's ugly when they have to close the lid on you.

Yeah, I hate funerals. Especially cop funerals, especially when it's mine.

CHAPTER 1

I came along way from a happy, chubby girl growing up in a big house on Long Island to a dead cop in Atlanta. Most New Yorkers move south to slow down, prosper and live. Not me, nope. I came down here, got in a whole bunch of trouble and got my ass killed. It's a long story so let's start from the beginning.

"How's my baby!" Officer Rohan Robinson sang as he came out of the bedroom dressed in his uniform. His east Indian heritage gave his skin a nice golden tone while his hair was almost straight. His dark skin wife Michelle knew the combination would make some pretty children but more importantly have good hair.

She envisioned a bunch of handsome, curly-headed boys, but all she got was one daughter. A pretty, little girl who would never need a perm but still, boys are not the same as girls. She came from a household of five boys and her being the lone girl. She saw how different her parents treated her from them. She went from wanting to be a boy to wanting nothing but boys.

"Hey, baby. I—" Michelle began but Rohan wasn't talking to her and scooped up their daughter Megan instead.

"Hey, daddy!" the little girl squealed in delight as he blew raspberries on her chubby cheeks. The happy child had skin tone exactly like her dads and big, black, bouncy curls for hair. Being an only child, spoiled by her father made her a fat but happy child. Michelle wore a jealous scowl at playing second fiddle but quickly erased it when Rohan turned her way.

"And my darling wife?" he greeted, extending his arm so she could join the group hug.

They had just quietly made love before he showered and dressed for his night shift. Their theme song 'just in case I don't make it home tonight' would play in the background to ensure their child didn't hear the moans and groans of her pursuit of another child. He could get some more when he got home since their daughter would be off to school.

"Last but not least," she quipped as she joined the embrace. Megan reached to squeeze her neck, as well. The gifted 7-year-old was smart enough to notice the temperature change whenever her father left. What she couldn't add, subtract or multiply but saw her mother was jealousy over her. She was too young to understand what it was but sure felt it.

"You know I love my ladies don't you?" he asked needlessly. He proved his love and devotion to his family on a regular basis.

He secured them a big house out on Long Island that seemed to be a million miles away from the south Bronx projects they came from. Two brand new cars in the driveway and closets full of clothes. Rohan made it his mission in life to protect and serve but that started at home with his family first. Being overextended forced him to work several double shifts each week.

"Yes!" they sang in chorus and squeezed him again. He closed his eyes and basked in the love before heading out into the dangerous streets of Harlem.

"Love you, guys. See you in the morning," he proclaimed and gave each a parting kiss. Michelle blushed knowing just how he would see her when he got in. Both smiled and waved as he exited the house and entered his car. They kept smiling and waving until he was out of sight.

"Wanna watch a movie with me?" Megan turned and asked hopefully before the temperature dropped.

"Nah," Michelle said, turning up the corner of her lip. It really wasn't the child's fault that she reminded her of the stuck up pretty girls who taunted her about dark skin and course hair. It definitely wasn't her fault that she gave birth to her and not the brood of sons she longed for. She just couldn't seem to get pregnant again even though they had sex daily.

Mother and daughter went their separate ways to do their separate thing. For the girl, that meant the daunting task of trying to figure out which toys to play with. She had Barbie this and Barbie that, not to mention every video game system available in those days. The smarts child's number one past time was the encyclopedia set. Just something else for her ratchet mother to talk about.

Michelle went and got on the phone with her friend Reese back in the Bronx. The two had grown up together in the same projects. They smoked the same weed, wore the same clothes and slept with the same dudes. Michelle happened to catch Rohan's eye in a club and the rest was history. She would have slept with him that first night but he had school the next day. He was so busy they didn't get a chance to hang out for a couple of weeks. Once the nerd from Queens got a taste of a hoe from the Bronx he was hooked. He proposed weeks later.

Reese was still doing the same thing resulting in four baby daddies and a case of genital warts. They didn't get to hang out much but spoke almost daily. Michelle loved to brag about her husband, house, car and life. Reese always congratulated her but secretly despised her.

"So, Rohan just upgraded my truck. You know you need an SUV out here in the suburbs. You're so lucky to still be in the projects. Bus stop right out in front and you can always catch a gypsy cab." Michelle bragged and dissed at the same time. Two fucked up people can never really be friends but they can relate.

"Mmhm," Reese hummed since she was holding in smoke from the blunt she was smoking. She laced it with powdered cocaine to make the high, higher and last longer. Some call it a 'Woolie' or 'dirty' but it should be called 'Strike one' on the way to striking out. Most crack heads start off light like this. Then, get a stripe and graduate to the pipe, aka strike three.

"So, what you been up to girl?" she asked, knowing there wasn't shit to be up to in the projects. Old folks still lived there because it was all they could afford. They just waited on their reservation to the upper room. The young ones with vision escaped and never came back. The others sold drugs and made babies, also waiting to die.

"Just chilling. My baby daddies coming through with that check so I been straight. Hitting the club err night," she relayed between tokes.

Michelle could hear her smoking and wished she could get a pull. Just one long toke and a line. Just one long, thick line of coke. Oh and a big swig from a 40 like back in the days. She twisted her lips ruefully, knowing that wasn't going to happen. Not with a cop for a husband. Not just a cop but one of Manhattan's best narcotic cops.

Meanwhile, Megan read two books at the same time. One was for school and the other just because she loved to read. Books were like an all-expense paid vacation to wherever. She'd already visited 15 countries on 3 different continents. Her actions and adventures were nothing compared to what her father had going on.

CHAPTER 2

"Sup 'potna. You love that monkey suit I see!" Rohan's much younger partner Jackson greeted as he entered the locker room. The light skin pretty boy dressed like the rapper/rock star he envisioned himself as.

"My daughter loves my uniform," he replied as he began to change out of it. It was partially true since Megan did love to see her hero in uniform, but he loved wearing it just as much. He was proud to be a New York City police officer. Even after his promotion to detective and plain clothes he still wore his blues every chance he got.

"I need to swing through and see my kid," he said like he only had one. He made almost as many babies as he did arrest but only counted the one by his main chick. A hot-blooded Puerto Rican with a hot head and even hotter vagina. Their tumultuous relationship revolved around fighting, fucking and shopping.

"Yeah," Rohan grunted and bit his tongue. He couldn't imagine not seeing his beautiful daughter every day. That's why he worked so hard to make sure he came home every night. Just another example of how incompatible he and Jackson were.

'Jax' was a cowboy. A rooting, tooting, two gun-shooting cowboy. They were in the middle of a big undercover operation that would get them both either promoted or dead. A win/win since either way he wouldn't have to work with the man anymore. He may have not seen the man take money but it was obvious. Unfortunately, it was the rule and not the exception. Why should the dope boys have all the fun with all the money, cars and women?

"So, Snake wants to meet us at Back Shots!" Jax cheered rubbing his hands together like dinner was served. It was a high-end strip club known for having the baddest bad girls in the city.

"Why not City Island? Lobster and crabs?" Rohan wanted to know. He was a married man and hated being around a bunch of women. Especially some of the baddest bad girls in the city completely naked. He could see himself speeding home in the morning to rush inside of his wife for relief. Michelle would of course complain about him smelling like baby oil with glitter on his face.

"Or...Back Shot, big titties and fat asses. Blowjobs and shit. Bet Michelle gives you killer blow jobs!" he cheered.

"Jax you obviously can't see it, but there's a line, and you crossed it." Rohan calmly explained. He knew his partner well enough to know most of his words came straight out his mouth without ever passing through his brain. A normal person's brain will filter inappropriate shit and allow a person to keep it to themselves.

"My bad! I know you married guys are sensitive. Tender dicks, nothing wrong with that." he offered. It was probably as close as he could get to an actual apology so Rohan let it be.

"No problem. You ready?" he asked after transforming into his street clothes and persona. His Indian looks got him called 'Tonto' as a child coming up. It was the wrong kind of Indian but he embraced it. He looked every bit the part in a tailored suite and chunky platinum jewelry.

Jax on the other hand lived the part 24/7. He didn't have to change clothes because he dressed like a dope boy every day. Complete with an easy hundred grand worth of jewels dripping from his neck, ears, fingers and wrist. He pushed a spanking new STS Caddie but had a Porsche parked at his Brooklyn condo.

"Gotta take a quick shit," he said, holding up a finger. He did that quite often making his partner assume he had a digestive problem. He had a problem alright but it wasn't IBS.

Rohan rushed into a stall and shimmied out of his skinny pants and silk drawers. He sat his bare ass cheeks down on the toilet and dug into his pocket. His pretty smile spread on his handsome face when he saw the glistening cocaine in a hundred-dollar bill. That smile turned into a grimace as he took a heaping scoop up each nostril.

"Argh! This shit is the shit!" he congratulated. He knew he came up on some fish scale when they busted a dealer in Washington Heights. The coke was so pretty he grabbed a few handfuls to keep for himself. That and twenty grand from the pile of money.

"Straight now?" Rohan asked when he returned. He noticed an extra ping and zip in the man but knew a good shit can do that.

"Super straight!" he shot back, super high. He followed his partner out of the precinct into the parking lot. A press of a key fob made a Lexus beep in response. "Piece of shit they got us riding in."

"The Lexus?" Rohan shot back in shock. He knew full well it started at ninety grand because Michelle just tried to talk him into buying one. Jax was right because she did have some killer head, she threw in that morning to help her campaign. In the end, she had to settle on a new truck but that was close to sixty.

"Jap crap! You gotta drive the new Porsche!" he shot back and climbed behind the wheel.

"Still, be easy," he recommended since he drove like a bat out of hell. The last thing they needed was to get pulled over by other cops, which could blow their cover.

"I got this," he assured him as he eased out of the parking lot. As soon as he hit the street he mashed the gas and drove like a bat out of hell out to the Bronx.

*****

"They just called. Said they on the way," XL announced to his boss. Despite being 6'5" and three hundred pounds he pulled double duty as secretary and bodyguard.

"Shit, we get a good Queens dealer and that's the whole city!" Snake cheered. His Columbian connect was dumping as much work on him as he could handle. He fancied himself the Amazon of cocaine, distributing it all over the city. He was mulling over the idea of using drones to deliver to the five boroughs. A few table dances later Jax and Tonto entered the club.

"That's what the fuck I'm talking about!" Jax said and literally clapped his hands at the wall-to-wall strippers. The club boasted almost every ethnic group on the planet. They even had an Eskimo shaking her flat ass on a side stage.

"Let's handle our business, and get up out of here," Rohan said seeing the same tits and asses but with the opposite effect. He wanted to get far away while his partner wanted to get deep inside.

"Bruh, don't be a tight ass. Don't act like a fucking cop!" Jax warned through clenched teeth. Being undercover meant becoming a criminal. Jax embraced it wholeheartedly while it was the part Rohan struggled with.

"There they are," he said seeing XL stand in the VIP section and raise his large hand. He hit an internal switch and became Tonto. Jax never had to turn on and off since he was always on.

Jax smiled and groped his way through a swamp of naked women. Rohan just knew their perfumes were rubbing off on him. Michelle would certainly have something to say about that. The bouncer charged with keeping the common folk from the VIP parted the velvet rope.

"Jax! Tonto!" snake stood and greeted warmly when they reached his table. XL stood back with a menacing scowl like a good bodyguard does. Luckily the phone didn't ring and expose his secretarial side.

"Sup yo!" Jax greeted with a pound and man hug. Tonto stepped up next and did the same.

"Ready to handle some business?" Tonto asked as soon as they sat. He almost got kicked under the table by his partner for moving so fast.

"In a minute. Let's have a drink. Watch some asses shake" Snake said being a good host. He raised his hand and the waitress made a beeline to his table.

"What can I get you baby?" the woman who looked like she could be on one of the stages herself. Her tiny shorts were pulled up into her crotch to show it off and a set of heavy breast gave a wife beater all it could handle. Big nipples strained against the fabric like a nosey set of eyes trying to get a peek.

"Henny. Bring the bottle," he suggested and she took off to fill the order.

"Bruh, I would bend her over the table and eat her from the back!" Jax vowed.

"You want to? You can," Snake offered raising his eyebrows. Jax opened his mouth to shout a 'hell yeah' but was interrupted by the DJ.

"Now coming to center stage...The one! The only! Pocahontas!" he said, throwing the record on.

A voluptuous brown woman with jet-black hair took the stage in full Cherokee regalia. Tonto squinted past the feathers and war paint. He overlooked the big brown breast with large browner nipples and saw his little sister Maria. He felt the urge to rush the stage and drag her home to their mother. Just like he'd done most of their life. His baby sister was addicted to the streets so there was no saving her until she wanted to be saved.

"That's your type. Ain't it, bruh?" Jax asked excitedly when he saw his partner stuck on the stripper on the stage. Usually the man lowered his gaze whenever they had meetings in strip clubs. Which was quite often since Jax usually set them up.

"You want her?" Snake offered raising his eyebrows again. He had already had her and could vouch for how warm and comfy she was inside. If not for her nasty pill addiction she would have made a nice addition to his rotation of side chicks.

"Huh? Oh, nah. I'm good. Let's get down to business," he replied once again. This time his partner did kick him under the table. "After we get our drink on of course!"

The waitress returned with a large bottle of cognac and poured each a drink. She looked to XL to see if he was drinking but saw he was in mean mug mode. She shrugged and handed the men their drinks.

"My partner here wants to eat you from the back," Snake snitched. She shot her head to the guest to see which one he meant. Jax was smiling and nodding while Tonto was still staring at the girl on stage. It was purely clinical as he watched his sister shake and shimmy for dollars. Maria was high as a kite and horny from men rubbing her vagina as they put money in her garter.

"He can!" she smiled and gave him a booty shaking display as she walked away.

"I will!" he shouted and laughed after her. Snake ordered a few strippers to provide table dances while they sipped the Henny. Maria finally left the stage and Tonto mentally joined the others.

"Let's slide into a private room," Snake said, ready to talk business. He gave XL a nod setting the extra-large man in motion towards the private VIP rooms. The men followed, followed by hand-selected strippers.

Rohan was on high alert as they entered the plush back room. This wasn't a buy, so they weren't expected to have cash but he stayed on point. Meanwhile his young partner was straight clubbing. He groped one strippers breast and the others ass. XL stopped at the door where he would remain while his boss handled business.

"Nile, why don't you take care of my friend Tonto here?" Snake asked even though he wasn't asking. The Egyptian woman quickly swooped between his legs and went for his zipper.

"Whoa!" Rohan protested and swatted her small copper colored hand away.

"You being rude!" Jax snapped in a tone matching Snake's expression. A Russian stripper knelt before him like an altar as he unzipped his pants and passed her his meat.

This was the part of the job that the happy husband hated. Being undercover required him to indulge in forbidden acts. He didn't drink in real life but had to as Tonto. Rohan didn't use drugs but Tonto had to smoke weed, snort coke and pop a pill from time to time. Now he had no choice but let the strange woman go down on him.

"That's better. Making me, mmm, feel some kinda way," Snake said as a sexy Honduran took him inside her warm mouth.

"I like to handle business and pleasure separately," Rohan explained trying to ignore what was happening below his waist. He could ignore it all he liked because his penis didn't need his permission to grow stiff. He looked to his partner slamming the woman's head up and down in his lap while thrusting his hips upward.

The room went otherwise silent, save the slurps and moans of the simultaneous blowjobs. One by one they came to grunting halts and gulps. Rohan held out as long as he could but even Superman wasn't immune to head. Likewise, head was kryptonite to many a married man.

A heaping dose of guilt chased the explosive pleasure like an early afternoon shadow. Rohan let out a heavy sigh as he put his deflating dick back where it belonged after being where it had no business. He sighed again thinking how to make it up to his wife even though she wouldn't know. She had quite a few gifts and trinkets from situations like this. She had a whole jewelry box filled from when they took down a prostitution ring out in Staten Island.

"Enjoyed that trip up the Nile?" Snake asked knowingly since he made that journey several times himself.

"Hell yeah. Now, about the dope?" he said as the strippers cleared the room.

"About the dope. Like I told ya boy Jax, we don't deal in ounces and quarters. Ten bricks, at 19, then we front you ten more bricks. This is weekly so if you ain't got the clientele say hell no," he said finishing the sentence in his Biggie Smalls voice from The Ten Crack Commandments.

"Shit we can do twenty bricks in a day!" Jax cheered getting a look from his partner. It said 'calm down' so he did. "Twenty bricks a week is no problem."

"None at all. The price is a problem. I can get it from the Mexicans or Dominicans for 17.5. Why would I pay extra?" Rohan asked even though he knew the answer. Snake was pretending to be thee man when in fact he was just a middleman. Once they slapped the cuffs on him he would eagerly trade up to his connect. The dope game is proof that shit rolls uphill too.

"We can do 18.5," he quickly countered hoping to hold onto his profit. He was scraping a grand or two off each kilo, which added up to a pretty penny with all the bricks they moved.

"To start, 18.5 on purchased. 17.5 on the consignment!" Jax tossed in. He was as shrewd as any real dope boy because he was a real dope boy. He swiped as much drugs as he could from every transaction and had a small team of dealers pushing his product.

"18 on the consignment and you got a deal," Snake agreed looking between the two men. The fifteen grand a week was cool but something didn't sit well. Why were the sidekick handling negotiations? He wished XL would speak up during a deal.

"Deal!" Rohan agreed and stood to shake on it. He locked eyes with the dealer as they shook. Eye contact is like a human lie detector. Sure some people can look you in the eye and lie but most can't.

"I hope you brought us a sample of what we're getting?" Jax asked hopefully. Half would go to evidence and the other half up his nose. Once they copped the bricks he would replace ten percent of the pure coke with cut and put it on the streets.

Rohan pressed his lips together to keep his protest inside as the dealer passed his partner what looked to be about an ounce of dope in a plastic bag. He was a vet and could weigh most drugs by eye. Had he been a betting man he would bet it wouldn't make it into evidence. As slick as Jax thought he was, Rohan was hip. He followed the cop code and kept silent knowing it would one day catch up with him. There was a special prison upstate for crooked cop, rogue judges and other officials gone bad. His partner was making reservations and it was time they parted ways. Once Snake was finally cuffed he could get his promotion and move on.

"You guys don't want to stick around? Sample some more flavors?" Snake offered.

"Sure. No thanks," the partners offered with equal enthusiasm. They both looked at the other wondering what the hell was wrong with the other.

"I got a thing, early," Rohan explained and begged off.

"Yeah, me too," Jax cosigned halfheartedly. There was a little cop in him and since they came together they would leave together. That didn't mean he couldn't come back later. The blowjob was a nice appetizer but he was eager for an entree. Who could blame him when women from thirty countries were on the menu. Hands were shook and they made their departure.

Rohan zoned in on the door just as eager to leave as his partner was to stay. His tunnel vision caused him to walk straight into the back of a stripper. He was definitely going to smell like baby oil and have glitter on his face now.

"Shit!" he fussed more at himself than the woman since he assumed correctly that he and his partner had eyes on their backs.

"Watch where the fuck you... Rohan?" the angry stripper began with alcohol on her breath. She cut the tirade short seeing her big brother. Her initial reaction was glee so she wrapped her arms around him and kissed his face. Her second thought was, "What you doing here? I'm grown and—"

"I'll have to talk to you later. I'll call you," he urged and resumed his mission towards the door.

"Yo, Tonto. We can both hit that! She was on your nut sack!" Jax said. She was high on his list from her performance on the stage. He wouldn't mind holding those long Pocahontas braids while digging her out from the back.

"Stay away from here! Far, far away from her!" Rohan grunted, getting in his face. He regained his composure a split second later and resumed his march to the door.

"OK, OK. I swear you Indian dudes don't like no black niggers messing with your women. But you married a black girl," Jax complained all the way out to the car. Rohan ignored his grumbles all the way back to the precinct.